DARK ANGEL

Gentlemen of the Order - Book 4

ADELE CLEE

More titles by Adele Clee

Lost Ladies of London

The Mysterious Miss Flint

The Deceptive Lady Darby

The Scandalous Lady Sandford

The Daring Miss Darcy

Avenging Lords

At Last the Rogue Returns

A Wicked Wager

Valentine's Vow

A Gentleman's Curse

Scandalous Sons

And the Widow Wore Scarlet

The Mark of a Rogue

When Scandal Came to Town

The Mystery of Mr Daventry

Gentlemen of the Order

Dauntless

Raven

Valiant

Dark Angel

Ladies of the Order

The Devereaux Affair

Dark Angel
Copyright © 2021 Adele Clee
All rights reserved.
ISBN-13: 978-1-8383839-0-9

Cover by Dar Albert at Wicked Smart Designs

CHAPTER 1

DANTE D'ANGELO MIGHT BE SLIGHTLY drunk, but he was not stupid. He was used to the fervent gazes of women caressing his masculine form as he sauntered through the ballrooms of the *ton*, yet the golden-haired snoop dressed in midnight blue silk watched his movements as if stalking prey.

No, those inquisitive eyes—he'd wager they were ice blue, cold and frigidly formal—had no interest in devouring his muscular physique. She didn't flash a coy grin. An invitation to slip into a dark room, slip into something warm and wet so he might banish his demons temporarily. So what did she want? And how was it he knew every woman in attendance tonight, every woman except her?

As an enquiry agent for the Order, a group of men who helped the weak and needy, those without funds or connections, those persecuted by the wicked, it was his business to know every person of quality. As the grandson of the deceased Earl of Deighton, he'd been fed on a hearty diet of genealogy.

A man must know his allies and his enemies, boy!

And yet he did not know her.

Intrigued beyond measure, and with a need to rid himself of the depressing ennui consuming him of late, he decided to play a game with this stranger. Lure her into Lucifer's lair, see if she could withstand the heat.

Excitement thumped in his chest. Hell. It made a change from the need to murder every man breathing.

Dante swallowed his champagne and placed the empty flute on a passing footman's tray. Now, where amid Babington's crush of a party might a man find a little privacy? With the house having the most extensive garden in Great Russell Street, outdoors was the obvious choice. And it was a little early in the evening to stumble upon couples fornicating in nature. A little cold, too.

Not too cold or too early for him. Not too cold or too early for the lady who grabbed his wrist as he strode towards the terrace doors.

"Dante, how dashing you—"

"Not tonight, Charlotte." He did not make eye contact.

"But you said—"

"Not tonight. I'm here on business." It wasn't a lie. And now the woman who occasionally warmed his bed knew to cross him off her long list of lovers. Had he bothered to glance back, he would find she had already set her sights on his replacement.

Dante descended the terrace steps, took a moment to warm his hands against the flames roaring in the brazier before stealing deep into the shadows. Through the arched arbour lay an evergreen jungle of dense foliage and high topiary hedges. If one knew where to look, one might find a secluded seat hidden amid the lush greenery. A perfect place to hide and wait.

He did not wait long.

The hesitant patter of footsteps on the path were those of a woman, though he prayed Charlotte hadn't followed him outside, intent on seduction.

He almost chuckled when he heard a swish of silk and a disappointed sigh. The moment he saw the halo of golden curls, he knew the stranger lacked sense when it came to her penchant for spying.

"Do you know me, madam?" Dante stepped out from the verdure.

The stranger gasped, sending a puff of white mist into the chilly night air. "Heavens above! Did you have to do that? I might have died of apoplexy."

"When a lady wanders through the darkness alone, she should be prepared for surprises. But I ask you again. Do you know me, madam?"

She seemed flustered by the question. "Know you? Well, yes and no."

Dante couldn't help but smile. "Your mother lied when she told you men find indecisive women attractive."

"And you're vain if you think every woman seeks to capture your attention. I spoke the truth. Both answers are correct." She stepped closer, close enough for him to notice the pretty little mole sitting proudly above her bow-shaped lips. "As I'm sure you're aware, we have never met."

"No, I would have remembered the determined set of your chin." He would have remembered the teasing, heart-shaped mole on the swell of her breasts, too.

"But I know who you are, sir. You're the Dark Angel. That's the moniker given to you by your colleagues at the Order—Mr Cole, Mr Sloane and Mr Ashwood. And while Mr Ashwood should be addressed as Lord Hawkridge, he despises the fact he inherited a title."

Cursed saints!

It wouldn't be the first time he'd attracted the attention of an obsessed debutante, though why she'd risked her reputation to attend this bawdy soiree was anyone's guess. Perhaps he should tell her why his friends chose the fitting moniker. Warn her not to dance with the devil.

"I am the Dark Angel. But make no mistake, I possess neither temperance nor virtue. Angel is merely a reference to my surname. It is the dark element you should fear."

Most women would quiver upon hearing his menacing undertone.

Not this one.

"Fear is a construct of the mind, sir."

Dante feared nothing except for failing to find the fiend who murdered his parents. "Either you have no experience of pain, or you've suffered so greatly you're indifferent to the emotion."

Her watery smile said the latter was true.

He decided to press harder, elicit a reaction.

3

"The fault lies with your mother. Did she not alert you to the dangers of attending a party hosted by a disreputable rake?" He glanced at the daring silk gown hugging her hips like a glove. "Did she not tell you a virgin maid should wear white, so those of us seeking a bed partner for the evening know who to avoid?"

"How could she? She's dead." The sharply spoken words sliced through his conscience. "My mother died many years ago."

"Mine too," he said, unnerved by the instant connection. "Though I doubt they met the same grisly end." To banish the horrific image of his mother's blood-soaked body, he focused on the maiden's breasts, lush and bountiful, large enough to fill his hands.

She glanced down. "Did I forget to remove the label?"

"The label?"

"The label informing you of my virginity."

He snorted. "Love, I can read your body like I read a book. Every movement tells a story. In your lavish gown, you're the heroine who wants to appear confident and worldly-wise. Yet from the stiff way you walk I know you've never parted your legs, never gripped a man between your soft thighs, never climaxed beneath the skilled strum of his fingers."

She should have gasped and blushed, gathered her skirts and darted back to the ballroom, but she arched a challenging brow. "So, you're a reader who skims the pages and misses vital parts of the story."

"You're saying I'm wrong?"

This was quickly becoming a rather interesting conversation.

She sneered. "Not entirely. While I know what it's like to have a man's filthy paws maul my flesh, to feel the disgusting weight of him pressing down upon me, squeezing the last breath from my lungs, I am proud to say I'm still intact. But while the bruises heal, Mr D'Angelo, the harrowing memories remain."

Damn. He didn't like the graphic vision bombarding his mind —an ugly beast of an abuser marring her porcelain skin. He didn't like that she might understand why nightmares plagued him, why he was scared to sleep, why he walked and walked and walked until he was too tired to stand.

"I admire your candour, Miss—"

4

"Sands."

What a shame she wasn't a widow or some ageing lord's wife. They might spend a pleasurable night keeping their demons at bay. He would make her come so many times she would never see the filthy devil's face again. Would fill his mind with the sound of her pleasure, try to remember her passionate cries, not his mother's haunting howls.

"Now we're acquainted, Miss Sands, might you explain why you've been watching me all evening? And if you are a virgin maid attending a party for the debauched, please tell me you brought a chaperone."

She peeked over her shoulder as if about to confess a government secret. "I am here in a professional capacity, sir, and do not need a chaperone."

"Damnation! Don't tell me you've sold your virginity to the highest bidder."

Babington enjoyed playing depraved games. Though if the bids were still open, Dante would pay a king's ransom for the pleasure of bedding this intriguing maiden. Once would be enough to satisfy his curiosity.

"Sold my virginity? Don't be ridiculous! I work for Lucius Daventry and Damian Wycliff. I'm an enquiry agent for the Order. I'm here tonight because I've been assigned to the widow Emery's case and am merely following a lead."

Dante froze.

An enquiry agent for the Order? The woman was a few cards shy of a full deck. There were ways to get his attention without making absurd declarations. Yet, his disappointment at not winning a coveted place in Miss Sands' bed proved equally puzzling.

"I don't know what game you're playing, madam, but *I* work as an agent for the Order. *I* have been assigned to the widow Emery's case." Dante firmed his jaw, for he did not appreciate being treated like a dolt. Though how she knew such personal details was a mystery. "If you know I catch liars and thieves, why invent such a ludicrous tale?"

Miss Sands frowned. "Surely Mr Daventry told you of his project."

"Project? What project?" As the master of the Order, Lucius Daventry kept many secrets, but never those that might hinder a case.

"Mr Wycliff wishes to help ladies who find themselves alone and destitute. Mr Daventry is his partner in a new venture, for he believes a woman's insight might be invaluable when solving cases. I live in Mr Wycliff's house for waifs and strays on Howland Street and am employed by Mr Daventry as an agent."

It was Dante's turn to frown. What the hell was Daventry thinking? Employing an innocent to catch cutthroats and villains? She looked as if she might hurt her fingers snapping open her fan.

He considered this delicate creature, with her smooth skin and magnificent breasts. "But you're no older than twenty. What could you know about chasing criminals through the rookeries?"

Miss Sands gave a disgruntled huff. "I am three-and-twenty and have survived in the rookeries these last six months. Have you ever lived amongst harlots and murderers, Mr D'Angelo? No, of course not. You own an impressive townhouse on the eastern side of Fitzroy Square."

Dante was about to speak, but Miss Sands continued berating him.

"Have you ever trusted someone implicitly, only to have him abuse his position in the most diabolical fashion? Have you ever wandered through stench-filled alleys worried you might not find a bed for the night? Discovered gainful employment means spending most of the evening on your back? No, of course not. You're a man. A man of wealth and means and the strength to murder anyone who steps in your way."

Anger bubbled in Dante's chest. "I know horror, Miss Sands. I know what it's like to be a victim of one's circumstances." He'd had everything precious ripped from him in one fell swoop.

The sudden flash of pity in her eyes said she knew a thieving blackguard had slaughtered his parents when he was a child.

Damn it all!

Had Daventry told her?

"You're plagued by nightmares." She spoke as if she were a silent visitor to his bedchamber and had witnessed his restless writhing. "And yet you're an extremely skilled agent with an ability to think logically. What I'm trying to say is we all have our weaknesses, Mr D'Angelo."

They fell silent, the hum of music and laughter in the distance reminding him this was a party, not a night to resurrect ghosts. Despite the fact he planned to conclude the evening with a few hours of rampant bed sport, he was here in a professional capacity, too.

"Then let us not dwell on the past, Miss Sands. Let us focus on the reason we've been assigned the same damn case."

He was more than interested to know what she had discovered, although he doubted she knew how an incident of fraud related to the murder of his parents. Did Lucius Daventry know? Was that why he'd hired this woman to interfere?

Dante gestured to the cushioned bench tucked away amid the shrubbery. "Would you care to sit? Perhaps it might be easier if we work together tonight, for our goal is one and the same."

Her wary gaze flicked over his black shirt and coat. "Your suggestion makes perfect sense, sir, but it causes a minor problem. While you're an extremely competent agent, and most certainly a man who takes command of every situation, this is my first case. If you fail to solve it, you will be assigned another. Should I fail to provide any evidence of a crime, I might find myself mopping up ale at the Bull in the Barn."

Standing before him dressed in sumptuous silk, he could not imagine her scrubbing floors in a tavern. Judging by her eloquent speech and dignified deportment, she'd been raised in a respectable household. And yet now she had no option but to chase blackguards for a living. Why?

His heart softened—just for a few fleeting seconds.

"Then, in light of this being your first case, and the fact I'm feeling benevolent, you may present our findings to Daventry."

Her grateful smile had an odd effect on him. A strange shiver rippled across his shoulders, which he quickly attributed to the chill in the air.

"It would help my cause tremendously." She caught herself. "Oh, but you must let me take the lead. I couldn't lie to Mr Daventry, couldn't make a false claim."

Devil take it. The women Dante entertained would lie and cheat and kick a starving child from the pavement to get ahead. Miss Sands wished only to be rewarded for her own honest achievements. Impressive.

"Very well. You take the lead." Dante was interested to know if they shared similar suspicions about the widow's case. "Perhaps we should sit, and you can explain what brought you here this evening, tell me what evidence you hope to find."

Having been rescued from the rookeries, she could explain how she could afford an extravagant gown, how she'd secured an invitation to a notorious ball. As a man of integrity, Lucius Daventry would never send a virgin to a party for degenerates.

"We can barter, Mr D'Angelo. One of my secrets for one of yours. Though I warn you, I have many."

He might have laughed and offered a witty retort were it not for the brisk patter of approaching footsteps echoing from the shadows.

"Damnation. Someone is coming."

He wasn't sure why he captured the hand of a woman who had no need to protect her reputation. He wasn't sure why he dragged her into a shady corner amid the overgrown shrubbery and high hedges and insist she hide. He knew exactly why he pressed her back against the greenery, why he shrouded her body, why he stood so close their energies collided.

"Don't move. We'll soon be rid of them."

Miss Sands inhaled deeply but struggled to find her voice. She placed her hands on his chest, a means for him to maintain some distance, not for her to explore the muscular contours.

"Quick, there's a seat here, love," came the masculine voice so thick with lust it dripped like treacle. "It's too far from the house for your husband to come looking."

"Hurry, Frederick." The woman's desperate plea said she would be astride the lucky devil in seconds.

Feeling surprisingly aroused by his virgin's peony scent and gasps for air, Dante focused on Miss Sands only to find she had squeezed her eyes shut and looked almost pained.

"I'm in a lush green meadow, yes, a meadow," she whispered,

pushing at his chest as if preparing to mount an escape. "There is space, space, so much space."

"Hush. If we're seen together, people will assume we're lovers. Gossip spreads like wildfire."

Not that he cared, but Daventry would be annoyed to find his first female enquiry agent was the talk of the *ton*. That said, in an attempt to gather evidence, Miss Sands would need to rummage about in Babington's bedchamber. Posing as rampant lovers might give them a reasonable excuse if caught inspecting the gentleman's smalls.

Dante turned, ready to accost the newcomers.

The couple dropped onto the cushioned bench and the gentleman set about freeing his lover's breasts from her bodice. Passion consumed them to the point neither heard Miss Sands' mumbled mantra. Neither knew she gripped Dante's coat as one clutched the mast of a sinking ship. Neither knew the effort it took to stand firm.

"Oh, quickly, Frederick." The woman fumbled with the buttons on the man's velvet breeches. "I need you inside me else I shall simply die."

Dante expected Miss Sands to gasp at the crude comment, but she did not. Having lived in the stews, she must have witnessed lewd displays in the back alleys.

Loath to spoil their fun, but fearing Miss Sands was about to dart out from her hiding place, Dante had to act.

"This seat is taken." Dante's menacing tone sliced through the shadows. He recognised the woman as the young wife of a doddering peer. "I suggest you move elsewhere unless you wish me to inform Lord Clements he's a cuckold."

Squeals and curses replaced the carnal grunts. Lady Clements jumped from the seat and covered her bare breasts. Frederick Wace, a young buck with less courage than chin hair, grabbed his lover's arm and fled into the darkness.

Dante might have breathed a relieved sigh had Miss Sands' ramblings not taken an alarming turn.

"Get off me! No! Get away!"

"Hush." He swung around and drew her out of the shrubbery. "Hush now. They've gone."

Tears streaked her cheeks, the droplets glistening beneath the faint slivers of moonlight. She fought to catch her breath, lacked the strength to raise her eyelids.

He hated seeing any woman in pain, preferred seeing them panting with pleasure and gasping his name. His stomach twisted into knots. Hard knots. Crippling knots. The urge to run, to seek amusing entertainment, to drink himself into oblivion, to banish the memory of his mother's tears, forced him to step back.

But then Miss Sands' eyes flew open. Fear marred the vibrant blue irises. Fear left its hideous etchings in every distressed line on her face. She looked at him, the realisation she had escaped her nightmare evident in her sudden exhalation. But then the tears came anew. The first like the trickle of water seeping through the cracks in a dam. It did not take long for the walls to collapse under the pressure.

Miss Sands rushed into his arms, buried her face in his neck and sobbed.

Dante stood rigid. He had nowhere to go, nowhere to hide.

CHAPTER 2

How odd it was to take comfort in the arms of a stranger. But then Mr D'Angelo was not a stranger. Everything about their meeting tonight had gone as planned. If he knew her real name, he would know of their connection. But Beatrice could not risk telling him yet. Not until they were better acquainted. Not until he'd learnt to trust her, to respect her opinion. And although she'd come expecting some surprises, she had not thought to fall into his arms, a quivering wreck.

For a moment, she forgot about the horrendous year she'd had—a lonely year spent struggling to survive—and took comfort in his warm embrace. Mr D'Angelo did not smell like a sweat-soaked monster. A devious devil in disguise. No. His spiced bergamot cologne reflected a man with an unmistakable presence. A sensual seducer, confident in his own skin.

"Miss Sands," he said, his voice strung as tightly as a bow. "Perhaps I should have my coachman take you home. I'm not sure what caused your sudden panic, but—"

"I have a fear of enclosed spaces, sir." It was not irrational by any means. She pulled away from him and accepted his proffered handkerchief. The silk square smelled as divine as his clothes. "When trapped in dark places, I fear I might not escape."

"Ah, I assume it has something to do with the licentious libertine."

"Sometimes, it is impossible to suppress the memories." She hated the fact she had a weakness. Hated the fact someone insignificant could still affect her so profoundly.

"I understand. Memories appear with the slightest provocation."

"They do." She felt oddly comforted by his remark. "Mr Daventry took a chance hiring a female agent. I cannot go home without proving Mr Babington is the criminal who defrauded Mrs Emery."

Wearing a curious frown, Mr D'Angelo considered her intently. "I, too, believe Babington is the culprit." He gestured to the red velvet cushions lining the bench. "Though I am keen to hear how you came to that conclusion."

Beatrice dried her eyes and returned the gentleman's handkerchief. "You agreed to barter. One piece of information for another. It wouldn't do to reveal all my secrets."

"We were interrupted before I gave my consent." He waited for her to sit and then settled beside her. "But we share a goal, both seek to catch the culprit, and so I accept your terms."

Their shared goal amounted to more than identifying a swindler. She wanted to find the person who murdered his parents as much as he did.

"Excellent. Let us discuss the facts." Beatrice managed a smile. "A gentleman professing to be a wealthy merchant purchased the widow's rare ormolu clock for two hundred pounds. Naively, the widow took his cheque and gave him the heirloom."

"And when presented, the cheque proved to be a forgery." Mr D'Angelo was frugal with his information and gave nothing away.

"It occurred to me that this wasn't his first crime," she said. "According to Mrs Emery, he exuded an aristocratic confidence. Must be highly educated because he professed to hail from Lancashire, yet had no accent. As you know, criminals often tell some semblance of the truth when inventing a tale. Mr Babington's parents hail from Rochdale, and while his father is a gentleman, his mother's family are wealthy wool merchants."

"Lancashire? The widow made no mention of it to me."

Mrs Emery had commented on Mr D'Angelo's dark, dangerous eyes, on the fact one should be wary of anyone of Italian heritage. "Mrs Emery found you intimidating. After her initial shock upon meeting me, she was grateful that Mr Daventry sent a female agent."

"Did the widow tell you anything else important?"

Beatrice grinned but resisted the urge to tap him playfully on the arm. "It is your turn to reveal information, Mr D'Angelo."

He inclined his head, conceding. "I believe Babington has committed many crimes. But where does one sell stolen items without leaving a trace? I discovered he uses numerous pawnbrokers, men willing to turn a blind eye to his misdeeds."

Beatrice knew Mr Babington had various means of profiting from his ill-gotten gains. But she had focused on another line of enquiry.

"I gathered information about a gang known to work from the London docks. They smuggle stolen goods abroad, expensive items that are too identifiable to be sold locally. A gentleman of quality arranged to hide items amongst the cargo—a diamond brooch, a topaz and chrysoberyl bracelet, and a gold-mounted tortoiseshell snuffbox."

Mr D'Angelo folded his arms across his broad chest and grinned. "You speak of Gilbert Stint's gang?"

"Perhaps."

His inquisitive gaze journeyed over her hair, her face, dipped to her breasts. "How did you gain that information when Stint refused to discuss the matter with me? Even after I delivered a swift upper-cut to the scoundrel's jaw, he continued to play dumb."

"I have many contacts in the rookeries, Mr D'Angelo." During her first few days in London, she had been lucky enough to find work at a tavern run by Alice Crouch—a formidable woman with a fondness for waifs. Luckily, Mr Stint had a fondness for the buxom proprietor of the Bull in the Barn. "But while their information proves useful, I cannot present it as evidence."

Beatrice would never betray Alice.

"Lady Giles lost her chrysoberyl bracelet at Mr Babington's masquerade in August," Beatrice continued. She had earned that priceless piece of information by befriending the lady's maid. "And Mr Winston-Jones lost his snuffbox during a private party at the Blue Jade, a club known—"

"For opium-fuelled orgies."

"You've been?"

"No, Miss Sands. I've never had the need to pay for pleasure."

"Of course not." A man oozing raw masculinity must have a host of willing bed partners. "Mr Babington is a regular patron of the Blue Jade. It cannot be a coincidence." Beatrice paused. "It is your turn to divulge a secret, sir."

Mischief glinted in his black eyes. "A reason I believe Babington is guilty, or do you wish to know something personal, Miss Sands?"

"While it's important we know each other better, sir, we should focus on our current case."

They had plenty of time to become acquainted. The only way to prove Babington's guilt was to catch him in the act. Once she had proven her worth, she would offer to help Mr D'Angelo find the man who murdered his parents. The man who murdered her father, too.

"The blackguard sold Mrs Emery's ormolu clock to a pawnbroker in Holborn," he said. "The owner's description—a man an inch shy of six feet, with brown wavy hair and a pasty complexion—confirms it's Babington."

"Mrs Emery described the merchant as having chalk-white skin." Beatrice had pressed the old woman, needing her to confirm what she had learnt from Mr Stint. "I believe Mr Babington uses a mix of wax and powder to cover the purple birthmark on his cheek."

Mr D'Angelo's full lips curled into a slow smile. "To say I'm impressed by your investigative skills would be an understatement, Miss Sands."

A sudden rush of excitement stole her breath. Earning Mr D'Angelo's respect was key to her plan. "When one has to fight for survival, it pays to be shrewd."

In truth, she was merely lucky. Lucky, Alice had found her when she did. Lucky, she'd not been stolen off the street and put to service.

"Oh, you're shrewd, Miss Sands." Despite his compliment, his intimidating aura left her slightly unnerved. "Shrewd enough to afford a gown that must have cost more than a few months' pay. Shrewd enough to gain entrance to a ball for degenerates when I know Daventry would not have secured an invitation."

"You sound as if you distrust me, sir."

"Do not be offended. I distrust most people."

Well, she would have to change that. Perhaps a good dose of honesty was the cure.

"The dress belongs to Miss Trimble. The lady employed to run the house in Howland Street." Miss Trimble owned an assortment of clothes and disguises, all items a lady might use when conducting an investigation. "She disapproves of me attending Mr Babington's ball, hence why she is waiting outside in the carriage Mr Daventry provided for our use. She told me a lady with poise and confidence could walk into a king's court without an invitation. And she was right."

"Did Daventry provide the coachman?"

"Of course."

Mr D'Angelo gave a knowing nod. "Then Daventry will know exactly where you've been tonight. I'll wager the coachman is skilled in combat and carries a brace of pistols, wager Miss Trimble is employed to keep Daventry informed of your whereabouts."

"Mr Daventry considers the safety of all his agents," she said. According to Miss Trimble, he was particularly concerned about the captivating gentleman of Italian heritage.

Mr D'Angelo narrowed his gaze. "What are you really doing here, Miss Sands? Another motive drives you, not the need to put food on the table or prove yourself in a man's world, but something else."

Panic forced Beatrice to her feet. The gentleman's insight was remarkable.

"Might I suggest we postpone any discussion of a personal nature until we've found something to incriminate Mr Babington? Time is of the essence, Mr D'Angelo."

"And what if we need to hide in a dark corner?" He stood, his countenance turning somewhat arrogant as he straightened to

15

his full height. "Will you tremble in terror? Will you claw at my back, gasp, and give the game away?"

Her hackles rose at the mere hint of condescension. "Do not press your body against mine, sir, and there shall be no problem."

"You should take it as a compliment. Most women would beg to have me thrust them up against a topiary hedge, and yet I chose you."

She laughed. "You did not choose me. I stalked after you along a moonlit path. I sought you out because it seems ridiculous not to work together when we're investigating the same case."

He bent his head, and in a husky voice whispered, "But if I could have chosen any woman from the ballroom to push against, Miss Sands, it would have been you."

Oh, the man was a devil and a tease.

Miss Trimble had warned her to stay on her guard.

"Well, I'm liable to attack any man who so much as tries, and I doubt Mr Daventry wants fighting amongst the ranks."

Wearing a rakish grin, he brushed his hand through his brown shoulder-length hair. "Then I'll have to see what I can do to help you curb your temper. Now, back to the matter of Babington. We should—"

"I shall search Mr Babington's study while you examine his bedchamber."

"I'm not leaving you to wander the house alone. Perhaps you're unaware, but there are a few rogues out to seduce you tonight."

Seduce her? And she thought she had blended into the crowd.

"We'll both search the study," she conceded, else they would be locked in a battle of wills until dawn. "Though after your needless attempt to protect my reputation, I don't suppose you'll want anyone seeing us together."

Mr D'Angelo moved to stand beside her. "I shall enter the study. Wait outside until I raise the sash."

"Outside? You expect me to climb through a window while wearing a ball gown?"

He seemed to find the thought amusing. "You're an agent of

the Order. If I'm to let you present the evidence to Daventry, I need to test your mettle. Besides, the rakes are watching your every move, waiting for an opportunity to pounce. The moment you slip from the corridor to the study, they'll be fighting for a chance to join you."

Beatrice might have challenged his observations. If men were so intent on pursuing her, why had no one followed her into the garden? Still, it was imperative she passed Mr D'Angelo's test.

"Then I bow to the weight of your experience, sir, and will do as you suggest."

The rogue moistened his lips as his gaze slipped to her ankles. "I'll escort you as far as the arched arbour. Babington's study is—"

"The third window to the left as one approaches the house."

"Precisely."

Beatrice refused to hold on to his arm as they walked along the moonlit path back to the house. It had nothing to do with wanting to prove herself his equal, and everything to do with the fact the man's magnetic presence made her nervous. Of course, as a female agent, one had to be a damn good actress, and she'd done a remarkable job so far.

Amid the rustle of silk and the groans of noisy lovers coming from the shrubbery, the five-minute wait near the study window left Beatrice's heart thumping and her cheeks aflame. When Mr D'Angelo finally raised the sash, she couldn't race to the window quick enough.

"You'll have to lift your skirts to your knees if you're to climb over the ledge, Miss Sands." Mr D'Angelo offered his hand along with a devilish grin.

"I might have to raise them higher than that," she teased.

"Be assured I've seen more than my share of stocking-clad thighs."

Heat flooded her cheeks for the umpteenth time this evening.

Beatrice surveyed the ledge, feeling rather thankful she had come prepared. Bunching her skirts, she thrust her head through the gap and tried to ignore the feel of Mr D'Angelo's hot hands as he gripped her waist and helped her inside.

"Be careful. Mind your head," he whispered, his shocked gaze fixed firmly on her legs as she edged through the gap. "What the devil are you wearing?"

"These?" Beatrice set about righting her skirts, covering the fitted white trousers. "Miss Trimble gave them to me. Decorum is an important factor when a lady has to scoop up her gown and run."

For the first time this evening—for the first time since watching him from afar these last few months—a genuine smile touched his lips. The deep amber flecks in his eyes glowed. Heaven help her. Mr D'Angelo was handsome when angry, but the rare glimpse of happiness made him appear utterly breathtaking.

"During my time as an agent, during my time witnessing women in many states of dishabille, I have never encountered a woman wearing trousers beneath her ball gown." He lowered the sash, drew the heavy green curtains and set about lighting the candle in the brass stick on the desk.

"Have I defiled your delicate sensibilities, sir?"

"No, Miss Sands, you've sparked my interest, and that's a damn sight more dangerous."

The air between them crackled to life. She could see why a lady might want to be thrust against a hedge and have him smother her body.

Beatrice cleared her throat and rounded the desk. Maintaining a certain distance made it easier to focus on the task at hand. "Miss Trimble disapproves of me chasing criminals for a living, but she knows my options are limited. Consequently, she tries to assist me in my endeavours, not hinder my progress."

Mr D'Angelo tugged the handle on the desk drawer only to find it locked. "Hence the reason she made you wear trousers to protect your modesty."

"Indeed."

"And yet some men find them more arousing than bare legs."

"I doubt that."

He glanced up from trying to pick the lock with wire and a thin metal instrument. Their eyes met—more a sensual tussle than a clash of swords. "I'm a man who thrives on intrigue, Miss Sands. You'll do well to remember it."

"There is nothing intriguing about me, sir. Wearing trousers is a logical decision if you think about it."

"And I am thinking about it, Miss Sands. I'm thinking about it a great deal."

"Then stop thinking and focus on opening the drawer."

Beatrice glanced around the room, looking for a place where a man might hide evidence of his crimes. The bookcase full of leather-bound volumes captured her interest. Her uncle had hidden the damning newspaper cuttings between the leaves of a book entitled *Farming Practices of the Middle Ages*.

Mr D'Angelo cracked open the drawer and sifted through the contents while she studied the gold embossed lettering on the spines of numerous books.

"Search under the seat cushions," came Mr D'Angelo's whispered command. "Open the bureau and look there."

But Beatrice was drawn to the row of books on the top shelf. She took the footstool positioned near the fireside chair, stood on tiptoes on the cushioned seat, but could not reach to pull a book from the shelf.

"Mr D'Angelo, might I borrow you a moment?"

He closed a ledger and placed it back in the drawer. "We haven't time to examine every book on the shelf."

"I merely need you to take the candlestick and read a few titles." Her intuition had served her well so far and would not fail her tonight. "You did say I might lead our investigation."

"Miss Sands, we—"

"There are four shelves, sir. There isn't a speck of dust on the highest shelf, look." Beatrice ran her gloved fingers over the walnut wood. She did the same on the third shelf, leaving one white finger covered in grey fluff. "Please, it will take a minute, no more."

He sighed as he captured the candlestick and rounded the desk. Muttering something incoherent, he stood on the footstool and held the candlestick aloft. "What am I looking for?"

"The least appealing title. The one you wouldn't touch even if you were bored beyond belief."

"The stool isn't made to take my weight. I'm liable to snap the legs." He wobbled on the stool for effect. "You'll need to hold me steady lest I drop the candle and set the room ablaze."

"When we're done here, you may go in search of a lady to caress your muscular thighs, sir. Now read the titles."

He chuckled to himself and then began his study of the leather spines. "*Fashionable Infidelity*. Most people would want to read that. *The Nunnery for Coquettes*. Hell, I might take that one with me. *Agricultural History*. *Rural Economy of Lancashire*. *The*—"

"Stop! Remove the last title."

Mr D'Angelo did as instructed. Paper fell out and fluttered to the floor. Beatrice scooped up various receipts and a dog-eared trade card. One receipt was for a ring pawned at Crockett's Emporium in Shoreditch.

"Perhaps the proprietor has no scruples when buying merchandise," she said, handing the chit to Mr D'Angelo. "Though one wonders why Mr Babington kept it when it's dated four months ago."

Mr D'Angelo scanned the receipt before slipping it into his pocket. "Is that a calling card?"

"No, a trade card for a goldsmith in Cornhill. There's a name scrawled on the back—Craddock, I think."

"Mrs Emery visited a goldsmith in Cornhill for an appraisal on her clock, though Mr Craddock informed her it was of inferior quality, hence the reason she sold it privately."

"Mr Walters did a similar thing."

"Walters?" Mr D'Angelo placed the book back on the shelf and stepped down from the footstool.

"Yes. It occurred to me that Mr Babington might have conned others out of their heirlooms. I visited modistes, gathered old copies of the periodical, searched for a similar advertisement to that of Mrs Emery's." It had taken two days to find what she needed, another two days to gain Mr Walters' direction from the publisher. "Mr Walters accepted the forged cheque but was too embarrassed to visit a police office."

Dark, sensual eyes held her pinned. "Miss Sands, your deductive skills leave me somewhat breathless."

"Why, thank you, sir." She offered a serene smile, but her

heart hopped about like a March hare. "Now we have proof of a connection, a visit to the goldsmith is necessary."

"Agreed. I shall call at Howland Street at noon tomorrow. Be ready."

Beatrice couldn't help but give a relieved sigh. "You wish me to accompany you to Cornhill?"

"Daventry was right. Your insight is a help, not a hindrance. Nothing matters more than catching Babington, so it appears you're stuck with me until we've solved this case."

She hoped to be stuck with him a little longer than that.

"Then I shall make myself so indispensable you might ask me to assist you again." Namely, in finding the murdering blackguard who'd shot his parents.

"Let's not get ahead of ourselves. Let us tackle problems as they arise." He held the candle aloft and gave her figure his full consideration. "The first being how you might slip outside without me gawping at your charming trousers."

CHAPTER 3

DANTE STOOD amid the shadows opposite Babington's house in Great Russell Street and watched Miss Sands climb into the carriage. It had taken sheer strength of will not to race across the narrow thoroughfare and punch the fellow trying to coax her back to the ballroom. Breaking the rake's clammy hands would draw undue attention. Still, Dante had been about to intervene when Daventry's man—a beast of a fellow named Bower—climbed down from atop his box and escorted the lady to safety.

With Bower acting as coachman, Daventry would receive a full account of Miss Sands' whereabouts. Hence the reason Dante insisted on using *his* conveyance to ferry her to Cornhill tomorrow.

Strange he felt a tug in his chest as the carriage rattled away.

Strange he felt an odd connection to an innocent.

But they had both lost their mothers long ago. Both suffered at the hands of a conniving devil, suffered lasting effects from their traumas. Both had secrets.

Dante strode to his carriage, parked on nearby Caroline Street. Sharp shook himself awake, surprised his master had left the soiree before midnight, but presumed Dante had a rendezvous elsewhere.

"To Mrs Stanworth's ball or Madame Babette's, sir?"

"Neither. Take me home, Sharp."

"Home?" The coachman's chin dropped. "Home, sir?"

Dante didn't venture home until his eyelids were heavy, his bones weak and weary, and he could barely stand.

He hesitated. The need to question Daventry about Miss Sands' background was like an itch he couldn't scratch. Gut instinct said Miss Sands had a hidden agenda, a compelling reason for stalking after him in the dark, and he'd not rest until he'd uncovered her secret.

"Take me to Little Chelsea. I wish to call upon Sloane."

Sloane lived in a palatial pleasure dome, a place where Dante might easily silence his demons. They often drank until dawn, laughed so hard the euphoria lasted until midday. But Sloane had recently married, and a scene of devoted domesticity would likely make Dante retch. The same was true of Ashwood and Cole—married men with no interest in drinking and gambling and tupping lightskirts.

And so—like the moment Miss Sands sobbed in his arms and every fibre of his being fought against the intrusion—Dante had nowhere to go, nowhere to seek solace.

Well, there was a place where a man might forget his troubles.

"On second thoughts, take me to the White Boar."

Sharp shifted nervously in the seat. "But you were there three nights ago, sir. Muscles take time to heal, to repair."

Dante snorted. "After winning twice, do you think I'm due a beating?"

The White Boar was a noisy backstreet tavern near Leicester Square, its dank cellar a fighting house lit by medieval-style sconces and supervised by toothless men with thick necks. The den remained open throughout the night and was frequented by drunken bucks out to settle stupid wagers and prize-fighters looking for any face to pummel.

"Sir, your hands are still bruised, and it pays to rest between bouts."

"I'll rest when I'm dead." He wouldn't have long to wait, not when he was one step closer to finding the bastard who'd shot a helpless woman in front of her eight-year-old son. "I'm confident that won't be tonight."

Sharp's sigh rang with concern. He gripped the reins and straightened in his seat. "One day soon I'll be ferrying your coffin to the cemetery, to an unconsecrated burial ground for doomed souls."

"The resurrectionists are always on the lookout for prime male specimens. I shall save you the trouble, have them collect my body before it's thrown into a pit."

"Happen you shouldn't tempt fate. One day you might find a reason to live, and then you'll be sorry."

"Hardly." Dante yanked open the carriage door. "I live for one thing and one thing only, Sharp, and it's not for the day you stop complaining."

No. Dante refused to die before finding the murdering bastard who killed his parents. And when he did, by God, he would make him pay.

The house on Howland Street shared common characteristics with Miss Trimble—the thirty-year-old manager of the sanctuary for waifs and strays. Both presented a rather plain frontage, the red brick building being as dull as the woman's brown dress and auburn hair. The black iron railings looked as rigid as the set of Miss Trimble's chin. And yet amid the austere facade stood an extravagant first-floor balcony, a glimmer of sophistication to match Miss Trimble's cultured air.

"Mr Bower must accompany Miss Sands during her investigations," said the woman with unforgiving eyes.

Dante inclined his head respectfully. "Miss Sands is to accompany me to Cornhill. You may inform Lucius Daventry that she will remain under my protection for the entire day."

Miss Trimble surveyed the cut of his coat as if he were an urchin begging for scraps. "Forgive me, Mr D'Angelo, but I cannot let Miss Sands leave without Mr Bower acting as chaperone."

Chaperone? Miss Sands had survived in the slums for six months. She stalked after rakes in the dark, had seduced him with teasing glimpses of her tight trousers. Daventry was taking his responsibilities a little seriously.

Dante straightened his shoulders. "Miss Trimble, I can kill a man with a single blow. Miss Sands will be perfectly safe in my care."

The woman glanced disapprovingly at the fresh gash above Dante's brow bone. "You're known for your recklessness, sir. You might not care if you live or die, but I have a duty to protect the ladies who reside here. Miss Sands will leave with Mr Bower or she will not leave at all."

Miss Trimble stared down her pert nose. Hell, Newgate's hulking guards were less intimidating. This refined spinster spoke as if Miss Sands were a timid wallflower, not a lady who caught villains for a living or embraced rogues in secluded corners of the garden.

"In light of the fact it will take hours to receive Daventry's permission, I have no choice but to agree to your demands, madam. Bower will accompany us to Cornhill so he might play nursemaid."

Miss Trimble's smile was as cold and crisp as a winter's morn. "Then I shall inform Miss Sands you're here."

Dante waited in the drawing room like an eager suitor— except he'd not come with a pretty posy, had sinful and downright wicked thoughts, not honourable notions of courting and marriage.

When Miss Sands entered the room, humming a country ballad and with a light skip in her step, her springtime smile proved infectious. Dante rarely found something to be joyous about at midday, yet he felt an alarming flicker of enthusiasm.

"Mr D'Angelo. I'm pleased to find you're a man of your word." Her smile faded the instant she noticed the slight cut above his brow. She rushed forward. "Good heavens! What happened to your eye?" Disregarding propriety, the lady grabbed his hands and examined his knuckles. "Sir, these are fresh bruises. Tell me you didn't confront Mr Babington with your suspicions."

Dante stared at her hands, so pale and delicate, while his were an autumn palette of purple and green. The obvious difference held his attention, as did the tenderness of her touch. Still, it brought to mind the memory of his mother's dainty fingers gripping his tightly while begging for their lives.

"No, Miss Sands. I worked through my frustrations at a fighting den in the cellar of the White Boar." Perhaps he would revisit the tavern tonight.

"A fighting den?" Cornflower blue eyes scanned his face. "Do you go there often?"

The hint of concern in her voice roused his ire. He did not want her worrying about his welfare. "Does it matter?"

She arched a coy brow. "If you do, and this is the extent of your injuries, perhaps it's worth me making a wager."

A laugh burst from his lips. It was the last thing he expected her to say. "A man looks for ways to cope with his demons. I would rather rise to a challenge than lounge about in a laudanum-induced stupor."

"Better to feel something real," she agreed, releasing his hands.

"Indeed."

Pain was real. Pain stoked the flames of vengeance.

"Let me know when you plan to return to the White Boar and I shall accompany you, assuming they allow women to watch men brawl. I cannot work as an agent forever. Gambling on you, sir, might help me secure a nice little nest-egg."

"You've never seen me fight, yet you sound sure I'll win."

"As you have no intention of dying just yet, logic says you won't take unnecessary risks. Therefore, you only fight if you know you can win."

"Exactly so, Miss Sands."

He wasn't an imbecile.

Just a man trying to contain the devil's wrath.

"We agreed to barter secrets, madam," he said, steering the subject away from the reasons he eased his distress in the boxing ring. "Now you know one of mine, it's only fitting you reveal one of yours."

She straightened the collar of her red wool redingote. "There is something I must tell you, but let us wait until we're seated in the carriage and you have no choice but to curb your temper."

Every muscle in his body tensed. "Then we should make haste, Miss Sands. A secret is one thing. A secret involving me is something highly disturbing."

Miss Sands sensed the shift in his mood, the black mist of resentment swirling in his chest. Most women would swoon beneath the weight of his stare, yet she reached out and touched his upper arm.

"Your eyes are as black as Satan's heart. Presuming the worst, experiencing negative emotions before I have made my revelation, is considered unhealthy."

"Unhealthy?" A smile formed before he could prevent it.

"Indeed. We should hurry to the carriage before blood rushes to your head and you take a turn." She led him into the hall, where she teamed her red coat with a black bonnet and gloves— a combination as striking as the woman herself. "No doubt you're keen for me to ease your misery."

He thought to tease her, suggest ways she could soothe his woes, but said nothing as he retrieved his hat from the butler, whose fists were meatier than any he'd encountered in the ring.

After a brief conversation with Bower, who explained he had to abide by Lucius Daventry's instructions, the man climbed atop the box to sit with Sharp while Dante assisted Miss Sands into the carriage.

The need to press her for information danced like the devil inside, but he waited patiently until they'd discussed the sudden drop in temperature and Miss Trimble's overcautious nature.

"Is this a form of torture, Miss Sands? Am I to wait until we arrive at Cornhill before you reveal your secret?"

Her watery smile faded. "I must be honest with you, Mr D'Angelo. After everything I've been through, I cannot abide deceit. If we're to work together, it's important you know the truth."

"Which is?"

She inhaled to bolster her courage. "I've been assigned two cases."

"Two?"

"I'm to find the villain who defrauded Mrs Emery, and I'm to discover why certain elements of the case are important to you.

Mr Daventry is concerned and believes you're keeping something from him."

Dante couldn't help but laugh. "I'm your second case?"

"You are, though I shall have nothing to report now I've made my confession. Mr Daventry will think me useless." She glanced out of the window as if the bleak weather reflected her future. "Perhaps I should wager on your next bout, for I doubt I shall make a good enquiry agent."

Something strange happened to him when in Miss Sands' company. She said things to dispel his anger. Did things to calm his inner inferno.

"Don't be annoyed with Mr Daventry," she continued when he failed to respond. "He feels a great responsibility to those who risk their lives in the name of justice. But he also thinks of you as his friend."

Dante would have let bitterness fester for hours until he reached the same conclusion. Miss Sands had saved him the trouble.

"As my friend, he should have come to me directly."

"Would you have told him the truth?" She didn't wait for an answer. "No. Because instinct says you've discovered something about your parents' murder and nothing is more important to you than that."

Dante sat back in the seat and observed this mystifying woman. It was as if she lived in his head and could hear every unspoken word. Like a silent thief, she'd entered his psyche and stolen his guarded secrets.

"Based on your insightful remark, you must have studied me for some time, Miss Sands." She must have watched him from a distance, followed him about town. Yet that did not explain how she knew of his recent discovery.

"I know what it's like to live with unanswered questions. Questions that burrow away like weevils until you're nothing but a host for them to feed on."

Any man listening to her weird ramblings might have her committed to an asylum. But Dante was no ordinary man. Everything she said made perfect sense.

"My father was murdered, too, Mr D'Angelo." She took a

moment to compose herself, to purse her lips and fight back tears. "My family kept it hidden for many years. I shall tell you more about it on the journey back to Howland Street. The details may be of some interest."

Why would he be interested in another man's death when he had enough misery of his own? But he knew from the tone of her voice this was a means for her to barter.

"The details? In exchange for what, Miss Sands?"

"For you telling me what you did not tell Mr Daventry."

Dante made no reply. All this talk of death roused unwelcome images, images usually suppressed by a bottle of brandy, a fistfight, or a good f—

"As your partner in this case, it is only prudent we—"

"Morbid talk leaves me restless, Miss Sands. Restlessness leaves me seeking stimulation. I agree to this bargain, agree to reveal yet another secret. But in return, I want something from you."

She clasped her hands to her chest. "What could you possibly want?"

"Permission to strip you bare."

Despite being dressed in a deep sensual red, despite the provoking black gloves that conjured erotic dreams of a silk-covered hand stroking his cock, Miss Sands' virgin lips trembled.

"Strip me bare?" She gulped.

"I speak metaphorically, of course." Yet he fancied playing games with this innocent, wanted to see her naked and vulnerable, as vulnerable as she made him feel. "I wish to ask questions of an intimate nature. To understand the woman, not the agent."

"Agreed," she said with surprising confidence. "A woman without experience can have little to impart."

"You may surprise yourself."

Oh, she underestimated the power of flirtation and lewd banter. Not that he had any interest in bedding a virgin—whimpering was not the sound he wished to hear when banishing his demons. But he could rid her of this stiff exterior, help relax those tight muscles, ease her trauma.

Noting they'd passed the Royal Exchange and were about to rattle to a stop outside the goldsmith shop near Birchin Lane,

Dante decided it was best he gave Miss Sands fair warning. As she'd rightly said, nothing was more important than catching Babington in the act.

"We're here. Should you do anything to hinder the case, anything to prevent me from gathering evidence against Babington, I shall terminate our working partnership. Is that clear, Miss Sands?"

Her strained smile failed to reveal the sweet dimples on her cheeks. "Crystal clear, sir. Though you might want to think twice before casting me aside. Particularly when I have something you want."

Damn. Miss Sands was a master puppeteer. She toyed with him as if he were a marionette, tugging his strings whenever she lost the upper hand, making him dance to her merry tune.

Perhaps he should take command of the controls, speak in the only way he knew would unnerve her. "Something I want? Daventry would likely banish me from the Order for bedding his only female agent."

A blush as red as her coat crept up her neck. "Must every conversation resort back to your sexual prowess? No. I have information you will find invaluable."

"Information about Babington?"

"No, sir. Information regarding the murder of your parents."

CHAPTER 4

THE PAINED LOOK on Mr D'Angelo's face tore at Beatrice's heart, as did the wavering light of hope that lasted mere seconds. Both were replaced by an icy stare capable of freezing one's blood.

The atmosphere in the carriage turned frigid.

He leant forward, resting his muscular arm on his equally solid thigh. "Do not toy with me in this matter."

Beatrice swallowed past the lump in her throat. "I would never make light of something so serious. But we will discuss it at length once we've questioned the goldsmith."

"You will tell me what you know now, Miss Sands."

The hint of breathlessness in his stern voice came from a lifetime spent searching for the truth. Beatrice had known of her father's murder for months, not years. Still, her lungs constricted whenever she envisioned his final moments, contemplated the injustice.

"Trust I will tell you everything once we've dealt with the goldsmith. I doubt you will be of a mind to work otherwise."

His snort of contempt sent a shiver to her toes. "Your memory fails you, madam. I trust next to no one, and certainly not a woman I have only just met."

Beatrice took a huge leap of faith and reached for his hand.

Mr D'Angelo flinched but did not pull away from her grasp.

"Then you must learn to trust me, sir. Rest assured, I shall give you every reason to have confidence in my character. There is nothing I want more than to help you find the devil responsible."

He stared at their clasped hands before looking her keenly in the eyes. "Then let me caution you on two points, Miss Sands. If you intend to stand on the battlefield with me, there can be no retreat."

Beatrice's heart thumped like the pounding of a war drum. "Like you, I am prepared to fight to the death to discover the truth. Like you, I have nothing else to live for." How could one forge a future when their past was a lie? "And your second point?"

His gaze slid from her eyes to her body with a slow appraisal. "We cannot be alone when you speak about my parents. I have but a few ways of dealing with my demons, and I would hate for lust to ruin what might be the beginning of a working friendship."

Lust? Good Lord!

Did he even find her attractive, or was that of no consequence?

"And I would hate for my inquisitive mind to take command of my senses, sir." Having had a bleak, lonely year since her aunt's death, she would likely submit at the first sign of affection. "I suggest we find a coffeehouse and discuss the matter there."

"Agreed." He glanced again at her dainty fingers entwined with his. "You may release me now, Miss Sands, for you have made your point."

"Yes, of course." She snatched her hand away. "And how shall we tackle the goldsmith? Gently? Or with a firm grasp of his jugular?"

Mr D'Angelo laughed. "As the lead agent in this case, the choice is yours. Whatever you decide, you must ensure we do not fail."

Panic flared. Thank heavens she'd learnt something from Alice Crouch. Criminals confessed when backed into a corner. Once trapped, escape was the primary objective.

Beatrice squared her shoulders. "Very well. I trust your acting skills are up to par and you're able to improvise."

"I'm accomplished in many things, Miss Sands, as you will soon discover."

As luck would have it, they were greeted by the proprietor and directed to the assistant, Mr Craddock, a barrel of a man whose fat fingers sported numerous sovereign rings, and whose name had been scrawled on the back of the trade card found in Mr Babington's study.

"Welcome!" The officious gentleman hurried around the counter to repeat his greeting. "Welcome." He smiled at Mr D'Angelo, revealing crooked, tobacco-stained teeth. "If you've come in search of a special gift for the lady, sir, you've come to the right place."

Mr D'Angelo placed his hand on Beatrice's back and guided her towards the counter. The brief touch sent her thoughts scattering, left her a little breathless.

"A special gift for a special lady," Mr D'Angelo said in a smooth drawl so opposed to his earlier icy tone. "Perhaps a pair of blue topaz earrings, though I fear you have nothing to match the vibrant sparkle of my beloved's eyes."

Mr Craddock took one look at Beatrice and gave a knowing wink. Ah, he believed her to be the mistress, not the wife. "She has the eyes of Venus herself, sir. Such beauty should be rewarded."

Beatrice leant closer and whispered, "Then I require a necklace to match. The most expensive you have, for it shall keep me fed and clothed when he tires of me."

Mr Craddock cast Mr D'Angelo a wary glance.

"Fetch a necklace, too, Craddock."

The assistant's paunch shook with excitement as he hastened to a display case and fumbled with his keys.

"A man never tires of a woman who stimulates his mind," Mr D'Angelo informed her. "A man never tires of a woman who holds him hostage and makes him wait to hear her secrets."

"That is good to know. And if you were to purchase a gift for me, sir, I would prefer something practical to something pretty."

"Practical?"

"A locket watch. Failing that, a donation to the orphanage."

Mr D'Angelo found her comment amusing. "You would prefer I feed an orphan than buy you a diamond and topaz necklace?"

"Benevolence is an attractive quality in a man."

"And yet I've never met a woman who said so."

"Perhaps you need to reconsider your social calendar."

His gaze dipped to her lips. "Perhaps I do."

Mr Craddock's return brought an end to their banter. "Here we have a diamond and topaz parure, sir." The stunning necklace and earrings sparkled in the black velvet box. "The necklace can be worn as two bracelets. The pendant removed and worn as a brooch. The rose-cut diamonds are of superb quality and together amount to twelve carats."

Beatrice gasped. "It's beautiful, Mr Craddock. But how can we be assured they are real diamonds and not paste imitations?"

Flabbergasted, Mr Craddock made an odd popping sound with his mouth. "Madam, I assure you, everything sold is of the highest quality, appraised by experts in the field. You'll find nothing finer."

"That is reassuring, sir, though one wonders why your appraisal of Mrs Emery's ormolu clock proved unfavourable. Or why you informed Mr Walters that the diamonds in his wife's ring were poorly cut, shallow, mere slivers."

Mr Craddock almost choked on his own spittle. "I beg your pardon?"

Beatrice glanced over her shoulder before leaning closer. "You lied, sir. You lied and informed them they should sell the items privately, encouraged them to place an advertisement in a certain periodical. You kept a record of the items, a record you sent to a gentleman whose face is marred by a purple birthmark."

Shock widened the man's eyes until they practically bulged from their sockets. "You must have me mistaken with some—"

"Do not test my patience, else I shall call the proprietor and discuss it with him." Beatrice firmed her jaw, imagining it was her aunt's odious husband standing behind the oak counter. Filthy scoundrel. "I stole evidence of your involvement from the gentleman's study last night. You made the mistake of signing your name on a document."

Mr Craddock's beady eyes flitted about as he scoured the shop for a means of escape.

"You cannot run. Not when you need funds to settle your debts. Run, and we're likely to find your bloated corpse bobbing in the Thames. I'm afraid your only option is to persuade us to turn a blind eye to your misdeeds."

Beatrice faced Mr D'Angelo, seeking his support.

"Should you doubt the lady's word, let me offer proof." Mr D'Angelo removed the trade card from his coat pocket. "This was attached to your correspondence. That *is* your name scribbled on the back?"

The man's ballooning cheeks flamed. "If it's money you want, you're out of luck. I haven't a penny to—"

"We want to know of your most recent correspondence." Mr D'Angelo straightened to his full, intimidating height. "I want the name and address of the last person you deceived, the person you advised to sell their heirloom privately."

Mr Craddock's bulbous lips quivered.

"Tell us now," Beatrice pressed, "else we shall be forced to call a constable. Both Mrs Emery and Mr Walker are willing to testify to your treachery."

After a few seconds deliberation where he scratched his head and mumbled like a madman, Mr Craddock took a pencil and piece of paper from a drawer beneath the counter and with shaky hands scribbled the details. He slipped it to Mr D'Angelo.

"Should the information prove false, I shall return after dark, drag you into an alley," Mr D'Angelo threatened. He snatched the note and scanned the man's scribblings before capturing Beatrice's elbow. "Come, let us leave Mr Craddock to contemplate his future."

"But what about the d-diamond and topaz parure?" Mr Craddock stammered as they made to leave. "The stones would complement the lady's eyes perfectly."

Mr D'Angelo cast Beatrice a sidelong glance. "Some women require men to give a little more thought to their gifts."

Beatrice smiled, though her stomach lurched when they stepped out onto Cornhill and Mr D'Angelo mentioned a coffee-house close by. He approached the carriage and informed Mr Bower of their intention before escorting Beatrice to a rowdy establishment further along the street.

Upon entering, he pointed to a particular booth occupied by four gentlemen, then slipped the waiter a few coins and waited while he ushered the men on their way.

"Do you always get what you want, sir?" Beatrice whispered as she settled into the booth. "Do people always do your bidding?"

"Usually," was all he said before ordering port wine, not coffee.

While a glass of port would calm her nerves, she ordered a cup of chocolate to settle her roiling stomach.

Amid the loud chatter of conversation and the bursts of laughter filling the crowded room, they remained silent. Beatrice thought to discuss what they had learned from Mr Craddock but knew the brooding gentleman opposite had but one topic on his mind.

When their drinks came, he downed his port and ordered another.

"I pray you won't prove a disappointment, Miss Sands." Tension radiated from every muscle, though his rich voice warmed her insides as much as the first few sips of chocolate.

"I'm not the sort to play coquette and give a gentleman false hope."

His coal-black gaze settled on her mouth. "No, I don't imagine you are, and yet you found yourself in a compromising position with a man who thought he had the right to take your innocence."

"I assure you, he received no encouragement from me."

"Tell me what happened."

Why did he not insist she speak about his parents' murder? Why was he avoiding the only question he wanted to ask? Fear, perhaps. She glanced at the cut above his brow. Sad that such a perfect specimen of masculinity might be unnerved by his emotions.

"It's not important," she said, gripping her cup to warm her hands.

"I wish to learn the identity of the man, so I know who to throttle should our paths ever cross. Someone must defend your honour."

"Beating him will not erase the nightmare. Besides, it's unlikely he will venture to town." John Sands was a gentleman of some standing in Rochester. Had he any intention of finding Beatrice, he would have paid men to hunt her down long ago.

"A beating cannot undo the past, no, but it will prevent a reoccurrence."

The bout of nausea came on suddenly, a gut-wrenching sickness at the thought of the devil touching her again. She would never forget his rancid breath and ugly grimace. Never forgive the betrayal.

Mr D'Angelo noticed her discomfort. "Tell me his name, and I shall ensure he never hurts you again."

What harm could it do? She had no family or reputation to protect, and Mr D'Angelo had better things to do than go traipsing to Rochester on a fool's errand. Indeed, when he discovered what she knew, avenging his parents would come before avenging her mistreatment.

"I have never told anyone what I am about to tell you now." She had told Alice snippets of the story but never mentioned the devil was a relation. "My mother died when I was two, my father when I was five. My aunt and uncle raised me, and I lived a relatively comfortable life until my aunt died last year."

Mr D'Angelo shifted on the wooden seat. "You've no siblings?"

"No, I am alone in the world, sir."

He finished his port and summoned the waiter to fetch another. "Please continue, Miss Sands."

The words got stuck in her throat, and her pulse raced as she mentally prepared for the uncomfortable revelation.

"In his grief, my aunt's husband began to behave differently towards me. Perhaps it was because I assumed her responsibilities." Beatrice often made excuses for him in her bid to understand the sudden change in character. "Weeks of improper comments preceded the drunken attack."

Mr D'Angelo cursed beneath his breath.

"I fled that night and have never returned." The panic and terror of it all bubbled acid-like in her stomach. "And so here I am today, sir, working as an agent because I happened to meet Miss Trimble at the Servants' Registry."

Through suspicious eyes, he stared at her for the longest time, his chest rising rapidly as if he had chased her uncle and already given him a good thrashing.

"Happened to meet Miss Trimble? Or did you seek her out?"

Even when struggling with emotion, the gentleman proved why he was considered an excellent enquiry agent.

Beatrice lifted her chin. "It was a chance encounter, though an extremely fortuitous one. I needed to meet you and knew you worked for the Order. Imagine my surprise when Miss Trimble told me of Mr Daventry's new venture."

"Ah, now we come to the denouement of your tale. The real reason you followed me along the moonlit path. The reason that has nothing to do with the fact we are investigating Mrs Emery's case."

She pushed her cup aside. "I wanted you to know me a little better before I told you about my father."

"Your father? I thought this was about the murder of mine."

"It is. My father was in the carriage with your parents the day they were all murdered by what most believe was a highway robber."

Mr D'Angelo frowned and snapped his head back. "I was in that carriage, Miss Sands. Besides my parents, the only other occupant was their steward."

Ah, her poor Papa!

Beatrice's throat tightened, almost blocking her airways, but she had to tell him everything while she had his undivided attention. "Yes, that is correct. My father, Mr Henry Watson, was shot first by all accounts."

With his elbows propped on the table and his bruised hands clasped, Mr D'Angelo studied her intently. "So, your name is not Miss Sands. You lied to me." Disdain dripped from those last few words.

"I did not lie. I took my aunt's name, for she wished never to remind anyone of the tragedy. Wished to keep it a secret, even from me, and so we moved to Rochester, and people assumed I was her daughter."

The muscle in his cheek twitched, and his lip curled into a sneer. "Rumour has it Watson stole from my father, that he arranged the robbery, but his accomplice betrayed him."

In a panic, Beatrice grabbed his arm. "That is a lie. A wicked lie."

He shrugged out of her grasp. "Is it? Then why would your aunt seek to relocate and change your name?"

"Out of fear. My father was not a steward. My father was an enquiry agent hired because your parents believed someone wished to kill them."

Beatrice rummaged in her reticule with trembling fingers and handed Mr D'Angelo the letter of appointment written by his father.

"This is proof, proof what I say is true."

Perhaps she should have waited until they had solved the widow's case before revealing the facts. But having lived for eighteen years believing a lie, she could not keep such vital information from Mr D'Angelo.

He snatched the letter as if she had the plague and the merest touch of her fingers would infect him too. His brusque manner softened as he read, though he cleared his throat and inhaled deeply when water filled his eyes.

"May I keep this?" His voice cracked, and so he reached for his port and swallowed the soothing nectar.

"Of course. I wish to assist you in any way I can and have other documents at home that might interest you. In her wisdom, my aunt kept them. Hid them in a chest beneath the silk gowns she inherited from my mother."

"Other documents?"

"Notes my father made regarding suspects. Details of a prior attempt on their lives. Though I am inclined to believe they knew their attacker and did not suspect him of treachery. My father would have been armed. Hence the reason he was shot first. I know it may be difficult for you to read—"

Without warning, Mr D'Angelo slid out of the booth. "Excuse me a moment." He marched to the rear of the coffee-house, spoke to the waiter who pointed to a narrow corridor.

A little shocked by his sudden departure, Beatrice waited. Perhaps he had downed his port too quickly and needed air. Perhaps the boyhood memories were too much to bear, and he was clutching the brick wall in the yard, casting up his accounts.

She sat fiddling with her fingers, not knowing what to do. Mr D'Angelo's pain was like a ferocious lion trapped in a cage. Angry. Savage. Should anyone step too close to the bars, he would likely claw and bite.

Minutes passed.

She motioned to the waiter who informed her the gentleman had thrust enough coins into his hand to pay for their drinks, that he'd asked about a rear exit.

Mr Bower appeared, his large frame towering above her as she sat hunched in the booth. "Mr D'Angelo has asked me to escort you home, Miss Sands."

"You've spoken to him?"

Mr Bower nodded.

"Where is he?"

A wince tainted Mr Bower's usually passive expression. "He remembered he had business in town and asked me to convey his apologies."

"Do not lie to me, Mr Bower. I'm not a chit making her debut."

"I beg your pardon, miss, but I am simply relaying the message. Mr D'Angelo insisted I see you safely back to Howland Street."

"I take it he is on foot."

A frown marred Mr Bower's brow. "If I may be so bold as to ask you to heed the gentleman's advice and leave him to his business."

Frustrated, Beatrice pushed out of the booth. "Very well. But I am not going home." She had to discuss the gentleman's odd behaviour with someone, and Alice was a fountain of knowledge when dealing with men's moods. "I wish to visit the Bull in the Barn tavern. Take me to Whitechapel, Mr Bower."

CHAPTER 5

THREE DAYS HAD PASSED since Dante made a hasty escape and left Miss Sands in the coffeehouse in Cornhill. She had sent letters, called at his house in Fitzroy Square and hammered loud enough to wake the dead. When all attempts to gain his attention failed, she resorted to contacting his friend and colleague Evan Sloane, worried Dante had ventured to the White Boar and taken a pounding.

He *had* gone to the White Boar to spar with his demons, though his bruised ribs failed to offer a much-needed diversion.

"Well?" Sloane relaxed back in the fireside chair, cradling a brandy goblet between his long fingers. "Do you not think you owe the lady an explanation? After all, she has something you want. And considering her father died while in your parents' employ, it is only right you include her in your plans for vengeance."

"I cannot deal with my own torment. How the hell am I supposed to deal with hers?" Time had not blurred the harrowing images but enhanced them. Bitter thoughts mingled with bad memories. They fed each other, two gluttons gorging on misery. "I watched her father perish. Am I to bear the guilt for her loss, too?"

"Guilt?" Sloane shook his head, confused. "You were a child. Why should you bear any responsibility for what happened?"

"I lived. They died." Dante drained the last drop of brandy from his glass. "Fate dealt me an ace card, why not them?" Although watching one's parents die could hardly be considered fortuitous.

"You lived because a coach approached and the blackguards fled. By the Lord's grace, you were spared."

Kill the boy last.

The two devils had argued about whether they needed to kill a child at all. The murdering bastard thought it necessary. Wounded boys grew into vengeful men. His accomplice lacked heart when it came to dimming the light in a youngster's eyes. Those few minutes had made all the difference.

"Did the Lord not spare the coachman, too? He lived despite taking a shot to the shoulder."

The servant died a few years later, drank himself into a stupor and toppled into the Thames. Had he been paid to stop the carriage at the roadside? Paid to aid in a murder?

"I think we both know why the coachman survived, and it had nothing to do with divine intervention," Sloane said, echoing Dante's suspicions. "Still, Miss Sands offers new information. There might be something written in her father's notes to lead you to the killer. Ought you not at least listen to what she has to say?"

"I will. I need a few days. A few days to calm—"

"You've had a few days."

Dante firmed his jaw and mentally darted behind his barricade. Sloane meant well, but if he did not retreat, Dante would haul out the canons, and he did not wish to attack his friend.

"Leave me be. Go home to your wife and let me drink away my troubles."

"Over the years, you've consumed enough brandy to fill a king's cellar, bedded women galore, beaten men to within an inch of their lives, and yet the pain is as raw as the day the bastard fired the shots. When will you realise your way of coping fails to bring the desired results?"

Every muscle in Dante's body tensed, fought fiercely against discussing the matter further. He craved peace, peace, not this incessant torment. But Sloane was determined to have his say.

"You've spent your adult life looking for the fiend. Miss Sands has the means to help you, yet it's as if you're teetering on a precipice and refuse to grab the rope."

Dante scrubbed his hand down his face. "And what if something should happen to Miss Sands? How am I to live with the fact I dragged her into this godforsaken mess?"

Sloane exhaled slowly. "Miss Sands is as determined as you when it comes to finding the man who killed her father. She intends to catch the devil whether you help her or not."

I'm prepared to fight to the death in the hope of discovering the truth.

Dante's temper cooled. Miss Sands was a kindred spirit, perhaps the only person who understood his internal struggle. One of the few who saw his weaknesses. But he did not want her compassion or pity. Didn't want her to see him as less of a man because he could not control his demons.

"Tomorrow you plan to catch Babington in the act of defrauding Mrs Monroe of her sapphire ring," Sloane continued. "Are you to follow him when he leaves? Attack him before he climbs into his carriage?"

"The plan is to wait for him inside his carriage." And then he would grab Babington by the throat and demand to know how he came to pawn a brooch ripped from Dante's mother's gown.

"Had you spoken to Miss Sands, you would know she is to don a disguise and take Mrs Monroe's place. She plans to corner Babington before he leaves the woman's house."

Dante shot to his feet. Blood pounded in his veins. "Has she lost her damn mind? Babington will see through her disguise." Dante needed leverage, something to trade if Babington were to spill his guts. "I need him to pay with a forged cheque, to leave the house with the ring."

"Miss Sands has other plans."

"Devil take it! Do you know what he'll do to her when he realises it's a trap? The man has no morals, no scruples."

"When you refused to answer your door or respond to her missives, she asked for my assistance. I'm to hide in the shadows and bear witness."

Dante released a torrent of curses.

"You only have yourself to blame," Sloane said calmly. "You

knew she'd been assigned the case. When you failed to inform her what you'd learnt on your trip to Cornhill, she visited that debt-ridden sluggard at the goldsmith shop and obtained details of Mrs Monroe's appraisal."

Admiration flickered to life in Dante's chest. He recalled her determination to have him inspect the books on Babington's shelf. Miss Sands had many fine qualities, but if he spent any length of time in her company, he was likely to corrupt her soul, ruin her for good.

"May I offer some advice?" Sloane said.

"Isn't that what you've been doing this last hour?" Dante mocked.

"Miss Sands is a rather unique woman. You cannot control her or cast her aside as you might do other women of your acquaintance. She will solve this case without you, likely find the man who killed her father. Vengeance will be hers, not yours."

"The woman has the will of the gods," Dante complained.

"Help her. Work with her. And I'm confident you will both find a way out of this nightmare."

Dante thought to fill his glass with brandy, but instead dropped into the chair and sighed. "Marriage has changed you, my friend, made you more philosophical, if not a little preachy."

Sloane smiled. "Love has changed me. Vivienne deserves a man of good sense, not a drunken buffoon who plays at being a pirate."

"Am I the only agent left who indulges in vices?"

"At present." Sloane's lips curled into a sly smile before he took a long sip of his brandy. "Though I doubt it will remain that way for long."

Having crept into the hall of Mrs Monroe's modest townhouse in Newman Street, Dante watched through the narrow gap in the door as Miss Sands invited Mr Babington to sit. She'd donned a white wig, a sheer black veil that blurred her delicate features, and widow's weeds—though the snug spencer had only drawn Dante's attention to the fullness of her breasts.

"You must forgive me, sir, but I had to let my housekeeper go when poor Wilfred died. My maid is so behind in her duties she is slow to respond to the bell." Miss Sands' voice quivered with nerves, but she brought her lace handkerchief to her nose and sniffed. "It is still difficult to believe he's gone."

"I understand, madam, but do not concern yourself. I took refreshment at my club." Babington was all kindness and consideration. "There is no need to trouble your maid."

"You are most obliging, Mr Greaves."

Greaves was the name Babington offered upon his arrival, the name he'd used to defraud his other victims.

"I would have preferred not to receive house calls, but needs must," Miss Sands continued, sounding desperately forlorn. "One must eat despite one's suffering."

"Indeed."

A strained silence ensued. Babington did not wish to appear too eager to make his purchase, and Miss Sands wished to drag more information from the unsuspecting man's lips.

"You must know that to part with such a precious item breaks my heart." Miss Sands made a little whimper. "Tell me your story, sir. Tell me you plan to give my beautiful ring to someone special who will treasure it as I have."

Babington cleared his throat. "It's a gift for my wife. A gift to celebrate the recent birth of our son."

Lying bastard!

"Then I hope it is to your satisfaction, sir, for I can rest knowing it will be a gift given out of love."

Miss Sands was somewhat naive. Gifts were given for ulterior motives. They were peace-making trophies. Objects to assuage a man's guilt. Bribes. Only once had he seen a gift given with honest affection.

"Indeed. Might I be bold enough to ask to see the ring, madam?"

"Of course, sir. You said your sister saw my small advertisement in the magazine at her modiste's."

Mr Craddock had advised all of Babington's known victims to place a discreet notice in the periodical distributed to modistes in town. Dante had spent days spying on the publisher until assured of his innocence.

"Yes, she noticed your elegant description and applied to the publisher for your direction. She believed it would make a perfect gift for my darling Anna."

Various women had applied to the publisher. Dante had traced all but one who had recently vacated a lodging house in Holborn. No doubt the woman sold favours for a living and knew when it was prudent to disappear.

Dante peered through the gap in the door and watched Miss Sands hand Babington the green leather box. The cad removed the sapphire fleur-de-lis ring and held it up to the light.

"Some consider it rather crudely made," she said, referring to Mr Craddock's appraisal, "but I've been told it's sixteenth century."

"I'm not sure I would agree," Babington replied. "I'm more inclined to think it a replica, albeit a rather convincing one. Might you have the original receipt or proof of purchase?"

Presumably, Craddock had informed him of the lack of provenance.

"Sadly not. Wilfred bought it in Stratford not long after we married but kept no paperwork." Miss Sands paused. "You should know I require two hundred pounds for the ring, sir."

"Two hundred pounds for a secondhand ring?" Babington sucked in a breath. "Be reasonable. I can give you a hundred in notes now, Mrs Monroe."

Dante's hands thrummed with the need to pummel the devious scoundrel. He wished they would hurry to the part where Babington gave the forged cheque and slipped the ring into his pocket.

"A hundred! Heavens. I cannot part with it for less than one hundred and eighty pounds, sir."

"Hmm." Babington fell silent while he continued examining the midnight blue sapphires. "That is more than I wished to pay."

"I have someone else calling to look at the ring later this afternoon," Miss Sands said, not wishing to make it too easy for

Babington. "Perhaps you should think on the matter, call tomorrow to see if it's still for sale."

No doubt Babington's heart raced at the prospect of losing such a valuable piece. By Dante's calculation, it was worth well over three hundred pounds.

"It is exactly what I'm looking for." Babington sounded resigned to the fact he would have to raise his offer. "Might you take a cheque written against Sir James Esdaile and Company? I took the liberty of writing it for one hundred and sixty pounds, presuming it was a fair offer for a ring of this description."

Babington delved into his coat pocket and presented the crisp note.

Miss Sands hesitated. "I'm afraid I must push you to a little higher, sir."

"You drive a hard bargain, Mrs Monroe."

"The money must supplement my paltry jointure."

"Then accept the cheque along with ten pounds. That's the highest I'm willing to go."

Based on the fact Babington intended to leave a forged cheque, he could have offered the full price, but he seemed to enjoy the cat-and-mouse game and did not wish to rouse his victim's suspicions.

"Very well." Miss Sands accepted Babington's payment, asked if he required written confirmation of the purchase, or if he would like to take tea. "A quiet house can be a depressing place, and I should like to hear more about your wife and son."

"Proof won't be necessary." Babington stood. "And I am eager to hurry home and present the gift to my wife. Perhaps I might arrange another time to call and take tea. I'm certain Anna would like to accompany me."

"That would be wonderful." Miss Sands clapped her hands. "But forgive me, I'm a little confused."

"Confused?"

"Who will you bring to tea when we both know you're not married?"

Good Lord! Dante thought he was to deal with Babington, prevent him from leaving and confront him with the truth. He'd not expected her to question the scoundrel's story.

Babington coughed. "I beg your pardon?"

"You've told me a tale, sir. You strike me as a man who indulges in all manner of vices. Your eyes are cold and hard and carry a selfish streak that is evident in the arrogant curl of your lips, evident in the way you grip your walking stick as if you might beat anyone who questions your intentions."

Walking stick? Dante had not witnessed Babington enter the house, and so this was Miss Sands' way of informing him the fiend had a weapon. Damn the woman for putting herself at risk when she could have let Dante deal with the matter.

Babington's rasping laugh was meant to intimidate. "A man must spin a tale to secure the best price. But the deed is done, Mrs Monroe. You have the cheque, and so I shall be on my way before you say something you may regret."

"Is that a threat, sir?" she said, raising her veil.

"Take it however you please, madam." He moved towards the door, blocking Dante's view. "Suffice to say, I shall refrain from calling again."

"When the magistrate discovers you've used fraudulent means to steal a sapphire ring, Mr Babington, you will struggle to make house calls from your cell in Newgate."

Babington remained motionless for a time, every muscle frozen, though in his mind he was surely plotting how he might silence the woman. A swipe with his stick would do the trick.

He swung around and raised his stick aloft. "You interfering old—"

Dante was about to rush into the room when Miss Sands cried, "Take one step closer, and I'll shoot."

Shoot? Shoot! She'd made no mention of a pistol.

Silence ensued—a stalemate.

Dante had no option but to make himself known lest Babington knock the pistol from Miss Sands' hand and bludgeon her to death.

"Lower your walking stick, Babington." Dante shoved open the door and blocked the exit. "Do not make a bad situation worse."

Babington took one look over his shoulder and cursed. "Dante D'Angelo. Should you not be catching villains instead of hounding innocent men? Are you so eager for work, you've taken to inventing crimes?"

"Inventing crimes? We've been collecting evidence against you for months. This little meeting is the culmination of our efforts."

Babington glanced at the drawing room window as if contemplating his escape. "You have me at a loss, D'Angelo. I saw Mrs Monroe's advertisement and wished to purchase her ring."

"But you've paid with a cheque drawn on Sir James Esdaile's bank," Miss Sands said, keeping her pocket pistol aimed at the devious gentleman. "We know you do not have an account there. Therefore, you used fraudulent means to steal from Mrs Monroe. It's a crime punishable by death."

Looking somewhat like a snared rabbit, Babington's beady eyes darted about in their sockets. There was only one way to save his neck, and so he charged at Dante, tried to knock him to the floor in a desperate attempt to flee.

Being used to brawling with much stronger men, Dante stood firm, looked for an opening and threw a punch that connected hard with Babington's jaw. Babington flew back, landing on Mrs Monroe's pink Aubusson rug.

Dante was at the writhing devil's side in seconds. He snatched his mother's brooch from his coat pocket, grabbed Babington by the throat and forced him to look at the decorative heirloom.

"You pawned this at McCarthy's in Holborn along with Mrs Emery's ormolu clock. You'll tell me how you came by it, or by God, I shall beat you to death."

Hatred surged in Dante's veins. Hatred tainted his blood.

Babington tried to prise Dante's vice-like fingers from his throat. "I've never seen it before."

"I don't care if you stole it, if you were given it in exchange for some other criminal deed. But you will tell me how you happened to pawn a brooch that was ripped from my mother's dress moments before she was murdered!"

Miss Sands' shocked gasp mirrored the surprise in Babington's eyes. He clutched Dante's hand in an attempt to catch his breath. "I—I cannot remember where I got the brooch."

"Tell him!" Miss Sands cried, darting from the chair to the floor. She aimed her pistol an inch above Babington's manhood. "Accidents happen during a scuffle. Tell him what he wants to know, else I shall pull the trigger. How will you service your mistresses then?"

The determination in her voice left Babington in no doubt she would follow through with her threat.

"Wait! Wait! I'll tell you. I stole it from a house in Wilson Street off Finsbury Square."

"Who lives there?" Dante's heart pounded so fast he could barely focus. Despite numerous trips to Italy to dig into his father's background, months of trawling through documents and estate ledgers, he had never found a motive for murder.

"A man I met at the Blue Jade. He hosts wild parties, keeps company with the scoundrels in the demi-monde."

"What's his name?" Miss Sands snapped before Dante could ask.

"Mr Coulter. Benjamin Coulter."

Dante committed the name to memory. "Tell me where you found it. Were there any other items of value? What made you steal this one? And why the hell has a man in your position taken to robbing trinkets?"

Again, Babington tugged at Dante's hand. "You're choking me." When Dante relaxed his grip, the rogue gasped a few deep breaths. "I found it in his desk, in a locked drawer. I stole the first things I found of any value, the brooch and a cheroot case."

Dante's blood ran cold. "Describe the case."

"I cannot recall—"

Miss Sands cocked the pistol.

"Wait! Wait! Black case. Gold trim. Lacquered papier mâché. A scene of a man on horseback surrounded by a pack of hunting dogs."

The description brought a vision of domestic bliss flashing into Dante's mind. He sat with his parents around the dining table, knowing his mother was about to present his father with a gift.

"I had it made in your likeness, my love." His mother's sweet voice filled his head, sending a warm glow to every cold corner of his heart. "And I know how you cherish those dogs."

His father captured her hand and brought her delicate fingers to his lips. "Not as much as I cherish you, *il mio amore*." He'd looked at Dante and smiled. "Cherish you and our beloved boy."

The heat in Dante's chest turned to gut-wrenching nausea. A sensation soon replaced by rage's red mist. "What the hell did you do with the case?"

Panic flashed in Babington's soulless eyes. "It was of little value. I sold it to the owner of a trinket shop in Bermondsey."

"Of little value?" Dante snarled. "Of little value!"

Lashing out was the only way to temper the devil's wrath burning in Dante's chest. His fist connected with Babington's nose, breaking the bone. Blood trickled from his nostril, the colour of claret, dark and dirty, not as clean and pure as Dante's mother's blood.

While Babington writhed and groaned, Dante pulled back his fist to throw a second punch, but Miss Sands grabbed his arm, tugged on his coat sleeve.

"No! Let Mr Daventry and the magistrate deal with the matter. Hitting him won't help you find the cheroot case."

She did not wait for a reply, but shot to her feet and hurried to the hall. Daventry, Sir Malcolm Langley—Chief Magistrate at Bow Street—and two constables were waiting in a carriage parked across the street. All four men followed Miss Sands into the house where she explained Babington's attempt to defraud Mrs Monroe.

"Mr Babington used the alias Mr Greaves, though he doesn't have an account at Sir James Esdaile's bank. Not only that, he admitted he stole items from a Mr Coulter who lives near Finsbury Square."

Damnation! Dante wished to keep that matter secret, at least until he'd visited Coulter and discovered how he'd come by the brooch and cheroot case.

"I shall have all the evidence we've gathered sent to Bow Street." Daventry addressed Sir Malcolm while the constables dragged the surprisingly quiet Babington to his feet and hauled him from the room. "Miss Sands and Mr D'Angelo will write a report and deliver it to your office this afternoon."

Miss Sands listened intently while Dante expressed concerns over Mr Babington's motive. The man had no gambling debts, no wife or mistress, could afford to host lavish parties yet seemed desperate for funds. It made no sense.

"The question we should ask is why Babington risked his neck to steal items worth paltry amounts." Blackmail was the only motive to spring to Dante's mind. "Babington must have spent a thousand pounds on champagne last week. So why risk the noose for a hundred and sixty pounds?"

Dante might have asked Miss Sands for her opinion were it not for the sudden shouts and screams in the street. His heart shot to his throat—every instinct warning they had underestimated Babington's cunning.

Dante raced to the window. "What the devil?" A crowd had gathered on Newman Street, a circle of people all staring at the same spot on the pavement. Men gawped. Women turned their heads, one gripping her companion's arm and pressing her horrified face to the sleeve of his coat. "I fear there's been an accident."

The thud of booted footsteps rang through the hall. A constable appeared, blood dripping from his nose, his lip split. "Come quickly, Sir Malcolm," he panted, supporting his arm as if it were broken at the elbow. "It's the felon, sir."

Sir Malcolm took one look at the state of his man and cried, "You let the bounder escape?"

"No, sir. Well, yes, sir, but he—"

"Which is it, Perkins?"

Dante caught a glimpse of a body, heard the cries of the crowd. "What your man is trying to say, Sir Malcolm, is that Babington is dead."

CHAPTER 6

It wasn't the sight of the wooden handle protruding from Mr Babington's blood-soaked chest that caused dismay. It wasn't the man's wide, lifeless eyes staring blankly at the heavens. Or that for one brief moment, Beatrice imagined seeing her father lying dead on the pavement. No. The tension radiating from Mr D'Angelo gave her the greatest cause for concern.

"I've seen it a hundred times before," Alice had said the day Beatrice returned to the Bull in the Barn tavern and asked for the woman's help. "The man's got bitterness in his blood. A sickness of the soul."

"What do you expect? His parents were murdered in front of him when he was eight years old. Witness accounts say he refused to let them wash his mother's blood from his face." Beatrice didn't know why she felt a need to defend Mr D'Angelo, not after he'd stormed out of the coffeehouse without explanation, left her sitting alone in a booth. "Miss Trimble thinks he'll be dead before spring. His coachman believes he'll be dead within a week of finding his parents' murderer."

Beatrice's heart ached at the thought. Sadness marred Dante D'Angelo's soul, not a sickness. And despite all reservations, she could not shake the feeling that her life's purpose was to drag him from the darkness.

"I can help him."

Alice disagreed. "Men like that don't change. They skulk about in the devil's lair, waiting for someone new to burn. Stay away. Leave him be."

"I can't."

She'd made an excuse, given her own need for vengeance as a reason to forge a friendship with the tortured agent. But during his brief bouts of weakness, she'd glimpsed the frightened boy locked in a mental prison.

"Then you'd best find a way of protecting yourself from the flames."

The whirring and clacking of a rattle tore Beatrice from her reverie. Amid the chaotic scene of men shouting and charging about the street, she snuggled beneath her blue pelisse and tried to focus on the gruesome spectacle.

"Gather witness statements!" Sir Malcolm cried to the numerous constables who had appeared upon hearing the high-pitched racket. "How does a man escape custody and end up dead within minutes? We need a description of the assailant. Fetch something to cover the body until the coroner arrives. And move these people along, Perkins."

Mr Daventry drew Beatrice and Mr D'Angelo aside. The man's dangerous aura made him almost as intimidating as Mr D'Angelo, except her heart didn't flutter every time she met his gaze.

"Return to Hart Street. I want to know exactly what happened during your time alone with Babington." He faced Mr D'Angelo. "No more games. I want to know why the hell you're keeping secrets."

"Perhaps Miss Sands can tell you. After all, you hired her to spy on me."

Mr Daventry slid Beatrice a look of displeasure, but said, "Good. I'm glad she told you. It means she's placed her faith and trust in the fact you will do what is right." He pulled his watch from his pocket and inspected the time. "I shall see you both in Hart Street at two o'clock. And I want the truth, D'Angelo, else I've no choice but to reconsider your position with the Order."

Mr D'Angelo mumbled his annoyance as soon as Mr Daventry was out of earshot. For a few seconds, he stared at the blood-soaked body while the constables jostled with dawdling bystanders. "No doubt you will tell him about my mother's brooch, about the mysterious Mr Coulter and the fact your father was an enquiry agent."

"Not if you don't want me to." She'd be a fool to cross Mr Daventry when he paid her wages and provided safe lodgings. But her loyalty lay with the man who'd spent a lifetime suffering. "My advice is we tell Mr Daventry everything, that we ask for his support in solving our parents' case. But I will respect your decision, will omit certain parts of the tale if that is your wish."

A curious look passed over his troubled features. "And risk dismissal? Risk going back to scrubbing vomit from the dusty boards of a tavern?"

Beatrice shrugged. "On the battlefield, one follows orders or men die. I just hope your deserting days are over. Hope you'll not abandon me to face the consequences alone."

The glance at his Hessian boots said he felt some remorse for his conduct at the coffeehouse. "Fight or flight. It's a common response to a threat, I'm told."

"I pose no threat. But I came to London to find my father's killer, and to escape the clutches of a madman. In the stews, people cannot afford to dwell on the tragedies of the past. I intend to follow their example, find the culprit and punish him—with or without you, Mr D'Angelo. Then I shall lay the past to rest and grant my father peace."

"I admire your spirit. The conscious mind strikes with steely determination. It is at night, when the devil resumes control, that one's resolve falters."

"The devil is in control when one tells lies and keeps secrets. Any pious man will tell you so. I'm sure Mr Daventry would let us use my father's notes to conduct an official investigation."

He made no reply but captured her elbow when the constables ushered them away from the scene. "Come. Let me escort you to the carriage. I shall meet you in Hart Street at two."

Panic tightened her throat. "You're not coming with me?"

Had the morbid events left him needing to drown his sorrows in a bottle of brandy? Worse still, did he seek satisfaction at the White Boar tavern? Did he intend to call on Mr Coulter without her?

"In the absence of the usual distractions, I find walking beneficial."

"But it's less than two miles to Hart Street, and we're not due for a couple of hours."

"I shall walk until our meeting with Daventry."

Her legs turned to lead weights at the thought of leaving him. Was it because she kept inventing sad stories, casting him in the lead role?

"May I accompany you?" She sounded like a desperate debutante keen to snare a husband. "You wished to strip me bare if I recall. I can walk with you while you delve into the dark recesses of my mind."

His rakish grin proved a welcome sight. "Intimate questions require an intimate setting, Miss Sands. A crowded, stench-filled street in London is hardly the place to expose your vulnerabilities."

"We can walk in silence if you prefer."

He hesitated.

If you want to help him, give him a reason to care.

Alice's words echoed in Beatrice's mind.

"Please, Mr D'Angelo. I cannot shake the image of Mr Babington's deathly stare, cannot help but draw comparisons with my father's last moments." It wasn't a lie. No doubt she would struggle to sleep tonight. "Let us talk about horses or hats or something other than what has occurred today."

"It's bitterly cold. Too cold to walk for hours. And you've no bonnet."

She thought to suggest stopping for a cup of chocolate, but refused to force herself on the man when he wished to be alone.

"I understand. There's no need to escort me to the carriage. I shall meet you at the office in Hart Street at two. Good day, Mr D'Angelo."

Without another word she turned and walked towards Little Castle Street where Mr Sharp and Mr Bower were waiting with the conveyance. She had the vehicle in sight before she heard footsteps pounding the pavement, heard the gentleman call her name.

"Miss Sands!"

She didn't stop.

"Miss Sands, wait!"

She pasted a smile and swung around, though the sight of his masculine form racing towards her stole her breath.

"Have you decided it's too cold to walk, sir?"

"Not at all," he said, practically skidding to a halt. "But it was selfish of me to dismiss your plea for help. If it's a distraction you seek, then I invite you to walk with me."

Beatrice suppressed the urge to clap her hands and celebrate her triumph. "Perhaps we could walk the length of Oxford Street and play a little game."

"I prefer playing games in private, Miss Sands."

"It's not that sort of game." Heavens, the man was an incorrigible flirt. "We examine the items in shop windows. You pick something to match my character, and I pick something to match yours. It's a much better way of getting to know a person than asking the usual dull questions."

His warm smile chased away the biting chill in the air. "It sounds like an interesting way to pass the time. No doubt it will help us both forget our troubles."

He instructed Mr Sharp to return to Fitzroy Square, said he would take a hackney from Hart Street later. "We've decided to walk, Bower," he informed Mr Daventry's man. "You may follow us if that is your instruction. Though it seems ridiculous that Miss Sands cannot walk with me when I was the one who stopped Babington bludgeoning her to death."

It was a slight exaggeration, but Beatrice held her tongue.

Mr Bower thought for a moment before climbing down from the box. "I'll inform Mr Daventry you're walking to Hart Street and meet you there."

The men exchanged glances, though nothing further was said.

When invited to do so, Beatrice slipped her hand in the crook of Mr D'Angelo's arm. The alluring smell of his cologne made her head spin, the scent evocative of pine forests in exotic locations, unreachable places halfway across the world. Or perhaps the heat of his body made her dizzy and caused the swirling in her stomach whenever they touched.

"Are you sure you want to walk?" He must have noticed her unsteady gait.

"I'm used to striding ahead, not promenading with a gentleman."

"We're in no rush," he said. "It will take but half an hour to cover the length of Oxford Street to the Tyburn Turnpike."

"In your ignorance, you have underestimated the lure of the game. It will take at least an hour to reach the turnpike."

He laughed, a sound deep and heart-warming. "I fight in dank cellars to suppress morbid thoughts, Miss Sands. You think you have what it takes to keep a scoundrel entertained for an hour?"

Beatrice grinned, though feared she'd soon be floundering. "Have I ever disappointed you, sir?" Heavens, it would take more than picking the right colour ribbon to keep this man expiring from boredom.

They began their journey into uncharted territory at the confectioners. An assortment of candied fruit, lemon drops, sugared almonds and liquorice squares filled the glass jars displayed behind the handsome window.

Beatrice brought Mr D'Angelo to a halt in front of the mouth-watering selection. "Well, sir, pick what you think suits my character best, and I shall choose something for you."

Mr D'Angelo looked highly amused as he rubbed his jaw and surveyed the delicious offerings. He studied the fancy labels, looked at her numerous times before saying, "For you, Miss Sands, I choose candied pineapple."

She arched a brow. "I have never tried pineapple."

"I know."

"How do you know?"

"Because I believe your aunt was rather frugal. You've spent months in the rookeries, and I doubt Miss Trimble lives life to excess."

Beatrice couldn't help but grin. "But what is it about pineapple that reminds you of me? Other than the fact they look prickly."

"There's nothing prickly about you, Miss Sands." He moistened his lips as if anticipating the flavour of the fruit. "Pineapples are rare. Highly coveted. The flesh tastes deliciously sweet, utterly divine. So divine, a man might gorge himself for hours."

Lord! He took flirtatious banter to new heights, was a master at lascivious discourse.

"Wait here, and I shall purchase our selection." A moment alone in the shop would help to cool her heated blood. "Then we shall see if I've chosen correctly."

He touched her arm. "Allow me to purchase our confectionary, Miss Sands."

"You may buy something from the next shop," she teased. "It's the silversmith's, and I cannot afford their extortionate prices."

He laughed again, but acquiesced.

She returned a minute later with a paper bag. "Now, who will go first?"

"Allow me." He reached inside the bag and retrieved a piece of candied pineapple. "Close your eyes, Miss Sands."

"What? Here on the street?"

"No one is paying us the slightest attention." His rich, sensual drawl stirred the hairs at her nape. "Open your mouth."

She shivered in anticipation, but closed her eyes and opened her mouth. Merciful heaven! The moment he ran the candied fruit over her bottom lip, her knees almost buckled.

"Bite down," he instructed. "Hard."

She did, tugging a small morsel with her teeth while he held the rest between his fingers. An intense fruitiness filled her mouth. Sweetness saturated her tongue.

She opened her eyes and met his amused gaze. "Hmm, you definitely made the right choice."

"I would suggest using your handkerchief to wipe the sugar from your lips, but you strike me as a woman who hates to waste anything."

"You're right." She swept her tongue over her lips without thought.

A hum resonated in his throat. "Perhaps an hour spent feeding you candied fruit might prove an entertaining pastime."

"But it's my turn to feed you, sir. Are you not curious to know what I picked?" She had chosen chocolate-covered marzipan for reasons she was about to explain.

"Chocolate?" He sounded disappointed when he removed the treat from the bag. "Why? Because my eyes are as black as my heart?"

"No, because the outside is hard and somewhat bitter, while the inside is softer and not at all displeasing."

"An interesting observation."

"Well, I am an enquiry agent and must look beyond what most people see. And I see you, Mr D'Angelo, with remarkable clarity."

He stared at her before closing his eyes and opening his mouth.

Mother Mary! She could have spent the entire hour gazing at his face, wondering if she might taste pain on his lips, if he was as skilled with his tongue as most ladies claimed.

"Bite down," she said, pushing the marzipan square into his mouth.

Mr D'Angelo bit through the chocolate, his pleasure evident in his groan of satisfaction. He opened his eyes and licked his lips while she gawped like a besotted fool.

"Rum-infused marzipan," he mused. "Why the rum?"

Because there was something intoxicating about him. Something that simulated her senses. "Because you often say or do things that surprise me." Lord, now he would likely ask her to explain. "Like today, when you changed your mind about walking with me."

And earlier this morning, when he'd called at Howland Street in an effort to make amends.

"Then, I hope you gain as much pleasure from my unpredictable nature as I did the rum." Before she could reply, he captured her elbow and guided her towards the silversmith shop.

Sun glinted off the array of silver plates, teapots and serving tureens, making it almost impossible to concentrate. Shielding their eyes from the glare, they spent a few minutes scouring the items in the bay window.

"Can you find anything suitable here, or shall we move on?" he said.

"No. I know what I would choose for you." She wasn't sure he would like her reasoning. "The silver tea tray."

"The tea tray?" His grin shifted from surprised to sinful. "Why, because you want me to play maid and service all your needs, Miss Sands?"

You may have to join him in the darkness, dearie. Catch him by surprise. Ease him slowly back towards the light.

"While I would like to see how well you stoke my fire—"

"Or how skilled I am at removing stays."

"Or how good you are at washing those hard to reach places, sir, that is not the reason for choosing the tray."

His gaze caressed the golden lock of hair grazing her cheek. "I could think of other duties I might perform when it's time for bed, but no doubt you wish to explain why I remind you of a cold metal tray."

"You don't remind me of a tray." She had to banish the image of him washing her back while she sat in the tub, of him pressing his lips to her damp nape. Oh, she had been lonely for far too long. "I would forge the tray into chest armour and insist you wear it whenever you went out. I worry you might take a lead ball to the heart and wish to alleviate my fears."

"Do not worry about my heart, Miss Sands. It perished a long time ago."

"The human body has a great propensity to heal. If there's one thing you should know about me, sir, it's that I never give up hope."

"I imagine you see the good in everyone."

"Not everyone. Just those worthy of redemption."

He did not reply, but turned to the window and scanned the items for sale. "For you, I choose the silver and agate letter opener. I would insist you keep it under your pillow at night, for once you start uncovering answers, the man who killed your father will most certainly hunt you down."

Fear threatened to steal her voice. If the veiled warning was supposed to act as a deterrent, then he had misjudged the strength of her conviction. She thought to remind him of the pact they'd made to stand firm on the battlefield, to work together to right a past injustice. But their meeting with Mr Daventry would stir his demons from their slumber, and so she decided to steer away from morbid topics.

"Why the agate and not the one with the silver handle?"

He grinned. "Because the rake in me would prefer you hold something warm in your palm."

Lord! The man knew how to elicit a reaction. When one was out of their depth, the only option was to keep paddling, and so she drew him to the next window, a shop selling silk fans, feathers and bonnets.

"The red masquerade mask," he said before she'd paused for breath.

"Why? Are you tired of seeing my face?"

Clearly he had a point to make because all evidence of amusement faded. "You're adept at hiding your feelings. You say you never give up hope, but the light in your eyes has dimmed. You speak of truths, but your words fail to reflect your inner struggle. You're terrified, terrified your life will end prematurely, terrified you'll suffer a similar fate to your parents, and so you pretend life has no value because it's the only way you can sleep at night. And so you take unnecessary risks, almost willing the gods to prove your theory."

Beatrice gulped.

Was she so transparent? Or was he simply a skilled enquiry agent?

"You sound so sure of my character, sir."

"It's like gazing into a looking glass, Miss Sands."

"We're alike in many ways," she agreed.

"Indeed, if this game has taught me anything, it's that we're kindred spirits. Like me, you thrive on passion and danger. Indeed, I fear your recklessness will get you killed."

CHAPTER 7

THEY ARRIVED in Hart Street promptly at two. While awaiting Lucius Daventry, Dante gave Miss Sands a tour of the house, introduced her to the housekeeper, explained why he worked for the Order, discussed anything to distract his mind from the conversation about the masquerade mask.

He had revealed too much. Spoken about the complexities of his own character, something he never did. But Miss Sands had a way of luring him out into the open, exposing every hidden facet.

I see you, Mr D'Angelo, with remarkable clarity.

He'd seen her, too. He'd seen the fire of hatred in her eyes as she aimed her pocket pistol at Babington's manhood. A burning need to punish all men who took advantage of the helpless. He had seen the woman busy constructing a life filled with intrigue and danger, a life as empty as his own.

"And so your work for the Order is a means of occupying your time," she'd stated while considering the picture of Themis hanging in the study. "Themis carries the scales of justice. After your experiences, you wish to ensure others do not suffer the same fate."

"And I hoped to hone my investigative skills."

"To aid in your bid to avenge the murder of your parents?"

"Indeed."

He knew what she was thinking—precisely what he'd been

thinking when he told her why he'd picked the mask—they shared similar goals, had similar motives. However, he'd had other reasons for making his choice.

The half-mask would draw attention to her mouth, to the pretty pink lips he wished to taste and explore. Red, because it spoke of everything primal—fire and blood, anger and danger. But red was the colour of lust and passion, and he suspected Miss Sands would embrace a romantic liaison with the same fervency she did most things.

The clip of booted footsteps in the hall dragged Dante to the present.

Lucius Daventry marched into the drawing room. "Forgive me for keeping you waiting. Sir Malcolm wished to take Craddock in for questioning, and I was keen to hear what the devil had to say."

"Did you learn anything new?"

"The names of two other victims. Babington promised Craddock that Mrs Monroe would be the last and had agreed to return the man's vowels."

"Did Craddock give a reason why Babington needed funds?" He wanted to ask if Craddock knew Mr Coulter but decided to avoid the topic of his mother's brooch.

"No, but Sir Malcolm's men will continue to probe for answers."

"Tea, Mr Daventry?" Miss Sands gestured to the silver pot and the plate of macaroons resting on the low table between the sofas. "I suggest you take one before Mr D'Angelo devours them all. He has a fondness for sweet biscuits."

"Thank you, but no. Mrs Gunning will bring coffee when the others arrive."

"The others?" she said.

Unable to hide his annoyance, Dante snapped, "He means Cole, Ashwood and Sloane. This is to be a family affair by all accounts."

Miss Sands cast him a mild look of reproach. "I'm sure Mr Daventry has his reasons for including them. It's unhealthy to jump to conclusions."

Too late. Dante's blood simmered. Every muscle in his body

tensed, ready for an argument. Perhaps Daventry wanted the men to investigate Babington, discover what drove a wealthy man to commit crimes. But gut instinct said the meeting was to discuss Dante's personal need for vengeance.

The sudden slam of the front door and the burst of lively chatter in the hall heralded the arrival of Dante's friends and colleagues—the gentlemen of the Order.

"Hmm, I smell macaroons." Noah Ashwood shot Dante a teasing glance. "Mrs Gunning has been spoiling you again, D'Angelo." He turned to Evan Sloane. "You know he squirrels them away in his pocket to nibble at his leisure."

Daventry noted the bruises marring Dante's knuckles. "Perhaps he saves them for when he's expended his energy at the fighting den in the cellar of the White Boar."

Hellfire!

Either Sharp had spilt his guts or Dante had a stalker.

Dante considered Miss Sands through narrowed eyes. Had she made notes on every conversation, informed Daventry in the hope of keeping her position?

"Do not think I betrayed your trust," she said, reading his mind. "Our private conversations are just that, sir, private."

"I followed you there." Daventry gestured for their colleagues to sit, though he remained standing. "I hid amongst the crowd and watched you brawl bare-chested. You fight as if you relish pain."

Miss Sands' gaze darted in Dante's direction, concern marring those pretty blue irises. "You fight bare-chested?"

A man didn't want his fine clothes stained with sweat and spittle and blood. "Clothes are cumbersome. They restrict movement."

Mrs Gunning entered carrying a coffee pot, the maid following behind, her tray laden with china. The housekeeper smiled when noticing there were but a few macaroons left on the plate.

"We will serve ourselves, Mrs Gunning," Daventry said.

The housekeeper knew from Daventry's tone that she should leave them to their business and so ushered the maid out into the hall and closed the drawing room door.

A heavy silence descended.

"Perhaps I should begin by introducing Miss Sands." Daventry smiled at the woman who'd slipped behind Dante's defences, then spent a few minutes justifying his reasons for hiring a female agent.

A blush stained Miss Sands' cheeks when Daventry mentioned women down on their luck, women needing to escape their tormentors, and Dante had a sudden urge to throttle the last breath from her uncle's lungs.

"Welcome to the Order, Miss Sands," Ashwood said in his suave voice.

"Thank you, Mr Ashwood. I hope to be an asset, not a liability."

Cole watched her through dark, intelligent eyes. "I think we can all attest to the fact that a woman's opinion has proven invaluable when solving our most recent cases."

Damn. Something foreign slithered to life in Dante's chest. Thank the Lord these handsome men loved their wives, for he did not want Miss Sands to find them intelligent or appealing.

"Miss Sands possesses remarkable insight," Dante said. Insight she'd used to delve deep into his psyche. "It was her idea to search the books in Babington's study, which resulted in us visiting the goldsmith and locating Babington's next victim."

Miss Sands' smile reached her eyes. "We worked together, Mr D'Angelo. Had you not given a helping hand, I might not have gained access to the study."

The memory of her white trousers raised a smile he couldn't suppress.

The other four men in the room stared.

"I'm sure we'll all get the chance to work with you, Miss Sands." Sloane had a mischievous twinkle in his eyes, but the man sought every opportunity to torment and tease.

Dante wondered how he would fare working with someone who knew so much about him. Someone who could elicit a host of odd reactions. "Indeed, one wonders why we've all been called here today."

Dante had been summoned to explain his actions.

Were the others summoned to bear witness?

Lucius Daventry moved to stand near the fireplace and clasped his hands behind his back. He faced Dante. "You may be an agent of the Order, but you're my friend. For that reason, I hope you understand what I'm about to do."

What the devil?

Dante's throat constricted. Was Daventry about to banish him from the Order? The rules were clear. No lies. No secrets. No personal vendettas.

Evidently fearing the worst, Ashwood sat forward. "We've all used vices to banish the demons. We've all seen things that make it hard to sleep at night. Fighting at the White Boar is merely D'Angelo's way of ridding his mind of harrowing images."

"I'm sure he'll agree to find other methods of dealing with his trauma," Cole added, making his plea to the judge.

Dante could not recall when he'd last felt a warm glow of affection. He couldn't think about his mother without a sudden pang of grief, and he'd spent his formative years with a grandmother who often grew tired of seeing his face. But these men were like brothers, as close as kin. Being expelled from the Order would be the second greatest tragedy of his life.

"I should have come to you," Dante said, knowing he only had himself to blame for his situation. "But I live to catch the devil who killed my parents. Vengeance is all-consuming."

He would die for his cause.

Nothing would deter him from his plan.

But for the first time, the thought of not being part of the Order, not seeing these men, never knowing the taste of Miss Sands' lips, made him question his reasoning.

Daventry nodded. "I understand. Nothing I say or do will stop you in your pursuit of justice." He turned his attention to those seated in the room. "Which is why I am assigning you all to the case of finding the fiend who murdered D'Angelo's parents."

Cursed saints!

Shock rendered Dante speechless.

A mix of emotions warred in his chest. Relief and anger battled like deadly enemies. What right did Daventry have to assume control? Dante would find the killer, would deliver the punishment. He'd witnessed the crime, suffered the loss, had his life torn apart. But it was a mammoth task for a man on his own. And if Dante died, who would play the avenger then? Miss Sands?

I intend to find the culprit and punish him.

The lady was not as strong as she would have people believe. In his absence, who would come to her aid? There were many ways a villain might silence a woman, some worse than death.

"D'Angelo will lead the investigation with Miss Sands' help," Daventry added. "You will do as he instructs, follow any potential leads."

Relief threw the finishing blow, relegating Dante's anger to the dust. "I've spent years searching for evidence, but to no avail."

Sloane cleared his throat. "But Miss Sands has her father's notes." He took a moment to inform Ashwood and Cole of the facts surrounding Miss Sands' connection to the case. From the look on Daventry's face, he already knew. "We will examine her father's findings and begin there."

Miss Sands shuffled in her seat. "I'm afraid I must offer a minor objection. Should Mr D'Angelo not read the notes first? He may need time to process the information, and we cannot discount his personal and emotional interest in the case."

Lord, this woman did not need to strip off her clothes to get Dante's attention. She stirred him to life with nothing but her thoughtful comments. Indeed, she might fool a man into thinking she cared.

"D'Angelo?" Daventry prompted.

"I agree with Miss Sands and wish to see what's written about my parents before we strip her father's theories apart."

"Mr D'Angelo may call at Howland Street and collect the notes," Miss Sands said. "Then he can plan a strategy, decide what information to use and what to discard."

"Agreed." Daventry moved to the low table and poured coffee into a china cup. "D'Angelo, you will call at Howland Street today once you've given Sir Malcolm your statement." He sat next to Sloane and sipped his beverage. "Now, perhaps it's best we all hear what happened with Babington and why a case of fraud has some connection to the death of your parents."

Dante sighed. There was little point in keeping secrets anymore. He explained how he'd located Mrs Emery's ormolu clock, how the pawnbroker in Holborn had purchased another item from Babington—a neo-classical cameo brooch with an image of a mother cradling her child.

"My father gave my mother the brooch when I was born. To make murder look like highway robbery, the man who shot my mother ripped it off her gown and shoved it into his pocket. From my father, he stole a pocket watch, seal ring and a cheroot case painted with a unique hunting design."

Miss Sands offered the plate of macaroons to the men. "Mr Babington stole both the brooch and the case from a Mr Benjamin Coulter who lives in Wilson Street, near Finsbury Square."

"Coulter hangs with a set from the demi-monde." Dante knew most scoundrels in the *ton*, but he did not know Coulter. The fact made him doubt Babington's word. "Though I can't say I've ever heard of him."

"Coulter?" Daventry frowned and repeated the name a few times. "Damian Wycliff knows every rogue who dances on the fringes of respectable society. I shall make enquiries, discover what I can about Benjamin Coulter."

Ashwood reached for a macaroon. "I suggest we gather here tomorrow afternoon to receive our instructions. In the meantime, I shall offer to assist Sir Malcolm. We should act quickly. Babington's death must be connected to the reason he defrauded vulnerable widows, stole precious belongings. He might have lied about Coulter."

"Cole will accompany you," Daventry instructed. "Sloane will interview those who work at the goldsmith shop and see if anyone knows Babington."

"And what shall I do, sir?" Miss Sands' melodic voice breezed through the room. "Perhaps I could visit Mr Craddock's home, make a list of his creditors, discover how Mr Babington came by the man's vowels."

Hell. The thought of her wandering the streets alone, probing into the louse's affairs, sent a shiver to Dante's toes.

"You have an assignment, Miss Sands." Daventry glanced at Dante. "You're to assist D'Angelo, ensure he behaves. Uncovering the truth will prove distressing. I trust you will be the voice of reason when he's battling his demons."

Damnation! He did not need coddling, but Daventry had a way of communicating silently, and it was clear he feared for Miss Sands' safety, too.

"Then I have a request." If he were to spend time with Miss Sands, he would do so without Miss Trimble's interference. "It is impossible to conduct an investigation while Miss Sands is still in leading strings. Inform Miss Trimble that the lady is perfectly safe in my care, and there is no need for Bower to play chaperone."

Daventry contemplated the request. "Miss Sands can decide if she requires Bower's assistance. I'll inform him and Miss Trimble of that fact. I take my responsibilities to Miss Sands seriously and hold you responsible should anything untoward happen."

Dante inclined his head in agreement.

Ashwood pushed to his feet and tugged the cuffs of his coat. "If there's nothing further, I shall call at Bow Street. See what use I can be to Sir Malcolm."

They all stood.

"D'Angelo, sit with Miss Sands when you read through the notes." Daventry spoke as if he'd read every traumatic line and could foresee how the night would end. "You may have questions, and she's the only person who can provide answers."

"While I agree wholeheartedly," Miss Sands began, "Mr D'Angelo should be free to make his own choice."

"It's a suggestion, not an order." The glimmer of compassion in Daventry's eyes spoke of a man who had struggled with his own difficult past and knew the importance of finding inner peace. "Rest assured, we'll catch this murdering rogue, but I warn you both, the truth is often different from the story we concoct in our minds."

"Greed is often the primary motive for killing innocent people," Miss Sands declared.

"Vengeance is another, Miss Sands, and you've made the classic mistake of presuming the victims are all innocent. Push personal feelings aside. Presume everyone in that carriage is guilty of wrongdoing."

Dante suppressed a sigh. He would have to treat this case like any other, too. "Unlike the law courts, we work differently in the Order. When it comes to vengeance as a motive, we assume the victims are guilty of some transgression and seek ways to prove the theory."

That said, the thought of a kind and caring woman like Daphne D'Angelo committing a sin was far beyond Dante's comprehension.

CHAPTER 8

NERVES MUST BE a familiar feeling for any woman awaiting Dante D'Angelo's arrival. Never had Beatrice experienced such a mix of emotions when in the company of a gentleman. The pulses of desire, the need to make him smile, to beat the demons from his door, had nothing to do with his handsome features or muscular physique. All the men of the Order were prime specimens of masculinity, yet she felt nothing when she looked into their eyes.

But it wasn't just the thought of being alone with Mr D'Angelo, alone in a candlelit room at night, that left her heart lodged in her throat. No. She feared how he would react when he read her father's notes, read his mother's statement where one could almost hear the ache in her voice as she made her heartbreaking confession.

A knock at the drawing room door made Beatrice jump.

Miss Trimble entered, her countenance carrying an air of disapproval which was only a mask to hide her deep concerns. "Mr D'Angelo has arrived. Shall I send him in?"

"If you would." Butterflies fluttered in Beatrice's chest, and he hadn't entered the room. "It's late. There's no need to bring tea. The gentleman will take port while scrutinising the documents."

Miss Trimble managed a weak smile. "You know to call if you need me."

"Thank you, but I assure you, I am perfectly safe with Mr D'Angelo."

The clip of his boots on the tiled floor raised her pulse a notch. He entered the room dressed in the immaculate blue coat and tan breeches he'd worn while throttling Mr Babington, and while teasing her senses with candied fruit. They'd parted after their meeting with Sir Malcolm. Mr D'Angelo had other business, hence the reason he agreed to call at Howland Street later, but she had the impression he needed time alone before delving into the secrets of the past.

"Miss Trimble seems more accommodating tonight." Mr D'Angelo's playful grin hid any reservations he might have about proceeding down this path, but his brief glance at the leather case on the seat beside her resulted in him swallowing deeply. "I know Daventry suggested we read the notes together, but you must be tired, and I prefer to study them alone."

Beatrice stood. She had been expecting such a reaction, a need to flee to a place where he could express his anger and frustration freely.

"Sir, may I call you by your given name?"

"Of course. It's—"

"Dante. I know. You're named after your paternal grandfather."

"He was extremely charming by all accounts."

"Then, your parents named you well."

Their gazes locked across a space that seemed cavernous. Indeed, there was every chance she might never reach him. And for a second she asked herself why she cared.

"I assume you will afford me the same courtesy, Miss Sands, or would you prefer I call you Miss Walton?"

Hearing her father's name spoken aloud brought to mind everything they'd both lost. "You may call me Beatrice. It seems ridiculous to adhere to formality when we know intimate details of each other's lives."

"Dante and Beatrice," he mused. "It's a tale of unrequited love."

"It's a Florentine tale of love at first sight, though to my knowledge we did not meet as children and you've not spent years pining."

"No." A light laugh escaped him, but his amusement died. "I've spent my life disconnecting, avoiding the intimacy of romantic relationships."

She shrugged. "In that, we are different, for I hope to fall in love and marry one day."

"You'd marry knowing life brings nothing but tragedy?" he said cynically. "You would risk experiencing the crippling pain of loss?"

"Every moment is a chance to learn, to grow, to love. We do our dearly departed a disservice if we do not forge ahead and create cherished memories. That's what I shall strive for when this is over—a life with more than fleeting glimpses of happiness."

He stood there, a silent observer.

"My aunt used to tuck me into bed at night and ask me to recall something special about the day," she continued. "The simple things like birdsong, the sweet taste of candied pineapple, witnessing the bonds of friendship that exist between a group of men."

"The sweeping stroke of your tongue when licking sugar from your lips." He spoke as if it were an erotic scene witnessed at the Blue Jade.

"Like a new and honest friendship where there is no need to hide behind a facade." She paused. "Let me sit with you, Dante, and help you decipher my father's scrawled notes."

Behind his proud countenance, she sensed an internal war raging.

"Miss Sands—"

"Beatrice," she corrected.

"Beatrice." The beginnings of a smile formed but faded. "You're a woman of virtue, and I'm a consummate seducer who will seek to corrupt you the second I witness anything remotely disturbing in those documents."

She straightened her shoulders, affronted he would think her so weak, so malleable to his will. "I'm not a child."

His rakish gaze traced a path down the column of her throat, stopping at the swell of her breasts. "No, you're by no means a child."

"And I'm quite capable of refusing your advances."

"Ah, now we come to the moment you call me a conceited fool." He closed the gap between them until he stood mere inches away. "Like me, you crave a distraction from your nightmares. Your body would betray you the second I slipped my tongue into your mouth."

"If you believe that, then you are a conceited fool." And yet her mind created a passionate scene, a wild and hungry mating of mouths, something to banish the loneliness and the horrid visions of a monster.

"Beatrice, were it not for the fact I promised Daventry I'd protect you, and the fact I enjoy your company immensely, I would invite you to put your theory to the test."

Why would she rise to the challenge when she was likely to fail? And so, she used one of Mr D'Angelo's escape tactics —avoidance.

"Does that mean you won't sit with me to read the notes?"

"It means I shall take the leather case and examine the contents in the privacy of my own home. Should I have any questions, I shall call on you in the morning, when the soft glow of candlelight isn't dancing over your lips. When the heat in the room isn't conducive to stripping off one's clothes."

Such seductive comments were a ploy to unnerve her.

"And yet one's body thrums with energy at sunrise," she teased, needing to gain some ground. "Alice said a man has a strong urge to make love in the morning."

"I'm not a man who makes love."

"You mean you avoid anything meaningful."

"Who's Alice?"

"The proprietor of the Bull in the Barn tavern in Whitechapel. She took me in when I had nowhere else to go."

"It must have been a difficult time."

"It was."

He held her gaze for seconds before capturing her hand. The brush of his lips against her knuckles sent heat pooling to the apex of her thighs. After the mad tussle with her uncle, she had never thought to feel anything but hatred for men. And yet something about this man held her spellbound.

"Enjoy the rest of your evening, Miss Sands." Offering a knowing grin, he reached past her and snatched the leather case. "Should I survive the night, we may discuss my findings over coffee tomorrow. Shall I come for you at noon?"

Survive the night!

For the next seventeen hours, she'd be beside herself with worry. What would he do when he discovered how his mother had suffered? Would he drink himself into oblivion, visit a haunt like the Blue Jade, attack some beast of a man in the cellar of a fighting den?

"Please, sir, you don't understand. Let me help—"

"I shall see you at noon tomorrow, Miss Sands."

Oh, the obstinate oaf!

She sighed but would have kicked the chair had she been alone. "Very well. Good evening, Mr D'Angelo. You know where to come should you have any questions. Call on me regardless of the hour."

He turned on his heel and strode towards the door, stopped to offer a bow before heading out into the night, to whatever wickedness would occupy him once he'd absorbed every harrowing detail.

Beatrice woke with a start. It was dark, and the fire had died to nought but glowing embers. She threw back the coverlet and leapt out of bed, followed her usual routine of pacing the room and wringing her hands until the horrible visions subsided.

Tonight, it wasn't visions of her uncle's lecherous grin that left her heart pounding. It wasn't the memory of Mr Babington's lifeless body, either, but that of Dante D'Angelo—blood-soaked and gasping his last breath.

The nightmare seemed so real. If she closed her eyes, she would be back in the fetid alley, the stench invading her nostrils, death's icy breath biting her cheeks. But she knew why she had dreamt about his mother, about Dante being the one who'd perished coming to her rescue—it was an account of an attack written in her father's notes.

In reality, some other man had died coming to his mother's aid, but Daphne D'Angelo had suffered terribly, had lost her unborn child in the fall.

Dante!

Was he reading that part now? Did he even know he'd lost a sibling along with everything else? Would the news be too much to bear?

Curse the devil!

She should have refused to let him leave with the leather case, insisted she sit with him while he absorbed the facts. Been a pillar of support.

Should I survive the night...

Beatrice stopped pacing. Fitzroy Square was but a five-minute walk, and men like Mr D'Angelo rarely tumbled into bed before dawn. She should go to him, try to prevent him from seeking solace in reckless pursuits.

While quickly dressing, other comments flitted through her mind. By his own admission he used lust to numb the pain, but he used brandy and port, too, and there were dusty bottles of liquor hidden at the back of the pantry.

Miss Trimble usually slept with one eye open, but Beatrice waited for the longcase clock in the hall to strike the hour before heading downstairs, thankful it was midnight, not one.

She hurried to Fitzroy Square, gripping a bottle and a pocket pistol beneath her thick cloak. Footpads lingered in affluent areas at night, though Mr D'Angelo's butler was the only mischief-maker Beatrice encountered.

"There is no one home, miss." The snooty fellow glared over his hooked nose. "Might I suggest you return at a respectable hour?"

He tried to close the door, but Beatrice wedged her booted foot in the gap. "Inform Mr D'Angelo that Miss Sands is here to discuss aspects of our current case. I am an enquiry agent for the Order."

"And I'm the Duke of Marlborough, miss."

"Good evening, Your Grace. Am I to understand you're refusing to inform Mr D'Angelo he has a caller?"

The butler sneered. "The master's instructions are clear, miss. No lady callers permitted day or night. A man's home is his sanctuary."

"But I am here out of concern for Mr D'Angelo's welfare."

"Yes, yes, you've come to soothe his woes. It's a story I've heard many times before. Now, if you will excuse me, I have—"

"Earlier this evening, I gave your master documents relating to the death of his parents. When he left me, he had the look of a man who might murder someone, if not himself. When a man dies alone at home, surely you know the butler is considered the most likely suspect."

The man rolled his eyes and was not the least bit intimidated.

"I shall tell the magistrate you refused me entrance, which is why I had no option but to brandish my pocket pistol." Beatrice aimed the weapon, and the poor devil jumped in fright. "If Mr D'Angelo wants me to leave, I will do so. You have my word. Now take me to him."

Fear and confusion marred the man's wrinkled features. Perhaps he thought her a spurned lover come to put a lead ball in Mr D'Angelo's chest.

Beatrice sighed. She lowered her weapon. "Take the pistol. Keep it until I'm ready to leave. I come with the intention of helping Mr D'Angelo through his torment, not harming him. All I ask is that you give him the choice."

He took the pistol from her outstretched hand but did not welcome her inside.

"If he does himself an injury, I shall hold you responsible."

With a huff of resignation, he said, "Follow me, miss."

She ambled behind, waited while he knocked on the drawing room door. Upon receiving no reply, she said, "Open it. I need to know all is well. Blame me if he's annoyed."

The butler inclined his head and pushed open the door.

Mr D'Angelo was sitting on the floor before a roaring fire, legs stretched out in front of him, his head tilted back against the sofa, his arms splayed wide. He wore nothing but a white open-necked shirt and tan breeches. Paper littered the floor, her

79

father's notes strewn about the rug. The leather case lay but a few feet from the door, as if he'd hurled it across the room in a vicious temper.

The butler cleared his throat. "There is someone here to see you, sir. I informed the lady you were averse to visitors, but she drew a pocket pistol and demanded an audience."

Mr D'Angelo did not move or open his eyes.

Panic seized her throat. She pushed past the butler and raced into the room. "Dante? Dante!"

"Miss Sands is here, sir."

Slowly, Dante opened his eyes and lowered his head. Thank the Lord! But her relief faded when he considered her through the eyes of a man who'd received a hundred lashes. Pain—raw and brutal—swam in irises as dark as death's door.

Beatrice placed the bottle on the floor, shrugged out of her cloak and thrust the garment at the butler. The servant glanced at her trousers and fine lawn shirt but kept an impassive expression.

"Leave us," she said, "and close the door."

"Sir?" The poor fellow was clearly conflicted.

"Do as the lady says, Bateson. Miss Sands may stay."

"Of course, sir."

The butler left, though Mr D'Angelo did not move or say a word.

Pull him out of the darkness.

"I brought liquor as I thought you'd need it." She snatched the bottle off the floor and wiped away the dust with her shirt sleeve. "Well, at least I hope it's liquor. I found it in the pantry." She pulled the stopper and sniffed. "It smells like brandy and cherries." She swigged from the bottle and almost choked when the fiery liquid scorched her throat. "Heavens. It tastes like brandy but not at all like cherries."

By some miracle, he managed a smile. "Let me try." He took the bottle, swallowed a mouthful and winced. "Two sips of this concoction and you'll lose sight of your inhibitions. Indeed, I'm surprised you trust yourself to get drunk with me."

She didn't trust herself at all in his company. "I thought liquor would be a tempting diversion. I feared you may have lost your mind and so sought a means to help you resist lustful temptations."

His laugh carried a hint of warning. "When I'm of sound mind I have to curb lustful fantasies of you, Miss Sands. If you know what's good for you, you'll take your brandy and hurry home."

He did an excellent job of masking his pain when in company, but she would not leave him alone with his nightmares.

"That's why I've worn trousers. I thought fiddling with a man's buttons might dampen your ardour." She couldn't help but look at the buttons on his breeches, at the muscular thighs fighting against the material.

"Madam, they're so loose on the hips I'd have them down with one tug. And I think you've forgotten the fact I find them as alluring on a woman as bare legs."

She sat on the floor amid the scattered paper. "Be that as it may, I came to offer my assistance. I thought you should have company when examining the notes. If you prefer, we can drink while you tell me of your wild escapades, and I shall tell you about my experiences in the rookeries."

Those black eyes softened. "I see. As a gentleman, you know I would never take advantage of a lady in her cups."

"Precisely." She grabbed the bottle from his hand and took a sip. "Though you may have to see me safely home. Mr Daventry will be most displeased if I'm arrested for disorderly conduct."

He watched her for a moment. "Were you always like this? Have you always looked to the injured and tried to heal them? Or has the time spent in the rookeries changed you in some inexplicable way?"

Life in the rookeries had strengthened her resolve. She had seen real struggles, good people forced to commit crimes. But like a ripple effect, one kind deed touched many, though it was often those with nothing who were most benevolent.

"In helping others, we help ourselves. Catching the murderer is important to both of us, and the darkness isn't so terrifying when you're holding someone's hand." She glanced at the discarded documents. "So, as the lead agent in our case, I—"

"You were the lead agent in Mrs Emery's case, not this one."

"Then if you wish to take charge of our new case, I suggest you give me instruction else I'm liable to ride roughshod over you, make you appear totally incompetent."

Any amusement in his eyes died. "Though loath to admit it, you were right. I can no longer deal with this alone. How can you read it and remain focused, objective?"

She had cried herself to sleep for weeks upon learning how her father died. Reading of Daphne D'Angelo's problems had touched her deeply, too. It didn't help that her aunt had kept it from her all these years, that she had no one but her depraved uncle to answer her questions.

"It gets easier. Like you, I dealt with it alone. But the need to unearth the truth and continue the work my father started is the only way to bring peace."

He fell silent for a time.

"So, as lead agent on the case, what do you propose we do, Miss Sands?"

"Lead agent?" Beatrice frowned. "But Mr Daventry said—"

"It will be our secret for the time being." He reached for the brandy and sipped from the bottle. "You can approach the facts objectively, whereas I often struggle to raise a rational thought. You've committed every word written in these documents to memory. You're logical while I'm irrational." He lowered his gaze and sighed. "Sometimes, a man needs someone to take his hand and lead him through the darkness."

CHAPTER 9

As a man who lived life as if it were worthless, Dante never asked for help. As a man free from the shackles of familial obligation, he did not rely on anyone for support. Distrust thumped in the hole left by his withered heart. Hatred lived there, too, hatred for the fiend who'd stolen more than a pretty brooch, hatred for the grandparents who'd mistreated a grieving boy.

The boy is of inferior stock. What use is he to me?

And yet Dante had chosen to place his faith in a woman who wore ill-fitting trousers and drank brandy that tasted like vinegar.

The reasons why were too complex to fathom, but she'd arrived at his darkest hour, her bright smile and witty banter like a ray of hope—a beacon of light.

"Then as the lead agent I wish to approach the matter using the fulcrum technique," she said, sitting beside him on the floor as if his pain were hers. "But Mr Daventry is right. There must be absolute honesty between us."

"The fulcrum technique?" Had she invented the term merely to raise a smile to his lips? "As in using a prop?"

"No. It's a matter of balance. We discuss something that may cause distress, memories you've buried and wish to avoid, followed by something unrelated. A topic of your choosing."

Ah, she referred to her earlier suggestion of bartering for

information. "And you will answer honestly when it's my turn to ask questions?"

"What was it you said? Intimate questions require an intimate setting?" She gazed around the candlelit room. "I have nothing to hide from you, Dante. Ask me anything if it will help you recall what happened the day our lives took a tragic turn."

She didn't wait for an answer but stood, set about gathering the strewn paper, recovering the leather case from where he'd flung it across the room in a fit of anger.

He watched every movement, studying her figure, examining the evidence. She'd dressed in a hurry, wore nothing beneath the unshapely white shirt she'd tucked into her trousers. Now and then, he caught the outline of her nipples, a sight that made his mouth water more than rum-soaked marzipan ever could.

"Are we to do it on the floor or shall we move to the sofa?" she asked.

The devil in his ear whispered, *Oh, I'd do you anywhere, love.*

"I've been here so long, I'm not sure I have the will to stand. And you should be careful with your phrasing when speaking to a scoundrel. A man might get the wrong impression."

Miss Sands glanced heavenward and tutted. "The floor it is, then." She sat down, clutching the leather case to her chest and ruining the view. "Now, I'm going to start at the beginning and repeat the events that occurred before the fatal shooting."

Nausea roiled in his stomach, but he nodded.

"Your mother met Alessandro D'Angelo at the opera. They were in adjacent boxes, and it's said they never took their eyes off each other all night."

Dante swallowed hard. "I do not recall reading that in the notes."

"No. While living with Alice, I made enquiries into their background." Her smile held a hint of pity. "They fell in love, madly in love. Lord Deighton intended his daughter to marry Lord Mooney's eldest son, but she eloped with her Italian lover, and her father never spoke to her again."

The evil bastard had disowned her, forbade her from using her title when she married a commoner. Above all, the earl liked donning a periwig, playing judge and delivering damning sentences.

"My grandfather took me in when my parents died and made me pay dearly for her error. You'll not have heard that while making your enquiries, Miss Sands, but I carry the scars, nonetheless."

She reached for his hand and gripped it tightly. "Trust me. It is better to expel the devil than bear the weight of his wickedness."

"Who told you that, the vicar?"

"No, Alice Crouch. When running a tavern in Whitechapel, one prays for salvation."

Dante laughed. Miss Sands had a way of calming his inner beast. He brought her hand to his lips and brushed his mouth across her knuckles. It was the only way he knew to say thank you.

"Your parents spent a few months in Italy but returned to live in Tidworth, Wiltshire," she continued but did not pull her hand from his grasp. "When you came of age, you sold the estate and purchased this property."

"Who wants to live in a house full of ghosts?" The horrific scenes of that fateful night haunted him whenever he ventured along that dark, lonely road.

"I believe the problems started a year before the fatal shooting. The housekeeper remembers a man calling at the house when your father was in Italy on business. Mrs Pickering said she heard your mother shouting and then crying and Daphne threw the fellow out."

Dante firmed his jaw and released her hand. "If you're implying my mother was involved in a clandestine affair, I suggest you think again."

Miss Sands took the fat-bottomed bottle, swigged the foul spirit and panted to cool the burn. "I'm not implying anything, but we must keep our minds open to all possibilities. Even so, I wrote to Mrs Pickering. She had nothing but praise for the couple, said they were totally devoted."

"They were."

"Then, we must presume this gentleman knew something damning. Something about your father's business dealings."

Dante found it hard to believe either of his parents had committed an offence that might have led to their murder.

"My uncle Lorenzo took control of my father's estates and business ventures until I came of age." He had wanted to take Dante to live with him in Italy, but the earl had used the full weight of his power to fight the decision. "Lorenzo examined every letter, every ledger. I've since sifted through the documents and found nothing incriminating. He interviewed stewards and housekeepers, concluded my father was a good and honest man whose life was snatched from him all too soon."

Dante's pulse raced as he battled with the memories, the injustice. The demons were stirring, getting ready to incite war. He needed to calm them if he hoped to make progress tonight.

"Then we must focus on your mother. In my father's notes—"

"Enough! Enough, Miss Sands. Please." He dragged his hand through his hair, softened his tone. "The balance seems heavily weighted on one side. It's my turn to probe your mind."

"Ask me anything, Mr D'Angelo." She sounded confident, but her long lashes fluttered wildly. He almost heard the portcullis come crashing down as she mentally withdrew to a place of safety. And one couldn't help but notice they both used formal address when battling emotions.

He might have asked if she'd had a good life until her aunt's death, if she remembered her father fondly, but it would bring them back to the case and he needed a moment to catch his breath.

"Tell me about life at the Bull in the Barn."

"There's not much to tell."

He suspected the opposite was true. "Did you feel safe there?"

The muscles in her cheeks twitched and distress lines formed on her brow. In those few silent seconds, he imagined a smoke-filled tavern where grubby men tugged at her skirts and made lewd suggestions.

"Safer than I felt huddled around a brazier in a dank alley. But it's loud and rowdy. One's nerves are constantly on edge."

She looked to the bottle on the floor between them. "Drink makes some men merry, some men monsters. But no one crosses Alice Crouch, and she took care of me."

For some reason, he felt immense gratitude to the madam of the tavern. "Did you not think to seek me out? Did you not think to approach me, explain our connection?" Would he have listened? Would he have treated her differently had she not been in Daventry's employ?

"I thought about it. I came to the Order's office and saw you standing in the street, laughing with Mr Sloane. But my uncle said people blamed my father for what happened, that I was the daughter of a traitor, and so I focused my efforts on reading the notes, trying to think of a way to prove his innocence." Her shoulders slumped. "Mr Daventry is right. My father is a suspect. I must assume he had a motive for not firing at the fiends, for not protecting your family, at least until I prove otherwise."

Damn!

Without realising it, he was back in the carriage, snippets of that dreadful night darting about in his mind.

"Your father is innocent, that much I do know."

She jerked to attention. "Innocent? Why? How do you know?"

Dante swallowed past the large lump in his throat. "Mr Watson gave my father his pistol and told him to wait in the carriage."

I'll distract them. Take the boy, Daphne. Take the boy and run.

"Watson climbed down and tried to reason with them, but they shot him." The bang, the sinister laughs, the screams, all filled his head. "So you see, your father died trying to protect my family. Despite the gossip, I believe he was an honest man, too."

Tears sprang to her eyes, yet she couldn't help but smile.

"Please don't cry," he pleaded ... begged.

Don't cry, Mama.

Bloody hell!

"Let's return to the topic of life in the tavern." He took a swig of the rotten brandy, for it was too much effort to stand and pour a decent drink.

She dried her eyes, seemed to understand what he needed,

seemed to understand him like no other woman could. The realisation left him wanting her more than he cared to admit. More than he'd wanted anyone.

"Are there any other rogues I need to beat for disrespecting you?" The stirring in his loins said he'd have to throttle himself if he didn't rein in his desire.

She managed a weak laugh. "You'd have to fight fifty men. In the rookeries, women make money any way they can. You cannot blame the men for making the usual assumptions."

When a man was at war with the world, he blamed everyone.

"You're three-and-twenty. Have you ever kissed a man?"

Her eyes widened, and he knew she had never kissed anyone freely, only the thieving reprobate who'd stolen a taste of her lips.

"Is it not time for me to ask you a question?" Her light tone belied the tension radiating from every muscle in her body.

"You may ask me a question when you've answered mine."

The resistance to confess was evident in her taut features. After exhaling deeply, she said, "I have felt but one man's lips on mine, but I would call it an assault, an assault on my person and my morals."

Oh, when he ventured to Rochester, Dante would knock her uncle's teeth down his throat and watch while the devil gnawed his own intestines.

"Have you ever met a man you wanted to kiss?"

She glanced at the open neck of his shirt. "Is this your idea of stripping me bare? Exposing my secrets? Revealing my scars?"

"Not all scars are visible." Dante wasn't sure why he stood, why he dragged his shirt over his head to reveal his bruised torso, but if this was to be a discussion about monsters, an exorcism of sorts, then it was only fitting he mentioned the deceased Earl of Deighton.

She sucked in a breath and shot to her feet. Her wide eyes settled on the purple bruises to his ribs. "Good Lord. Did you get those at the White Boar?" She moved to touch his marred skin but pulled her hand back as if she might scorch her fingers.

"The devil had fists like mallets." He captured her fingers, pressed them to the red scar crossing his pectoral muscle. "This,

I received when I was ten, punishment for slouching. Bruises heal, but this scar carries the truth of my grandfather's disdain."

He released his grip on her hand, expected her to step away, but she continued to trace the mark as if she had a magical ability to heal.

"You fight hard," she whispered, her fingers slipping lightly down his chest to his ribs—an examination and a caress. "Too hard. Save your energy for when we find the real culprit."

Her tender touch hardened his cock. "You didn't answer my question. Have you ever met a man you wanted to kiss?"

She gulped. "Only one."

"Then I shall have to beat him half to death, too."

She raised her head and met his gaze. "If these bruises are anything to go by, you've hurt yourself more than enough already."

The heat in her eyes encouraged him to be bold. "Is this where we barter? After your veiled confession, know that I've thought about kissing you for days. But I value your friendship, and Daventry is firm about such matters."

"As colleagues, there is a line we cannot cross," she agreed.

Then why did she continue stroking his chest?

Would it hurt to kiss her once? Did Daventry not suggest they support each other when remembering the traumas of the past? Perhaps it would prove a disappointment, and they could sidestep this attraction and concentrate on the case.

"And I imagine you're frightened, frightened any contact with a man might rouse memories you wish to forget."

She nodded. "I pray my fear amounts to nothing more than a problem with enclosed spaces."

"There's only one way to know. You've helped me tonight. Let me help you forget your troubles. One kiss. One kiss to banish the ghosts. One kiss from a man you desire."

He wasn't conceited. From her shallow breathing, the softness of her tone, the gentle sway of her body, he knew she craved his attention. He welcomed the distraction, too.

"The choice is yours." He glanced at the documents on the floor. "We can return to the matter of why a man attacked my

89

mother in an alley, why he killed the poor fellow who came to her aid."

Her gaze shifted to the scar on his chest. "You've suffered enough heartache tonight. We can meet at a coffeehouse in the morning and make a list of likely suspects. Begin there."

"And now?" If the sensual thrum of energy in the air was any indication, he'd be inside her mouth in seconds.

"Now? Perhaps you should kiss me, Dante, just so I might test a theory, you understand. There's every chance we'll both feel slightly underwhelmed."

Not if he could help it.

He brushed the backs of his fingers across her cheek, reached up into her loose coiffure and pulled the pins. Long, golden locks came tumbling down around her shoulders. *Hmm. Much better.* He slid his hand into her hair, welcomed her sweet sigh, gently cupped her nape and drew her close.

"This will be a kiss to satisfy a desire, not a theory," he whispered, tilting his head. "A kiss from a man whose only aim is to please you." He brushed his lips softly over hers, not wishing to frighten her with the depth of his experience. And for some inexplicable reason, he wanted to make every second last a lifetime. "We'll begin slowly."

He nipped her plump lips, sipping, not drinking, not yet.

Beatrice seemed to find his chest fascinating, or maybe she wasn't sure where to place her hands. He might have gathered her tight to his body, might have enveloped her in a steely embrace, let her feel the thick length of his arousal through the flimsy trousers. But he suspected she'd panic. And so he captured her hand and held it to his chest. A means to calm his pulse, temper his lust, but it only served to deepen his need to conquer and claim.

He fought it. Rained kisses along her jaw, down the column of her throat to distract him from wanting to thrust his tongue deep into her mouth. The plan might have worked had he been kissing any other inexperienced woman, but this temptress spoke to his carnal needs.

"Oh, Dante," she breathed, tilting her head and moaning her pleasure.

"You like that?"

"A great deal."

Damn. His body burned to push inside her warmth and he'd not yet explored the delights of her mouth. So much for a slow tutoring, for easing her gently into the wonders of a physical relationship. Too late. His lust had escaped its leash.

She'd have all of him. And she'd have it now.

"Forgive me."

"For what?" She was panting slightly.

"For rushing you."

He kissed her open-mouthed, possessing her as he'd wanted to do the first night they met, slipping his tongue over hers and feasting on her innocence.

She faltered, took a moment to find a rhythm, but when she did—holy hell—every sweet stroke left his cock throbbing, throbbing to push into her tight channel, to feel her hugging his hardness, to make sure she remembered being stretched and full long after they'd parted.

His control slipped. It didn't help that the minx moaned into his mouth, that he could feel her breasts pressing against his chest. It didn't help that he gripped her thigh, raised it over his hip and ground his erection against her sex, that everything about her was so bloody intoxicating.

Blood surged through his veins like a fast-flowing river. He was in danger of being swept away, of tugging off her damn trousers, spreading her wide and plunging deep.

With the wild roar of passion ringing in his ears, he'd failed to hear the knock on the front door, but whispers of Evan Sloane's voice drifted into his head, so close his friend could be standing in the hall.

"Move aside, Bateson. Don't pretend your master has a woman here as we both know he never entertains ladies at home."

"But, sir, you can't go in there without—"

Hell! Dante tore his mouth from Beatrice's luscious lips. She gasped for breath, stumbled back, but he caught her hand just as Sloane stormed into the drawing room.

Sloane came to an abrupt halt. He assessed the scene through the narrowed eyes of a skilled enquiry agent and grinned.

"Bateson was right. You do have company." He bowed, his gaze skimming the lady's unconventional attire and dishevelled appearance. "Good evening, Miss Sands. Forgive me, I expected to find D'Angelo alone. Indeed, I feared he might be about to head to the White Boar and have some lout pummel him senseless. I thought he might need a friend tonight."

Damnation.

Dante wasn't finished sampling Miss Sands' delights. But he supposed he should be grateful. Without Sloane's timely intervention, he would have struggled to temper his lustful cravings.

"I thought the same, Mr Sloane." Her cheeks glowed red. "Mr D'Angelo wished to read the documents alone, and I woke in a sudden panic, fearing this new information might be too much for him to bear."

Sloane glanced at Dante's bare chest. "There is no need to explain."

No, because it was obvious they'd been devouring each other, were seconds away from stripping off their clothes and writhing on the floor in a naked frenzy.

"Mr D'Angelo wanted to show me his scars."

"Indeed. One must be thankful they're all on his chest."

Dante grabbed his shirt and dragged it over his head. "I'm to see Miss Sands home. Why don't you pour yourself a drink and study the notes while you wait? I'll be ten minutes, no more."

"Ten minutes?" Sloane mocked.

Dante firmed his jaw and gave an inconspicuous nod, a sign for Sloane to cease with the teasing comments. Could he not see Miss Sands fought to hide her embarrassment?

"I shall fetch my cloak and meet you outside," she said, keen to make a hasty escape. "Good night, Mr Sloane. I'll be interested to hear your thoughts on the case."

Sloane inclined his head. "I shall give the matter my full attention."

She tucked her golden hair behind her ears and left the room. Having retreated to the hall, no doubt she took a moment to catch her breath, to close her eyes and chastise herself for succumbing to primal urges.

"I'll be back shortly." Dante tucked his shirt into his breeches.

Sloane stopped him before he reached the drawing room door. He lowered his voice. "Beneath the bravado, you're a good man, D'Angelo, and I love you like a brother. Miss Sands has struggled these last twelve months, and I'm sure you don't want to hurt her."

"Trust me. That's the last thing I want."

"Then have a care. She's not a courtesan, not someone to use and discard."

Dante resisted telling his friend to mind his own damn business. "I know who she is." A woman who brought calm to his chaotic world. A woman who affected him like no other woman had before. Someone rare. Someone special. Someone who deserved more than he could ever give.

He left the room, snatched the package from the console table in the hall, remained lost in the memory of her sumptuous mouth while Bateson helped him shrug into his greatcoat.

The brief walk to Howland Street was plagued by an uncomfortable silence. For the first time in his life, he wasn't sure what to say, what to do. He supposed he should apologise, but he was not sorry.

When the silence became deafening, he gripped her elbow and brought her to a halt. "Beatrice, about what happened before Sloane arrived."

"When I asked you to kiss me, and you did, so thoroughly?"

He could see through her feigned confidence. She didn't know how to deal with these odd emotions either.

"The kiss, I did not intend for it to be so ... so ..."

"Wild and passionate?"

He smiled. "I did not mean to overwhelm you, yet I got caught up in the moment. And I—" Hell! Why could he not construct a simple sentence?

"You don't want me to presume it was anything more than an experiment to see if my uncle's attentions have caused irreparable damage."

He could not reply.

That's not why he'd kissed her.

"One thing is clear," she said, a little choked. "I'm not frightened when I'm with you, Dante."

Her words touched him in a dormant place. He reached into the inside pocket of his greatcoat and removed the leather box. "I want you to have this. It's not a bribe, or a means to make amends for mistreating you tonight, but—"

"You did not mistreat me, Dante."

"It's a gift, a gift given from a desire to keep you safe."

Curiosity danced over her delicate features. She accepted his gift, smiled when she lifted the lid and stared at the object inside.

"A silver and agate letter opener."

"A practical gift to keep under your pillow."

"When did you have time to make the purchase?"

"I went before returning home this evening. I hammered the door, dragged the proprietor from his supper and paid over the odds for the inconvenience."

He had never given anyone a gift, yet the sheer joy on her face played havoc with his heart.

"Thank you. I shall treasure it always." She cupped his cheek with her cold hand and pressed her lips to his. It was a chaste kiss—an intimate thank you—but he felt the essence of the woman infuse every aspect of his being.

"Good night, Miss Sands. I shall wait here and watch until you're safely inside. Perhaps it's unwise for us to meet at a coffeehouse tomorrow."

Her smile slipped.

"I mean, we must insist on privacy when discussing the case," he explained. "I suggest we meet at the office in Hart Street at noon, command use of the study."

They needed to begin their investigation despite the fact he found the evidence distressing, regardless of the fact he couldn't concentrate in her company.

"That's an excellent idea. Until tomorrow, Mr D'Angelo. Good night."

"Good night."

Dante watched until she entered the house. He ignored the tug in his gut that would have him racing after her, sweeping her up into his arms and carrying her to bed. Indeed, he'd struggle to be alone with her without thinking about that kiss. In Hart Street, his colleagues would be flitting back and forth, making it impossible for him to devour her mouth with the same reckless abandon. At least he prayed that would be the case. Above all else, he did not want to hurt a woman who'd suffered enough.

CHAPTER 10

To Beatrice's surprise, she found Mr D'Angelo sitting behind the desk in the study when she arrived in Hart Street. She'd come half an hour early, needing to focus her mind on their investigation, needing to maintain a professional air after their intimate interlude last night.

But the sight of him roused thoughts of his bare chest, scarred and bruised, of her need to press her mouth to his bronzed skin and kiss his wounds. Similar thoughts had kept her awake most of the night, as had the memory of his tongue slipping into her mouth and luring hers into an erotic dance.

He looked up from whatever he was reading, and her heart lurched. "Miss Sands? Forgive me, I didn't hear you come in."

She might have challenged him. How could a skilled agent not sense her presence? But there was something different about him today, as if his muscles were restrained by a straitjacket worn beneath his expertly tailored coat.

She motioned to the papers littering the desk. "You've started without me, I see."

"I am merely reading through your father's notes."

Was that why he seemed so stiff, so reserved, so formal? Was he battling to keep his emotions at bay? Was this his way of coping?

"Did Mr Sloane have a chance to study them?" She began

unfastening her pelisse, but her fingers seemed incapable of gripping the buttons. "Did he offer an opinion?"

From Dante's awkward pause, she knew Mr Sloane had discussed the reason he'd almost found them in a passionate embrace, and not his thoughts on the case.

"Something occurred to me after speaking to Sloane last night."

"It did?" Her pulse thumped in her throat. Would he advise they keep their distance? Did he regret offering to help her forget her trauma?

Oh, he'd made her forget everything but the taste of him.

"You said my parents hired your father because of a previous attempt on their lives. They believed someone wanted them dead. Correct?"

"That's what my uncle said when I confronted him with the evidence I found in the chest." She was relieved he wanted to discuss the case and not their intimate exchange. "He seemed shocked and clearly had no notion my aunt had kept the leather case."

John Sands had tried to take the documents and read them for himself. But Beatrice had already switched her father's notes with letters she had stolen from her uncle's study. And so she'd emptied the contents into the fire blazing in the hearth before he could offer any protest.

Dante pushed a letter across the desk. Beatrice took it and peeled back the folds, though she knew it was the letter of appointment she had given him in the coffeehouse six days ago.

"My father hired Mr Watson in the December of 1804, three months before someone attacked my mother in an alley. Now, unless there was a prior attack, we must assume he had another reason for seeking the services of an enquiry agent."

Beatrice studied the date scrawled on the page. "Though Mrs Pickering's statement isn't dated, she said the man who called at the house in Tidworth came when your father was in Italy. Evidently that's when the problems started, and so the attack must have had something to do with the reason your mother threw him out."

"My father was away in Italy in the October of that year. I've seen a letter written by him promising to be home for Christmas. I've spent the morning examining these notes, and there's an obvious discrepancy, a discrepancy easily overlooked when one has a personal interest in every harrowing detail."

Guilt surfaced, along with a sense of inadequacy.

What had she missed?

"Give me a moment. Let me sit so I might concentrate and take notes." She managed to undo the buttons and shrug out of her pelisse.

"Shall I ring for Mrs Gunning to bring tea?" he said.

"No. Once we begin, I'd rather not be disturbed."

"Indeed." He watched her intently as she draped the garment over the chair, his gaze roaming over the lilac day dress she'd worn because it flattered her figure and gave her a boost of confidence. "Perhaps you should close the door."

"Of course."

He waited for her to sit, for her to take her black notebook and pencil from her reticule and give him her undivided attention.

"You spoke of a discrepancy," she prompted.

"It's more an inconsistency." He motioned to the papers spread out on the desk. "Clearly this isn't a year's worth of work. When we work on a case, we record every comment, every statement, every description given. We date the records and file them." He gestured to the walnut drawers lining the wall at the far end of the room. "Daventry insists on keeping meticulous records."

Beatrice knew how important it was to keep accurate accounts. Men had been hung from the gallows because of misplaced evidence.

"You mean pages are missing. When I showed my uncle the contents of the leather case, he said my aunt must have taken it as a keepsake, a memento. But I find that odd, unless she took only what she could find."

Why hadn't Aunt Margaret cut a lock of her brother's hair, or kept his signet ring? Beatrice remembered sitting on her father's lap and tracing her tiny finger over the initials engraved into the gold. Had he been buried with the ring? Because she'd not seen it since.

"Precisely. So what happened to the rest of your father's work?"

"I have no idea."

Beatrice knew very little about her life before moving to Rochester.

"It's not just that. Mrs Pickering's statement lacks basic information. There's no description of the caller, no mention of the name given. We don't know how long he stayed, if he came on horseback, by foot or by carriage. We don't know what my mother did when he left."

Beatrice grew a little defensive. "I'm sure my father asked those questions. His notes on the attack in the alley are extremely thorough."

"Indeed, so thorough they contain an important piece of evidence." He took a few calming breaths. "The brute attacked my mother in White Cross Alley in the parish of Shoreditch. One might ask what she was doing there alone and on foot, but Sloane said the alley leads off Wilson Street."

"Wilson Street? Mr Coulter lives on Wilson Street."

"Exactly. The question is, did Mr Coulter live on Wilson Street in the spring of 1805? If not, perhaps we're looking for a relative."

Beatrice's heart raced. It couldn't be a coincidence and was the first new piece of evidence they had. She made a note of it in her book before looking at Mr D'Angelo. His expression remained impassive, but his heart must be pounding too.

"I shall add Mr Coulter to our list of suspects."

He propped his elbows on the desk and steepled his fingers. "We need to go back to the beginning, unravel every tangled thread in this web of deceit."

"Then we should visit Mrs Pickering and take her statement." Beatrice was desperate to know if her father had asked pertinent questions or if he'd deliberately avoided recording anything that might identify the villain. "And we must discover why Alessandro D'Angelo sought my father's help."

At some point she needed to take Dante's statement, too,

have him relive that dreadful carriage ride. He might hold a vital clue to the mystery and be totally unaware. But he wasn't ready to make the journey, not yet.

"Agreed. You said you wrote to Mrs Pickering. Did someone in Tidworth give you her forwarding address?"

Beatrice frowned. Did he not know what happened to the housekeeper? "Mrs Pickering is still the housekeeper at Farthingdale. When you sold the estate, the new owners wanted someone with experience."

Dante closed his eyes briefly, pinched the bridge of his nose, heaved a sigh. "When I inherited, I told Lorenzo I wanted rid of Farthingdale, wanted to sell it intact, and he dealt with the matter on my behalf."

"I see."

And she did see. Dante didn't wish to hear of people haggling over his parents' belongings. Had he kept nothing from the house? Did he regret the decision? Was that why he clung to the brooch, or was it nothing more than a useful piece of evidence?

"Perhaps I will take coffee," she said, pushing to her feet. "I shall nip and ask Mrs Gunning to make a pot, as we're likely to be here all day. I won't be long."

Beatrice left him alone and went in search of the housekeeper.

"You must ring if you need anything," Mrs Gunning said.

"Mr D'Angelo is studying evidence, and I didn't want to disturb him."

Mrs Gunning gave a sad sigh. "He's been here for hours, said he couldn't sleep, said that by reading about what happened to his mother in the alley, he hopes to become numb to the words."

Beatrice touched Mrs Gunning's arm. "Once we find the culprit, I'm certain he will focus on building a bright future and not wallow in the memories of the past." She wasn't certain at all, but lived in hope.

The woman offered a weak smile. "I pray you're right, miss. But I'm not sure it's good for him, reliving it day after day."

No. Most people would break under the pressure.

Beatrice returned to the study to find Dante staring at the wall, lost in thought. "Mrs Gunning will bring coffee and biscuits shortly." She smoothed her skirts and returned to sit in the chair opposite the desk. "I thought we might send Mr Sloane to Farthingdale. He has a manner most women find appealing. No doubt Mrs Pickering will melt beneath the richness of his voice and the warmth of his emerald stare."

"You find Sloane's manner appealing, Miss Sands?"

"In a brotherly way. I had the pleasure of meeting his wife two weeks ago. Vivienne came to Howland Street to help me with Mrs Emery's case." She'd suggested Beatrice meet Dante, thought they'd have a better chance of success if they worked together.

"Sloane vowed never to marry, but he fell in love."

"They seem happy."

"Ridiculously so."

While Dante gave no cause to think he was anything but delighted for his friend, those dark eyes held a hint of sadness.

"Are we agreed?" she said, concentrating on the matter at hand. "Mr Sloane will go to Farthingdale and take the house-keeper's statement?"

"Yes."

"And I thought Mr Cole could investigate Mr Coulter. It's best you're not seen in the vicinity of Wilson Street. If Mr Coulter knew your mother, then there's every likelihood he knows you."

"Agreed."

"Have you thought where we might begin our enquiries?"

Silence descended like a hazy mist of suspicion.

"Your father struck me as a man of means. When he died, what happened to his property?" Dante must have realised he sounded quite blunt, and so softened his tone. "There's a chance the attacks are unrelated. Perhaps the culprit wished to silence your father and had no choice but to dispense with the witnesses. Was he working on another case before Alessandro hired him?"

What? He suspected Henry Watson was the intended target? Surely not. No. She couldn't bear the thought of innocent people losing their lives because of her father's profession.

"I know very little about my father. My aunt and uncle rarely spoke about my parents. They found it too upsetting."

Equally, the question of her father's property raised an important issue, one she had been struggling with for some time. One she hoped to solve with her newly acquired skills as an agent and her contacts within the Order.

Beatrice cleared her throat. "I have reason to believe I inherited my father's house, though I have never seen the will, never received any communication from his solicitor, and have no proof the property belongs to me."

Dante frowned. "Where is the house?"

Heat rose to her cheeks. "I don't know."

"You don't know? Where did you live before moving to Rochester?"

She shrugged. "I was but five years old and remember next to nothing. Aunt Margaret avoided the topic, said there was no point dredging up old memories. But I believe we moved from Hampshire."

"Hampshire?" The chair creaked as Dante sat back. He considered her through narrowed eyes, and it seemed like an age before he spoke. "It's time to switch roles, Beatrice." The fact he'd uttered her given name with some tenderness caused alarm. "We have one obvious line of enquiry, a matter we must address before we can proceed with our investigation."

"Which is?" Her heart stopped for a beat or two.

"This is where I ply you with brandy to numb the senses. Where I take your hand and lead you through the darkness."

The darkness? But the only wickedness she'd encountered was—

Fear took command of her senses as she came to the obvious conclusion. "Please tell me you're not suggesting we question my uncle?"

"You know it is the only logical course of action."

Beatrice shot from the chair. She had to grip the desk for balance as blood rushed to her head. "No, Dante." No! No! Please, no! "I cannot go back there."

Tears sprang to her eyes. Sheer terror gripped her throat.

"No," she reiterated. "There must be another way to find the information. Perhaps Mrs Pickering knows where my father lived." When one was swept away by a raging torrent, one clung to any blade of grass sprouting from the riverbank.

Dante stood, rounded the desk and took hold of her arms. "I know how hard it is to confront your nightmares, but you must see we have no option."

"No, no. I need more time." A lifetime would be insufficient.

"There is never a right time. But you can meet him in a public place, the taproom of the local tavern. I doubt he will speak honestly to me, so you must drag the truth from his lips by any means necessary, lie, make false promises. I shall watch from the next table. We'll take Ashwood. He can search your uncle's house while we keep the devil occupied."

Her whole body shook in response. She had stopped listening when she realised she would have to sit with the scoundrel.

"Dante, what's logical is me taking your statement, is you recounting every minute of that carriage ride eighteen years ago. But I would not ask it of you. Please don't ask this of me."

Without warning, he pressed his lips to her forehead—a reassuring gesture, though her stomach flipped when he kissed her temple and inhaled the scent of her hair.

If she looked up, gazed into his eyes, she sensed there would be a repeat of what happened last night. And while she wanted nothing more than to feel the heat of his lips, to draw in the earthy essence of the man she cared for more than she should, Mrs Gunning was likely to knock on the door at any moment.

Instead, she fell into his arms, pressed her cheek to his chest and listened to his erratic heartbeat.

"Dante, my uncle has a way of manipulating me, of making me pity him. That's how he lured me into his trap, how he hurt me." The pain of betrayal went deeper than sore lips and bruised thighs. They'd healed within days. "I'm too weak to—"

"You're strong, courageous." He kissed the top of her head and stroked her hair. "You've helped me more than you know, and I believe confronting your uncle will help you, too."

The more he spoke, the more she thought of slanting her lips over his and exploring the warm, wet depths of his mouth. Now she knew why he used lust as a distraction. Lust had a way of commanding one's senses, of emptying the mind of anything but the clawing need for pleasure.

The brief clip of footsteps in the hall preceded the study door bursting open. Beatrice shot back, would have stumbled again had Dante not gripped her elbow. Upon hearing a cough too deep to be that of Mrs Gunning, she dared to glance at the door.

Mr Ashwood stood in the doorway, wearing a grin similar to that of Mr Sloane's the previous evening. Now they just needed Mr Cole to catch them in a clinch, and all the gentlemen of the Order would know of her attraction to their colleague.

"Miss Sands is a little distraught." Dante did not turn around but kept his gaze trained on her. He seemed annoyed by the interruption. "We're both finding aspects of this case difficult to deal with."

"Indeed," came the only smooth word from Mr Ashwood's lips.

Thankfully, Mrs Gunning appeared, carrying the tea tray. Mr Ashwood relieved her of the heavy burden, and she hurried back to the kitchen to fetch another coffee cup.

"Perhaps I can help," the gentleman said, pushing aside the papers on the desk to make room for the tray. "Let's sit, and you can explain the problem."

Dante dragged another chair closer to the desk.

Having taken the extra china from Mrs Gunning, Mr Ashwood closed the door and took to playing maid.

"While it's traumatic to witness the horrors of some criminal cases," Mr Ashwood began as he poured coffee into a cup, "crimes that affect us personally prove infinitely more disturbing."

He gestured for Beatrice and Dante to sit together, while taking a commanding position behind the desk. Dante explained the dilemma but avoided any mention of her uncle's attack.

"So, your uncle is the only person who can shed light on your father's work in the years preceding the shooting," Mr Ashwood stated. "Equally, based on the fact there has been no mention of an inheritance, and you've passed the age of majority, one presumes your uncle has something to hide."

Mr Ashwood was right on both counts, but that didn't make the thought of seeing John Sands any easier.

"I left Rochester because my uncle attacked me, Mr Ashwood. No doubt he holds a wealth of information in that twisted mind of his. While I try to tell myself he acted out of character when he made his lewd remarks, I believe I saw the real man that night."

Instinct said John Sands knew something about Dante's parents. It's just she didn't want to be the one to drag it from his lying lips.

"And you're frightened to confront him?"

"I fear I lack the experience to coerce him into any sort of confession." She feared she might pull a blade and stab the devil in the heart.

"But you did a remarkable job with Babington." Dante's tone brimmed with admiration. He leant forward, took a cup of coffee from the tray and handed it to her. He held her gaze as she gripped the saucer. "Let me help you. Let me help you punish the rogue, so you never have to think of him again."

His words echoed the statement he'd made last night, though this time he meant to accompany her to Rochester, meant to keep her safe, not devour her mouth and set her body ablaze.

But the thought of meeting John Sands again sent her stomach roiling, roiling as if she were on a ship amid a violent storm, a ship destined to crash into the rocks and plunge to the depths of the sea. She sipped her coffee, though it did little to allay her anxiety.

"And Miss Sands made a valid point," Dante said. "As an eyewitness to the shooting, I need to make a statement about what happened on that road."

Despite Mr Ashwood sitting opposite, she reached for Dante's hand. Oh, she knew how difficult it was for him to make the declaration. She knew he'd done it to show he understood her pain, too.

Mr Ashwood's expression turned solemn. "A few weeks ago, I applied to the local magistrate for information relating to the shooting. He could not locate the paperwork and said it must have been lost when they moved offices. Suffice to say, anything you can remember, D'Angelo, would prove useful in finding those responsible."

They'd reached a point in the road where they must decide whether to continue along the treacherous path full of thorn bushes and brambles, or remain in no-man's-land forever. But they had come too far on this perilous journey to turn back now.

Ignoring the voice of caution, she released Dante's hand and straightened. "I shall meet my uncle, though I want to know you're close by, Dante," she said, forgetting that calling him by his given name would raise eyebrows. "I shall do this once, and if I fail to gain what we need, we must find another way to gather the information."

"I have every confidence you'll succeed, Miss Sands. And once we've dealt with your uncle, you may take my statement."

Beatrice nodded. She looked at Mr Ashwood. "Sir, might you be free to assist us? We thought you could search my uncle's house while he is distracted in the tavern. I can draw a map of the rooms, tell you where to look. But you would be taking a significant risk."

Mr Ashwood cast a mischievous grin. "As your uncle is a suspect in an investigation, I have an excuse to be there. As a man who upholds the law, one must enter a building when they encounter a door left wide open. And as few men are brave enough to question a member of the aristocracy, it will be one of the rare times I'll be glad I have a title."

CHAPTER 11

THE SIR JOHN FALSTAFF coaching inn in Higham stood on a popular road running past Gravesend and Rochester. A route used by merchants and seafaring men travelling to Dover, by lovers fleeing controlling parents and seeking sanctuary across the English Channel, by thieves and crooks who knew those heading to the port carried all their precious possessions.

The inn was but a two-mile ride from her uncle's house. If Mr Ashwood had played his part in this charade and delivered the note without arousing suspicion, John Sands should arrive at the Falstaff inn at around seven o'clock.

Beatrice sat at the round oak table in the bay window, staring out into the darkness, dreading the moment she saw the face that haunted her dreams.

In the rowdy taproom, men shared stories, laughed, clinked mugs, sang songs and drank themselves silly. One man sat in silence, his back mere inches from hers, so close they would bang chairs if one of them stood. So close, she could feel the power of his aura enveloping her like a steely cloak of protection.

Occasionally, men glanced in Dante D'Angelo's direction, but no one approached his table. Two men had approached hers, a local tenant farmer and his labourer.

"Why, if it ain't Miss Sands," the fair-haired young man had said.

"So it is," added the farmer, whose weather-beaten face reminded her of an old leather boot. "Your father said you'd taken a job as a governess in a fancy house in London."

Beatrice had smiled despite being reminded these people believed she was John Sands' daughter. It was just like her uncle to make everything appear respectable. She had wanted to say she'd washed mugs in a grimy tavern, kept company with crooks, now caught fraudsters for a living and kissed handsome rakes without giving a thought to her reputation.

"Yes, I'm travelling to Dover with the family and took the opportunity to see my father." She'd tried not to retch upon uttering the last word.

The men had glanced around the taproom, looking for a well-to-do couple and their prim brats.

"The family are staying with friends in Chatham, but their coachman will return for me within the hour."

The men simply lifted their chins in recognition. Left her to drink her hot punch and watch melted wax trickle down the candle in the table lamp.

Dante fidgeted behind her, then whispered, "He should be here soon."

She didn't reply but closed her eyes and said a silent prayer, a prayer for courage, for strength, a prayer to keep the devil from her door.

With the stable yard located at the rear of the hostelry and accessed via a narrow lane, she did not see John Sands sitting tall and proud astride his stallion. She knew nothing of his arrival until he came bursting through the entrance adjoining the yard.

Beatrice glanced up and saw him striding through the taproom as if he were master of all he surveyed. He carried his riding crop, ready to beat back lesser mortals, had to duck his huge head to avoid the low beams. People stopped the impeccably dressed deceiver, passed pleasantries, offered to buy him a mug of ale, lick his boots.

"My uncle is here."

"He's popular in these parts," Dante muttered.

"Satan often disguises himself as an angel of light."

A stick-thin man standing at the oak counter gestured to her table, and for the first time in months, Beatrice locked gazes with her uncle. John Sands' beady eyes honed in on his prey. A slow grin formed.

Beatrice raised her hand in acknowledgement, but the knot in her stomach tightened so hard she thought she might heave.

"Breathe," Dante whispered. "He'll never hurt you again."

The words resonated. This was her one opportunity to gather evidence—this was to be the last time she'd sit at a table with this imposter—and she had to do everything in her power to make it count.

Wearing his smug expression like a well-worn coat, John Sands dropped into the chair opposite and plonked his crop on the table as a means of intimidation.

"Beatrice." He lowered his voice for he did not wish the locals to hear any hint of panic. "Where the devil have you been?" That wicked gaze raced over her face and body, searching, assessing, trying to grope its way through the dowdy, high-necked dress she wore as armour. "I've been out of my mind with worry, thought you were dead."

Wished she were dead, truth be told.

Dead people did not tell tales.

"I moved to London, took employment as a governess to three young children," she said so calmly Dante would be proud. "The family are staying with friends in Chatham, and I wanted to see you before we sail to France." If he believed she'd left the country, he would not need to venture to London.

The wrinkles on his brow deepened, and he shook his head. "But this is ridiculous. You have a home here. You've no need to work. No need to make perilous journeys."

Beatrice clutched her hands tightly in front of her chest. "After what happened between us, I think it's unwise for me to return to Rochester."

His Adam's apple bobbed. "Can a grieving man not make a mistake? Can a sinner not repent? I'd drunk too much that night and behaved as no decent man should."

This was how he roused her pity, by admitting his failures, pleading for an opportunity to make amends. But there was never a truer word spoken than when he was in his cups. And he had made his real intentions clear.

We're not related by blood. I can take care of you. No one need know of our cosy arrangement.

Her hand burned to slap his face. How she longed to scream "liar", show the good people crowding the taproom that John Sands was not an upstanding member of their community.

"You've been like a father to me all these years."

"But I'm not your father, more of a close friend who cares about your welfare. The man who helped your aunt raise you into the fine woman you've become. In my grief, I forgot you saw things differently."

Beatrice snatched the opportunity to discuss her inheritance. "You must understand, I feel as though I've been betrayed twice. By you, the man who raised me, and my father, who named me beneficiary to his estate yet left me without a penny to my name. Aunt Margaret told me about the house in Hampshire, but there are no documents to support my claim to the property."

Her uncle developed a sudden tic at the mention of her inheritance. "Margaret spoke about Hampshire? What in blazes did she say?"

Beatrice swallowed a sip of fruit punch to chase away her nerves and the autumn chill. Fortune tellers in fair tents used various tricks to convince people they had the magical ability to see the future. They knew how to lead the conversation, how to draw information from unsuspecting victims.

"Aunt Margaret said we moved from Hampshire when my father died. She said you wouldn't let her take anything from the house, even though my father named her my legal guardian."

He jerked back. "Why the devil would she say that? She sold everything of value to pay for the move to Rochester."

So, there was a house in Hampshire.

Her father had been murdered in Hampshire, on the London Road, near Hartley Wintney Common.

"Aunt Margaret said you lived in the same village as my parents." The siblings were close, and she was sure her aunt mentioned something about living a short walk away, about Beatrice staying with them when her father worked out of town.

"That we moved because of the terrible memories, what with my father being murdered near the common."

His face turned ashen, so white she feared he'd stopped breathing. "The blighters must have known Henry was heading home and practically shot the poor man dead on his doorstep."

Beatrice's emotions danced between happiness at discovering her childhood home was in the vicinity of the common, and a deep sadness for the loss of her father, for the loss of what might have been a better life.

Asking more questions might rouse her uncle's suspicion, and so she retreated, hoping to draw him closer to enemy lines.

"It must have been a terrible time for you and Aunt Margaret. You gave me a comfortable home, took care of me all those years, and I shall be forever grateful."

The comment brought life back to his cheeks. "It's not been easy. I never wanted children, but could not leave you out in the cold."

Oh, now he wanted her gratitude and her pity.

"What happened to my father's house? Why is it I've never heard from his solicitor? As my guardian, Aunt Margaret must have had control of the property until I came of age."

They were not the questions Dante wanted her to ask, but knowing she had a home somewhere would make a world of difference when considering her future.

John Sands reached across the table and touched her clasped hands. "There seems to be some confusion. Henry left Margaret the house so she would always have the funds to care for you. She sold it when we moved to Rochester."

Beatrice froze. Her stiff limbs had little to do with her dashed hopes, more to do with this snake's touch. Even when he snatched his hand back, she felt his fingers slithering over her skin.

"I see." All was lost. Unless the man was lying. "But where are my father's books, the records he kept of solved cases? Aunt Margaret said he might have been the intended target in the shooting because of a previous investigation, that those poor people in the carriage died because of him."

He scowled with irritation. "Margaret shouldn't have said

anything. We told Henry it was no sort of profession for a man with a young child and always feared he would meet a tragic end."

Tragic was one way to describe the events of that day.

"There might be something in his notebooks, a clue to what occurred that night." Or was the clue hidden amongst the notes they'd read? And why had Aunt Margaret kept a few documents and not all the files relating to the investigation? "Do you know what happened to them?"

"Forget about Henry Watson," he snapped. "Return home with me where you belong, for no good will come from dredging up the past." Concern marred his tone, maybe even fear. "You've created a fairytale picture of the father you lost, and it's probably best you leave it that way." He glanced over his shoulder briefly. "We made a bonfire of his notebooks and files, and I suggest you never mention them again."

"Yet Aunt Margaret kept a handful of notes. Why?"

He shrugged but seemed agitated by her constant prying. "Perhaps she felt pity for the poor woman who lost her life. It was a tragic case, a case your father was close to solving. Perhaps Henry hid them in the trunk, and Margaret knew nothing about them. Who can say? But my advice is to burn them, let those people rest in peace."

Peace? Dante D'Angelo would not rest until he had answers. But Beatrice was no wiser than she was half an hour ago, and could feel Dante's frustration whipping the air.

"Yes, the account of what happened to Daphne D'Angelo is heartbreaking." Her comment would stir Dante's demons, but she had to press her uncle harder. "The fact her son was made an orphan because of my father's misdeeds makes it even more harrowing. Perhaps I should seek him out, see if—"

"No! No. There's no need for reparation." He sounded a little breathless now. "The boy is the grandson of an earl and has lived a privileged life. Besides, they were likely killed by someone in her family."

Her family!

Why would he think Daphne might have been killed by her kin?

Dante jerked in the chair behind her.

"As chance would have it, the gentleman I work for is acquainted with Daphne D'Angelo's son. By all accounts, the earl despised his daughter for marrying her Italian lover. But I cannot believe a peer would hire someone to murder his daughter."

John Sands slapped his hand on the table in a fit of temper. All conversation in the room died. He turned to the men gathered at the oak counter and laughed.

"What does a man have to do to order a drink?" he joked.

After some jostling behind the counter, a serving wench appeared and hurried to their table. "Beggin' your pardon, Mr Sands, but you were chatting away to Miss Sands, and I didn't want to disturb the reunion."

The wench glanced at Dante D'Angelo as if he were a meringue trifle in Gunter's window and she'd pay a month's wages for one lick. The action caught John Sands' attention. He craned his neck and stared at the back of Dante's head.

"I'll have another fruit punch," Beatrice said to distract her uncle.

"And I'll have a mug of ale, Daisy. Leave them on the table as we're stepping outside for a breath of air."

"Yes, Mr Sands."

As soon as the wench was out of earshot, her uncle leant forward and whispered, "I'll not discuss it here. Come outside for a moment."

Every muscle in her body tensed.

She'd be a fool to accept. Was it a ploy to persuade her to leave with him or a means of divulging a secret? But she was not alone tonight and would not have to fight this fiend if he overstepped the mark.

Beatrice stood, her chair hitting the toprail of Dante's chair. "Forgive me, sir," she said, swinging around to meet his gaze.

Looking into his dark eyes settled her racing pulse. Seeing him brought a sense of calm, a peace she had never known. The words she'd spoken to him that night in Howland Street entered her mind.

I'm not frightened when I'm with you, Dante.

She meant every word.

"There's no need to apologise," Dante said, then mouthed, "I won't let him hurt you."

John Sands stood, too, and snatched his crop from the table. He opened the front door, waited for Beatrice to gather her cloak around her shoulders and squeeze past him before following her outside.

The wind whipped strands of hair from her chignon. The biting chill nipped her cheeks, an attack she hoped wasn't a prelude to something more destructive. Worried he might lead her into the shadowy recesses of the garden, she hurried ahead, staying close to the red brick wall before stopping beneath the boughs of an old yew tree.

"What is it you couldn't tell me inside?"

He turned his back to the inn and faced her, his broad frame blocking her line of vision. "You've been busy concocting stories while you've been away. But no good will come from prying into the lives of powerful men. That's what I told your father and look how he suffered."

"If you're referring to the Earl of Deighton, he's dead."

"The son inherited, did he not?"

Beatrice jerked back in horror. "Are you saying Daphne D'Angelo's brother had something to do with her death?"

"Leave the matter alone, love." He gripped her upper arm, his fingers sinking into her flesh. "Come home with me where I can keep you safe. The house is so cold, so lonely, so quiet without my little Bea busying about the place."

Beatrice tried to shrug out of his grasp, but his hand clamped around her arm like a vice.

"Did my father have evidence that Daphne's family were involved?" Panic swept over her, a tidal wave threatening to drag her under, but she needed more information before Dante came charging to her rescue. "Tell me, and I shall consider returning to Rochester with you."

Satisfied, he released her arm. "It was so long ago, but it had something to do with a man claiming to be the illegitimate son of the countess."

The countess, not the earl?

"What was his name?"

It was one question too many.

Her uncle frowned and took to tapping the top of his boot with his riding crop. "Tell me those notes haven't fired more than your curiosity. Tell me you'll not use this information to try to find the devil who murdered your father."

She should have told him what he wanted to hear, but blurted, "Someone must fight for him. Someone must fight for justice."

The atmosphere changed, the wind blustering in from the north, whipping up leaves and twigs, a far more threatening presence that mirrored the sudden shift in her uncle's countenance.

"Now listen here." He pressed the tip of his crop to her chin, forcing her back against the brick wall. "Foolish talk will get you killed. Loath me to spoil your fantasy, but your father was a scoundrel who lost his way when your mother died. I wished to save you from this, love, but we sold the house in Hampshire to pay your father's debts to Manning. There's every chance Henry betrayed his clients, turned traitor, and it all ended badly."

Beatrice gulped. "That's a lie."

It didn't matter what this rogue said. Until presented with the truth, she refused to believe her father had caused the death of innocent people.

He snarled as he jabbed the crop at her throat. "You're coming home with me before your mouth runs away with you and we're both found dead on the roadside."

She tried to catch her breath, but he was suddenly surrounding her, a large ominous figure pressing her to the wall, trapping her, preventing her escape.

Familiar smells invaded her nostrils—the clawing scent of his shaving soap, the pomade he used to tame his unruly mop of hair, the musty pong of damp clothes. Aromas as suffocating as waking underground and inhaling nothing but soil.

Her knees would have buckled were she not forced upright by the tip of the crop. Her vision might have blurred were it not for the deep cough and the voice of the one man she didn't fear.

"If you wish to walk away from here unscathed, I suggest you release the lady, give her some air."

John Sands froze before pasting an arrogant grin and

swinging around to face the man foolish enough to offer a challenge.

"Be on your way, boy," he said, brandishing the crop as if it were a knight's steely sword. "Keep to your own affairs, and I shall keep to mine."

Dante stood like a Roman god, strong, solid, capable of bringing the heavens crashing to earth with a single strike. "Miss Sands' well-being is my affair. And I'll throttle any man who hurts her."

John Sands laughed. "I'm her father, fool, and may do what I please with my own daughter."

"You're her uncle by marriage, a man who would force himself upon her to satisfy his own deviant pleasures." With a quick whip of his wrist, Dante grabbed the crop from her uncle's hand. "I am Dante D'Angelo. Son of Daphne and Alessandro D'Angelo." He slapped the crop lightly into the palm of his hand. "Henry Watson came to my father's aid, and I've waited a lifetime to repay the debt."

John Sands blinked rapidly. "D'Angelo? You're the boy? The b-boy in the carriage?" Panic coated every syllable. He shook his head as if the vision before him were a mirage, a cruel trick of the mind.

With Lucifer's arrogance, Dante splayed his arms wide. "No longer a boy, but every inch a man. A man ready to wreak havoc to uncover the truth."

John Sands was at a sudden loss what to do. He shuffled back and forth, his eyes darting every which way like those of a hare snared in a trap.

"Imagine my surprise upon discovering my friend's governess is the daughter of the man paid to protect my parents."

Her uncle mumbled, muttered something about the earl slitting his throat, about him paying the price for his loose tongue.

Beatrice presumed he would plead for clemency, offer excuses for mistreating her, use methods to incite Dante's pity. But in true cowardly fashion, John Sands made a dart for the thicket of spindly shrubs and trees opposite.

Dante's sinister laugh pierced the chilly night air. He was about to take flight, too, no doubt thrash the lout with the riding crop until he begged for mercy, but she grabbed his arm to stall him.

"Wait! He's told me everything he knows. We have two new lines of enquiry. More than enough information to keep us busy for weeks." And she wished to be rid of John Sands, hoped he ran as far as his legs could carry him, hoped he stumbled into a poacher's trap and perished in the cold.

But the need for vengeance lived inside Dante. Wild and feral. He might have charged after her uncle for the pleasure of hunting a predator, had it not been for Mr Ashwood's timely arrival.

The coachman pulled the team of four to a halt outside the Falstaff inn. The carriage door swung open, and Mr Ashwood vaulted to the ground. Spotting them instantly, and sensing something was amiss, he broke into a jog.

Beatrice quickly explained what had occurred. "My concern is not for my uncle, sir. Beating the man will not ease Mr D'Angelo's suffering."

"No," Mr Ashwood agreed.

"You speak as if I cannot hear you," Dante countered, practically snarling as he scanned the road, waiting to catch sight of his prey.

"We must focus on the case," she said, eager to leave the inn before the serving wench came to remind them they had drinks waiting. "We must discuss what I've learnt tonight and how we might proceed with the investigation."

Mr Ashwood nodded. "Pursuing Mr Sands may rid you of this pent-up anger, D'Angelo, but Miss Sands has suffered enough and wishes to be away from here, free of the devil."

Dante glanced at her, his black eyes softening.

"Please, Dante. Let us leave now."

He glanced once more at the open road and sighed. "Very well."

A brief conversation ensued where Mr Ashwood informed them he'd found nothing of interest in her uncle's house. Dante muttered his frustration as he climbed into Mr Ashwood's coach. Beatrice hurried to the inn, paid for their drinks, and explained that the family's coachman had arrived to take her to Chatham.

A shudder of relief passed through her when she settled into her seat and Mr Ashwood's carriage pulled away from the Falstaff inn. But a few minutes spent amid the heavy silence had tension coiling its way around every muscle.

Dante sat rigid, staring out at the sprawling darkness, at the never-ending void, the vast emptiness that daylight merely masked. He had heard every word spoken in the inn and knew to add at least one member of his family to the suspect list. Yet she had so much more to tell him, but didn't know where to begin.

Mr Ashwood watched his friend intently, his frown softening when he glanced at Beatrice.

At this time of night, it would take the best part of four hours to reach London. Amid the bleak silence, it would feel more like a day.

Dante must have found the atmosphere unbearable, too, must have seen the lanterns lighting the entrance to the hostelry yards ahead, for he suddenly thumped the carriage roof and called for the coachman to stop at the inn.

"I shall spend the night here." Dante fixed his gaze on Mr Ashwood. "See Miss Sands safely home and we will reconvene in Hart Street tomorrow afternoon to discuss the investigation. Send word to Sharp, have him come for me in the morning."

Beatrice knew what troubled him. He didn't want to return home, not to an empty house, not to sit alone and relive past events. But if he stayed here, a mere five miles from the Falstaff inn, would he visit her uncle in the dead of night, take his vengeance too far.

She shuffled to the edge of the seat. "If they've rooms available, I shall stay too. We can dine together, discuss the things you wish to avoid."

He looked at her. "I doubt I shall be good company."

"You were dreadful company when I arrived at Fitzroy Square the other night. Look how quickly your mood changed." It was unwise to allude to their passionate exchange, but she knew of no other way to drag him from the doldrums.

"Then I shall stay, too," Mr Ashwood said, taking her by

surprise. "D'Angelo, if we're to catch the villain who killed your parents, you need to stop running. You need to hear the facts, deal with them, and then give Miss Sands your statement."

"I have done everything you've asked of me, Dante." Indeed, she had pushed all fears of her uncle aside, and was just as worried how she might react once she closed her bedchamber door and found herself alone with her memories.

Dante nodded. "What's the odds we'll find three vacant rooms?"

"Based on your winning streak at the White Boar," Mr Ashwood began with some amusement, "I'd say they're favourable."

CHAPTER 12

DANTE SPLASHED cold water over his face, grabbed the linen towel from the washstand and dried the rivulets running down his neck and chest. He glanced at the poster bed he'd have to share with Noah Ashwood and decided he'd sleep in the wing-back chair instead.

Beatrice and Ashwood had remained downstairs in the private parlour, discussing everything she had learnt this evening. No doubt it was a sensible conversation, two intelligent people plotting, making wise assumptions, not two people so attracted to one another they often used the case as a means to grow close.

That wasn't why Dante suggested he sit in Beatrice's chamber to give his statement. But something happened when they were alone. She chased away the ghosts, unlocked the chains shackling him to the past, made him feel unburdened. Free.

Having spent a third of his life surrounded by love and being too young to appreciate the majesty, a third living in a mire of hatred and distrust, he'd struggled to make sense of the world. Had latched on to the hope that solving the crime would bring absolution. Now he was another step closer to finding the villain, yet something else, someone else, held his attention.

A light knock on the door brought Ashwood. "Miss Sands is waiting for you when you're ready, and I'll be here if you need me." An uncomfortable pause ensued. "D'Angelo, about Miss Sands."

Dante grabbed his shirt and dragged it over his head. "She's a good friend, kind and selfless, and I would not hurt her for the world."

"I'm glad to hear it." Ashwood laughed as if recalling something she'd said earlier. "Miss Sands is excellent company, amusing, witty, not afraid to voice her opinion."

"She's exceptional in every regard." Dante remembered her sitting on the floor in her silly trousers, swigging brandy as she tried to pull him out of his dark mood. "And she deserves better than this."

"This?"

Dante shrugged. He meant she deserved better than working for a living, better than having to risk her life in the pursuit of justice. Better than him.

"She shouldn't have to live in fear."

"No." Ashwood watched Dante quickly knot his cravat. "Like you, I pray it won't be long before someone notices her worth. I know her options are limited, but I'm not sure I agree with the idea of female enquiry agents. At least not when they're working alone in dangerous parts of town."

The thought of Beatrice out scouring the rookeries at night, questioning unscrupulous villains, made Dante feel sick to the pit of his stomach.

"You should speak to Daventry," he said, for someone had to. "Suggest he thinks carefully about the cases he gives his female agents." And yet Beatrice would argue that chasing criminals was a respectable way for a woman without means to earn money. And considering Dante was her current case, he had no gripe with Daventry. "I should go and give my statement."

The thought left him cold to his bones.

When Dante made to leave, Ashwood caught his arm. "We will find the person responsible. You might not think it now, but you will go on to live a happy and meaningful life."

Dante appreciated the sentiment, even though it was a stretch too far for his imagination. "Perhaps I might take up poetry when this is all over," he teased, for his friend had published a book of erotic verse. "Write a humorous poem about a man who shunned love."

But Ashwood didn't laugh. "It sounds like a tragedy to me."

Ashwood's words rebounded in Dante's head as he crept across the landing, careful there were no witnesses to his late-night rendezvous. He let himself into Beatrice's room and found her sitting in a chair by the hearth, gazing at her notebook and tapping the tip of a pencil to her lips.

She looked up, her blue eyes twinkling like sapphires against the firelight, her hair hanging loose like locks of spun gold. Her brown, high-necked dress posed a stark contradiction. Plain. Dull. Yet her inner beauty shone as if she were draped in diamonds.

He almost chuckled upon noting the two glasses of brandy positioned on the small table next to her chair. He'd need a damn sight more—a quart at least—to tell the tale buried beneath a weight of guilt and pain.

"Dante," she uttered in a tone that said she welcomed his company. "Please, come and sit by the fire. It's so cold tonight I cannot get warm."

He could solve her problem in seconds. They could forget about the case for a few hours, do something to calm this damnable attraction.

"Perhaps it's not the weather affecting you." He came to sit in the chair opposite hers, stretched his legs and crossed his ankles. "Perhaps it's the chill of fear, the distress you hid so well while extracting information from your uncle."

She'd gone to her chamber to wash before dinner. But Dante had taken one look at her hands beneath the light in the private parlour and knew she'd spent an age scrubbing them raw.

"How is it possible?" She shook her head. "I lived with him all these years, and not once did he make me feel uncomfortable. Yes, he was always aloof, disinterested, but it's as if he woke up one morning a different man."

"You said things changed when your aunt died."

"Drastically so."

"Having heard your uncle speak tonight, it's evident he thrives on power. After your aunt's death, he needed someone to control." Dante wished he'd thumped the devil. "You should have let me chase after him, warn him never to darken your door again, give him a reason to stay away."

She exhaled deeply, the sound like a form of cleansing. "By hurting him, you would have hurt yourself, and I couldn't let that happen."

"You placed my welfare above your own?"

A bubble of emotion rose to his throat. It had no name he could place, not respect, not admiration, though he could think of no woman he respected or admired more.

She gave a half shrug and glanced at the notebook resting in her lap. "Helping you has become a passion of mine. Alice said kindness rids us of negative emotions. Acts of kindness leave us warm inside, and I'm tired of feeling cold."

"Alice is a fountain of wisdom, by all accounts."

She laughed, and he couldn't help but laugh, too.

"Alice speaks her mind. Nothing is left festering inside. You get to hear her opinion whether you can handle it or not."

"Perhaps we should adopt her attitude," he said, yet fear raised its head, warning him he would likely lose this friendship if he spoke openly. Like all good things, he would likely lose it anyway. So shouldn't he make the most of every moment?

"I thought we'd already agreed to be honest," she said.

"Honest about the case, not honest about the reason you think about me more than you should. Or why I feel at peace when I'm with you. Why I'm thinking about the night I kissed you instead of the dreadful task ahead."

A blush touched her cheeks. "We're attracted to each other. There's no secret there. Perhaps it's my inexperience, but the merest touch of your lips has a profound effect."

A sense of masculine pride reached around and gave him a hearty pat on the back. "Passion can be overwhelming." His mind conjured an erotic fantasy, a host of wicked things he would do to her given a chance.

"I wouldn't know. Passion is not something I've encountered before."

And therein lay the crux of the problem. She needed someone who could make love to her, hold her close and chase away the darkness. She needed a man who could love her with all his heart, not a rake seeking the euphoria of sexual release.

"Perhaps you should take my statement before this conversation reaches a point where our desires take command of our senses," he teased.

Her gaze drifted over his white shirt and poorly tied cravat, came to settle on his mouth. "You seem calm now, unfazed by the fact your grandfather or uncle may have had a hand in your parents' murder."

"I'm always calm when I'm with you," he said, yet he felt the stab of familial betrayal deep in his gut. "Let's begin before I change my mind. We can discuss my family's treachery and our mutual affection later."

Devil take it!

He'd said affection, not attraction.

Oblivious to his mistake, Beatrice took hold of her pencil and scribbled something at the top of the page. "Would you care for a sip of brandy before we start?"

"No. I'll wait until the beast needs sedating."

She smiled, though seemed nervous. "Do you remember where you were, what you were doing before you journeyed through Hampshire that night?"

Dante relaxed back in the chair and stared at the flames dancing in the hearth. Some people closed their eyes to recall memories, but he could not bear to watch the disturbing scene.

"We rarely ventured to London, but my father took me to a book shop in New Bond Street, then to Gunter's in Berkeley Square. My mother and Mr Watson met us there." His mother had been flustered, had tried to listen when he rambled on about eating a lemon ice when it was so cold outside, but couldn't focus. "She seemed agitated. When she sat down, they all spoke in whispers."

"Do you know where she'd been?"

"To visit my grandmother, the countess." Dante had begged

to go, was desperate to meet the sweet woman with whom he was estranged. Experience had altered his opinion, poisoned his fantasy. *Sweet* was no longer a word he associated with the Dowager Countess of Deighton.

"Of course, the earl has a house in Berkeley Square," she said.

"It belongs to my uncle, but my grandmother lives there."

"And you say my father accompanied Daphne?" She sounded surprised. "Why would an enquiry agent meet with a countess?"

After what he had learned tonight, the meeting clearly had some relevance to the case, had some bearing on the unfolding tragedy.

"I thought Watson was a steward or man of business and always assumed the meeting had something to do with inheritance or some other legal matter."

"Dante," Beatrice said, prompting him to look at her. "Based on the fact neither of us believe in coincidence, and until we prove the countess had nothing to do with the murder of her daughter, we have to consider her a suspect."

"I understand."

He understood only too well. Like the earl, the countess reigned with an iron hand, but the lash of her tongue delivered the deadliest blow. The matron had banished her daughter. Had ripped the soul from the chest of a grieving boy. It wasn't hard to believe she might hire cutthroats to get rid of the problem.

Sensing his disquiet, she said, "Do you want to continue?"

"No." He wanted to jump ship and swim to shore. "But I have to tell you what happened." He needed to confess, beg for forgiveness.

Silence ensued while Beatrice quickly made notes in her book, the sound like the faint scratching of mice trying to claw their way out of the darkness.

"And so you left London and journeyed to Hampshire," she clarified. "It's at least five hours to the common. Can you recall how many times you stopped en route?"

The simple question amounted to more than a desire to create a timeline. It acted like water, dousing his fiery emotions. Indeed, Beatrice Sands was perhaps the most skilled agent he'd ever met. Instinctively, she knew when to advance, when to retreat.

"I cannot recall. But my mother wanted to stay the night in Bagshot." A year ago, Dante had ventured as far as the inn, had made enquiries about highway robberies in the area during the autumn and winter of 1805. "Your father wanted to leave, but said he would hire a horse."

She swallowed deeply. "Evidently, you didn't stay."

"No." Guilt churned in his stomach. If he could travel back in time, he would tan his own backside for being a brat. He'd drag himself from the carriage by the scruff of his coat, put himself to bed without supper. "I cried and complained until she agreed to go home."

Beatrice said nothing. She stared at him, eyes glistening with unshed tears. The gravity of the decision was not lost on her.

"Had we stayed at the inn, we might—"

"Don't!" She dabbed her eyes with her fingertips. "Don't say you were to blame. Don't torture yourself—"

"We should have stayed, should have made the journey during daylight, when there were more people on the road."

"Whoever did this would have found another way to silence our parents. There's every chance someone followed them from London. Every chance the villain would have murdered you in your beds had you stayed at the inn."

He wanted to believe her. "What if it amounts to nothing more than highway robbery? What then?" He did not give her an opportunity to answer. "I'm the reason they were on the road that night. I'm the reason they were in the wrong place at the wrong time."

And while he'd spent years searching for a motive, searching for the fiend who fired the shots, part of him wanted to hide from the truth.

"Dante, the evidence suggests it has something to do with the man who visited Farthingdale. And if my uncle is correct, we must assume this man believes the countess is his mother. Vengeance seems a likely motive, as does the need for the countess to silence anyone who knew her secret."

He reached for the brandy glass, cursed the dowager to the

devil, and then downed the contents. "Then we must visit Mr Coulter as soon as we return to town. The man had items stolen from the scene, and so we could be looking at a conspiracy."

They would have to visit the countess, too, though Dante had not spoken to the matron for ten years. Not since he'd run away to live with his Uncle Lorenzo.

"Yes," she said softly. "There are many things we need to clarify. But what I know with all my heart is you had nothing to do with what happened to them. You need to stop fighting the world. Stop punishing yourself."

His instinct was to mock, tell her she couldn't possibly understand, and yet he said, "I don't know how to be anything but angry."

"Yes, you do." She placed her notebook and pencil on the side table. "You know how to be a good friend, can show kindness and compassion. You went out of your way to purchase a letter opener so I might sleep easier at night."

He shook his head. "Hatred lives inside me. Dark. Ugly. A living thing that grows more monstrous by the day."

She shot off the chair, came to kneel beside him, captured his hand and gave a reassuring squeeze. "That's not true. You care deeply for your friends. Love lives in your heart, I'm sure of it, and one day you will learn to share it with the world."

His chest grew warm, a swirling heat that infused his whole being. It had nothing to do with the words spoken, everything to do with this angel of deliverance who knelt on the dusty boards, repenting on his behalf. The angel who had faced the devil in a coaching inn because she wished to rescue him from a living hell.

Dante pushed a lock of hair behind her ear with a tenderness he didn't know he possessed. "I didn't thank you for what you did tonight. This may sound strange, but I don't think I have ever felt so proud."

"Proud?"

"You faced your fears, though I know it came at a price." Sore hands, eyes rimmed red from shed tears, nightmares that would plague every restful hour until dawn.

Beatrice glanced at the bed as if it were the rack or some other implement of torture. "I doubt I shall sleep tonight. No matter how hard I try, I shall see my uncle's smug face, not a field full of sunflowers."

"Would you like me to stay with you? I can sleep in this chair."

He'd offered because she did not deserve to suffer, because he hoped he would dream about something pleasant when in her company, and because he had a desire to watch her sleep.

"No one need know," he added.

She glanced at the door. "Mr Ashwood would know."

"Yes, Ashwood would know." But he'd not say a damn thing.

"I cannot ask you to sleep in a chair, Dante."

"You didn't ask, I offered."

"I'm not sure I would settle, knowing you're a few feet away, cold and uncomfortable."

Tired of skirting around their mutual need for affection, he took a huge risk and said, "Then let me climb into bed with you. Give you something pleasurable to think about. Touch you until you're sated, so exhausted you'll struggle to stay awake."

Her eyes widened, and her breath came a little quicker. "Sleep with me?" She jumped to the obvious conclusion. "Dante, I do not want to have a child out of wedlock."

"And I do not want to give you a child out of wedlock." Though for some reason unbeknown he wished to empty himself inside her. "There are ways to enjoy each other and keep your virtue intact. Ways to banish the demons tonight."

She swallowed. "What about your statement?"

"We can discuss it later." He sensed her nerves. "Tell me what you're thinking. Speak from the heart. Make no allowances for my feelings. Beatrice, put your own needs before mine."

She smiled. "I don't know how to do that."

Dante gripped her elbow, guided her to stand. Then he dropped to his knees before her. "I should be the one crawling on the floor, the one worshipping at your feet, for you are without doubt an angel here on earth. You deserve better than to have a rake proposition you in the grubby bedchamber of a coaching inn."

"Not so grubby. I checked the bed, and it's clean." She took hold of his arms and forced him to stand. "I cannot afford to lose my position with the Order. As much as I like Alice, I cannot go back to living above a tavern."

Rejection hit him hard. More so because he had never wanted a woman the way he wanted her. But he'd asked for the truth and had the utmost respect for her decision.

"I understand."

She placed her hand on his chest to soften the blow. "I cannot afford to lose my freedom, but I would risk everything to feel your lips on mine again."

Every nerve in his body sparked to life. "You would?"

"I won't pretend to know what exists between us, Dante. Maybe it's lust and it will fizzle away to nothing. Maybe we're just two people seeking comfort, respite from our nightmares. I ache for your touch, but need some reassurance before we proceed."

"Love, I'll not take your virtue."

"Not even if I ask you to?"

The question caught him off guard.

She laughed. "Dante, I value your friendship, but fear things will be different if we indulge our passions."

"Beatrice, we kissed like rampant lovers, and it only strengthened our bond. But I'm reckless and rash and rarely think about tomorrow." Yet he knew one thing with striking clarity. "Despite that, I need you in my life, more than I've needed anyone, and so a night spent banishing our ghosts will have no bearing on our friendship."

"You mean that?" she breathed, pushing her hand up over his chest.

"I give you my word."

"Then kiss me, Dante. Kiss me, so we might forget our troubles."

CHAPTER 13

GOD MOVED IN MYSTERIOUS WAYS. Or that was the sentiment Cowper used in the opening line of his poem. It came as no surprise that Beatrice recalled the title—*Light Shining out of Darkness*—for the first touch of Dante's lips was like an epiphany. Somehow, amid the trauma and strife, she had fallen in love with the damaged agent of the Order.

She should have fought against the powerful emotion, told him they should not complicate matters, expressed the importance of solving the case, been sensible. Professional.

But every part of her longed to join him in bed.

I'm reckless and rash and rarely think about tomorrow.

She didn't want to think of anything beyond this quaint room, either. Couldn't think about anything but the heat coiling low in her belly, the potent taste of brandy on his lips, the arousing scent of his bergamot cologne.

Dante D'Angelo seemed to be everywhere at once, devouring her mouth, stroking her back, squeezing her buttocks. The skilled sweep of his tongue sent her pulse soaring. Every masterful movement spoke of his impatience to reach the point where pleasure obliterated pain.

"Slow down, Dante," she panted, tearing her lips from his. She wanted this to be more than an opportunity for him to banish his demons. "We have all night unless you're worried what Mr Ashwood will say."

"I'm not worried about Ashwood." He sucked her lobe, nuzzled the sensitive spot below her ear. "But I feel like I've waited a lifetime to kiss you again."

Merciful Lord!

His teeth grazed the delicate skin, sending ripples to her core.

She could have given herself over to him, let him ravage her senseless, seduce her to the point of madness. Evidently, this man knew everything about sex, nothing about love.

But oh, how she wanted to love him tonight.

"Wait, Dante." She hadn't a clue how to please him, but this burning need inside gave her the courage to continue. "Let me kiss you, touch you, find my way around your body, set the pace."

He pulled back, considered her through eyes heavy with desire. "No doubt, my eagerness is overwhelming. But my intention is to pleasure you, make you come so many times you'll sleep like a babe."

"And I want to please you." She wanted him to sleep peacefully, too, not be ravaged by his nightmares. "Let me try."

He captured her hand, kissed her knuckles. "Do what you want with me, Beatrice. I am yours to command."

"You're happy for me to take control?"

"If that is your desire."

Nerves threatened to ruin the minor victory, but she pushed them aside, decided the best way forward was to confront her fears.

"Perhaps I should undress first," she said. "Perhaps I should—"

"You're thinking like an agent." His eyes glinted with amusement. "We're not looking for a logical way to perform a task. I should be tripping over my breeches in a passion-fuelled frenzy."

"We're not supposed to be plotting and planning?"

"No." His grin faded. "Beatrice, be honest with me. Do you want me to return to my room? We can explore our growing attraction some other time when we've—"

"No! No, I want to continue. It's ... it's just ..."

"Tell me."

Her shoulders sagged. "I haven't a clue what to do, Dante. You're used to women skilled in the art of seduction, whereas I'm skilled in deduction." She threw her hands up. "And now look at us. We're trying to solve a problem instead of enjoying the moment."

He slipped his arm around her waist, his hand dipping down to cup her buttocks. "I don't remember ever wanting a woman the way I want you. I have no memory of anyone else but shall remember the sweet taste of your lips until I draw my last breath."

Emotion bubbled to her throat. She would never forget how the strokes of his tongue set her body ablaze. Never forget the way the amber flecks in his dark eyes glowed with pleasure.

"You can be quite charming when the need arises." He could be rugged and masterful, too, and she loved the combination.

"Beneath the hard, bitter exterior, you'll find the inside is softer and not at all displeasing." His gaze dropped to her mouth. "We stood in the street, and you seduced me with confectionery. You came to my house and seduced me with rotten brandy and a fine lawn shirt that left little to the imagination. So you see, you're as skilled in seduction as you are most things. Indeed, I was utterly seduced the moment we met."

As if his words weren't enough to arouse her, he rubbed his hand back and forth, cupping and lifting her buttocks. Her sex pulsed in response. Her breath came quick and hot, expelling in little pants.

Their gazes remained locked.

The power of his magnetic pull held her spellbound.

"Don't go, Dante. Stay with me tonight."

Take all of me. Leave no part untouched.

Their lips met. This time they kissed slowly, deeply, a lazy, languorous exploration that tightened the muscles in her abdomen, left her sex aching.

"Feel what you do to me," he breathed, taking her hand and guiding it over the solid length bulging in his breeches. "That's the power you wield. I've never been so hard."

Fascinated, she couldn't help but caress him. "You're so large it's impossible to think we might—"

"We'll fit, love. But I'm not taking your virtue."

Disappointment flared. She wanted to give everything of herself, wanted to fuse their bodies, crawl beneath his skin, ease her obsession.

"Then pleasure me as only you know how."

His mischievous grin said he welcomed the challenge. "Would you like to see how hard I am, Beatrice? Would you like to touch the impudent devil desperate for the stroke of your hand?"

He was tugging off his boots before she found her voice. "Very much so."

She watched him undress, gloried in the way the flickering firelight danced over the muscular contours of his chest. Her heart sank the second she noticed the scar. But he unbuttoned the waistband of his breeches, tugged them down over his hips, sending all morbid thoughts scattering like petals in the wind.

Dante D'Angelo might be damaged inside, but he was a perfect specimen of masculinity. Strong. Formidable. Confident in his own skin. So aroused, she couldn't help but stare.

"You're like a statue in a museum, though rather more endowed." Inadequacy reared its head, for she was hardly Venus. Her calves were too thin, her belly too rounded, her left breast a little bigger than the right.

"Tell me what you like best," he teased, palming his erection.

"All of you."

She liked the arrogant seducer and the tortured hero, the bold warrior and the frightened child. She wanted to embrace them all. Never let go.

"Would you like to see my body, Dante?" she said, despite being choked with fear. The need to press her skin to his meant she had to overcome her insecurities. And Alice said men were blind to imperfections when faced with a confident woman.

"See it? Love, I wish to devour every inch."

Heat pooled between her legs, but she set to work on the ugly brown dress she'd worn for protection. Braced herself because she knew his eyes would widen in surprise when her petticoat hit the floor.

He did jerk back in shock. His eyes did protrude.

"You strapped your breasts? Strapped them over your chemise? I knew they looked different and assumed it was that dreadful dress."

She shrugged but experienced the aching throat that always preceded the onset of tears. "Not tightly, just enough so as not to draw my uncle's eye. The bindings irritate my skin."

His expression was unreadable, but he closed the gap between them and drew her into an embrace. "Forgive me. Forgive me for asking you to do something so distressing."

"It was necessary. And I couldn't run forever."

"Let us pray this is all over soon." He stroked her hair, unaware her anxiety amounted to more than dreadful memories.

The future was her primary concern. After the visit with her uncle, she'd come to realise she would always live in fear. But she would rather suffer these traumas, take comfort in this gentleman's embrace, than solve the case and part ways.

Overcome by a sudden desire to live for the moment, she looked up at the man who had stolen her heart. "Alice said there are ways to make love without the risk of a child."

He cupped her cheeks. "There's always a risk, love, but I imagine she's talking about sponges soaked in brandy or a gentleman withdrawing."

In a move bolder than anything she had done before, Beatrice reached down and stroked his manhood. "Make love to me, Dante."

He didn't make love, she knew, but she had enough love for both of them.

"I'm not asking for a commitment." She continued to fondle him. "But I need you to chase away the cold tonight."

Dante looked conflicted. "One day you'll marry and will want to give your husband—" His head fell back. "Hell, love, that's so good."

"Life is precarious. We both know that. I want you, Dante. Here. Now."

It took less than a heartbeat for him to surrender.

His mouth came crashing down on hers with an urgency that stole her breath. The ties of self-restraint snapped, leaving them both consumed by a form of carnal madness. So much for slowing down. Their tongues filled each other's mouths, but still, they could not get enough.

"Quickly, unbind me."

Dante set to work on the strappings, unravelling her like an eagerly awaited gift, throwing the material to the dusty boards. He pressed her back against the bedpost, dropped to his knees, raised her chemise to her waist and rained kisses over her thighs.

"Let me worship you, love, like you deserve."

"Yes," she breathed, not really understanding what he meant.

With him distracted, and before she lost her mind completely, she dragged her chemise over her head and discarded it to join the rest of their clothes.

But he'd parted her sex, slipped his tongue between the folds. *Merciful Mary!*

"Dante," she managed to say before he hooked her leg over his shoulder.

She pushed her hands into his hair, held onto him as he continued to devour her intimate place. Like a wicked wanton, she couldn't help but jerk her hips in response. The tension built, an urgency pulsing in her core. He'd once said he could read her like a book. He was right. Somehow he knew exactly when to slip his fingers inside her, knew she would splinter into a hundred pieces, knew her inner muscles would clench around him as she gasped, shuddered and called his name.

The devil looked smug as he met her gaze.

Slowly, he pushed to his feet. But not before kissing the softness of her belly, sucking her nipples, licking the mole on her breast.

"How was that, love?"

She couldn't find the words.

"That good, eh?" He caressed her cheek with the backs of his fingers. "Come to bed."

She gulped. "I'll need instruction."

"No, you won't." He offered his hand. "You know how to please me."

Emboldened, she entwined her fingers with his, went with him. She would follow him anywhere.

He threw back the counterpane and sheets. "Are you sure you want to feel the weight of me pressing you into the mattress? Once we start, I imagine we'll both struggle for breath."

A vision of her uncle flashed into her mind, but it left as quickly as it came.

"I'm not afraid of you, Dante." She ran her hands over his chest, relishing the hardness beneath her fingers. She pushed up on tiptoes, kissed his neck, inhaled the uniquely masculine scent that was as calming as it was arousing.

"You'll tell me if you want to stop?"

"I will," she whispered against his bronzed skin.

"I don't want to hurt you."

"You won't."

She sensed his confidence falter and so kissed him hotly on the mouth.

His arm snaked around her waist. His hand dipped to grip one buttock. And they were lost again. Gasping, moaning, tongues tangling, writhing in each other's arms. One minute they were standing, the thick length of his arousal pressing against her abdomen. The next they were in bed, the swollen head of his shaft at her entrance.

He laughed lightly. "I've not done this before."

"Neither have I."

Heavens! She would never forget the look on his face when he eased into her body. It went beyond the lustful glint in his eyes, beyond the rakish grin of satisfaction. He wanted her. Her. Not just her body. She could see it clearly. He was the book, and she could read this particular page.

"Wrap your legs around me, love."

She did, the movement drawing him deeper inside her. When he withdrew, she felt bereft. But he knew how to read her, too, knew she liked feeling full, liked the way he edged deeper each time.

"One long thrust, and you're mine," he panted. "There'll be no going back."

She didn't want to go back, only forwards with him.

"Do it now, Dante."

"I imagine it will be easier if I kiss you, if I distract you momentarily, but for some reason, I want to watch you when you take me to the hilt."

"Watch me, then." It was the least she could do after the pleasure he'd given her, and she wanted to watch him, too.

He fixed her with his heated gaze as he withdrew, pinned her to the bed as he thrust so hard she took all of him, every delicious inch.

For a second, she thought she might cry. It wasn't the sharp pain that brought a rush of emotion, for it soon subsided. It was the overwhelming feeling of love for this man.

"God, Beatrice. Everything about you is divine."

He started moving, slow pulses of his hips at first, but soon he was pumping fast and hard. The bed creaked. The frame hit the wall. Mr Ashwood could probably hear their passionate moans across the hall.

Dante didn't treat her like an incapable virgin. Perhaps it was his huge appetite for pleasure, but he couldn't seem to get enough of her. And she certainly couldn't get enough of him.

She came again, jerking beneath his expert strokes.

He withdrew, groaned in ecstasy as he emptied himself on her abdomen. He fell onto his back, dragging breath into his lungs, a grin filling his handsome face.

They lay there, slowly climbing down from dizzying heights. And yet her need for him had not abated. She laughed aloud, for she could not contain the euphoria.

Dante looked at her and laughed, too. "Was it what you imagined?"

"So much better." Insecurity surfaced. "I doubt you'd say the same."

He rolled onto his side, draped his leg over hers. "Beatrice, I've never made love, but I made love to you. I usually gather my clothes and leave, but I want you again so desperately I can hardly think straight." He brushed her hair from her cheek. "You touch me like no one has before. You reach places I didn't know existed."

Her heart soared. "We don't need to sleep. We might indulge ourselves again. There must be more you can show me."

He explained she would be sore, then climbed out of bed, fetched a damp linen square from the washstand and wiped her clean. She caught his hand as he washed traces of blood from her sex, took the linen and cast it aside.

"Touch me, Dante."

The first stroke of his fingers was their undoing.

It was some hours later when they finally fell asleep in each other's arms, their nightmares a distant memory.

CHAPTER 14

LUST THRUMMED IN THE BLOOD. It stirred every nerve to life, sent one's heart galloping. The internal sensations were only evident when one spoke or glanced at the object of their desire. Yet the memory of the night spent with Beatrice sent it powering through Dante like a team of wild horses, trampling over every other emotion in its wake. Surely those seated in the drawing room in Hart Street heard the thundering beats, felt the ground tremble and shake.

"D'Angelo?" Cole's voice penetrated Dante's inner chaos. "Did you hear what I said?"

Dante dragged himself from his reverie, though his body reacted as if he were still buried deep inside the woman who occupied his thoughts.

"Mr Sloane rode to Farthingdale yesterday to speak to Mrs Pickering," Beatrice said so calmly she wasn't thinking about ravaging him senseless. "He should return with her statement tomorrow."

"Excellent."

The weight of Lucius Daventry's stare bore down upon him. "D'Angelo, I know how difficult it—"

"I'm tired," Dante interjected. "That's all."

Tired, and craving Beatrice's touch. Who would have thought making love to her would have such a profound effect on him?

Ashwood's lips twitched. "You hardly slept last night. Perhaps when we're finished here, you should return home." He glanced at Daventry. "We were forced to share a bed barely big enough for one man, let alone two Herculean specimens."

Dante forced a light laugh. "You neglected to mention the fact you snore."

"Amid all the grunts and groans at the inn, I'm surprised you heard me."

Teasing devil!

"Did you sleep well, Miss Sands?" Daventry was by no means a fool and could read the implicit meaning disguised as gentlemen's banter.

"Very well, once I recovered from my nightmare." Beatrice's innocent smile seemed convincing. "Indeed, I pray I never have to set eyes on my uncle again."

"I wish there had been another way to gain the information we needed. While his tale of Lady Deighton's infidelity is plausible, I find it hard to believe a respected enquiry agent would borrow money from a cutthroat like Manning."

"Most men would rather do a stint in the Marshalsea than borrow from Manning," Cole added. "Manning harasses the family of those who cannot pay their debts, although whether the moneylender was as powerful eighteen years ago is something we need to investigate."

"Manning is in Newgate awaiting trial," Ashwood informed them. "However, he's still capable of ordering a man's murder from behind bars, and would have had no issue instructing his men to shoot everyone in that carriage."

Dante recalled the argument between the two villains. One had fired without compunction, his steel-grey eyes cold and lifeless. During his childhood nightmares, he'd imagined the fiend ripping off his mask to reveal a mouthful of razor-sharp teeth.

"It doesn't make sense," Beatrice said. "If my aunt sold the house to pay my father's debts, why move to Rochester? Unless they didn't pay the debts and were hiding from Mr Manning."

"Or moved because they didn't want you to learn of your inheritance." Dante wished he'd tortured the truth from the devil. "It could be another case of fraud. One we can investigate once we've dealt with Mr Coulter and my devious relations."

Dante shivered at the memory of the time spent with his maternal grandparents. The depth of the earl's hatred had been evident from the outset. Did it have something to do with Dante's Italian heritage, Daphne's elopement, or did the earl know of his wife's betrayal?

Cole sat forward. "Coulter has lived in Wilson Street for twenty years and is in his early forties now. He hails from Lancashire, inherited a substantial sum when his parents died."

Beatrice jerked to attention. "Mr Babington hailed from Lancashire."

They all fell silent, no doubt wondering at the connection.

A light knock on the door brought Mrs Gunning. She approached Ashwood. "A letter arrived for you, sir, from Bow Street."

Ashwood took the note and broke the seal. "Thank you, Mrs Gunning."

The housekeeper left them to their business.

"It's from Sir Malcolm." Ashwood read the missive. "Someone broke into Babington's house last night and ransacked the place, emptied every cupboard and drawer, yet stole nothing of value."

"Surely his staff heard the commotion." Dante suspected someone had got wind of Babington's penchant for stealing expensive trinkets and hoped for the return of their heirloom. "Can they identify the intruder?"

"Apparently, no one heard a thing."

"You mean no one wants to be embroiled in a criminal investigation while seeking new employment." Dante wondered if it might be worth questioning the staff about their master's light-fingered hobby.

"You may all disagree," Beatrice began, "but I think we should call on Mr Coulter. Mr D'Angelo can question him about the brooch and his connection to Lancashire. If Mr Coulter believes he's a suspect in Mr Babington's murder, he may be forthcoming with information."

It was just like Beatrice to suggest they confront the fellow rather than skulk about in the shadows gathering evidence. She had done a remarkable job of gaining information from her uncle —an even better job of extracting Dante's secrets.

"Miss Sands should question Mr Coulter," Dante said, struggling to hide his admiration. "I shall accompany her and offer assistance where necessary. She has a remarkable ability to bring calm to a volatile situation, whereas I'm likely to punch the cad should he prove uncooperative."

Daventry considered the request. "Agreed. You will go there directly. Ashwood, speak to Sir Malcolm about Manning, find out what you can about the moneylender's history. Cole, study Henry Watson's notes in case we've missed something. And see if there's any connection between Babington and Coulter. I'll talk to Babington's servants."

They arranged to meet the following day to discuss any new developments, but as they made to leave, Daventry pulled Dante aside, his expression pensive.

"Take Bower with you. Let him wait in Coulter's hall if you think he might prove too intimidating, but I feel the need to exercise caution."

"I can take care of Miss Sands." Dante lowered his voice. "I would sacrifice my life to keep her safe." It was not a flippant remark made to appease Daventry. The moment Dante uttered the words, he felt the truth of it deep in his bones.

"My concern is not for Miss Sands. Your parents were murdered because of a secret, or because Manning sought revenge on Watson. Babington stole your mother's brooch, and now he is dead. Slain in the street like a dog." Daventry gripped Dante's arm in a rare gesture of affection. "My greatest fear is that whoever's responsible will seek to silence you, D'Angelo."

Ordinarily, Dante would have reacted to Daventry's warning with a snort of contempt. He would have welcomed the challenge, invited the devil to his door with the arrogance he wore like a second skin.

But something had changed.

One day you might find a reason to live, and then you'll be sorry.

The coachman's warning echoed in Dante's mind. He glanced across the carriage, studied the woman who'd piqued his interest the moment he saw her across a crowded ballroom. Since then, he'd come to rely on her opinion, depend on her witty remarks, need her tender touch. The last thing he wanted was to miss the chance to discover what it meant.

She continued to stare out of the window, though he doubted she was interested in the hawkers offering their wares, or the street sweepers shovelling horse dung.

"Are you thinking about how you will approach the interview with Coulter?" Dante asked. "Or, like me, can you think of nothing but the passionate way you made love to me last night?"

Hell, he'd give anything to be back in that dismal room. Yes, Beatrice had gifted him her virtue. But he'd had a few firsts, too. He'd made love to her, not taken her just to sate his carnal cravings. He'd cradled her in his arms and talked for an hour, not dressed in a hurry and made a lame excuse to leave. He'd lay in bed exhausted, a sheen of sweat coating his chest, yet had to fight the irresistible urge to make love to her again.

She gave him her full attention. "It's time to confront Mr Coulter with our suspicions." A slow smile formed. "And yes, Dante, there's barely been a moment today when I've not thought about you."

That's what he liked about her, no games, no pretence.

"Might you like to indulge your passions again?"

"With you?"

"Damn right with me." Jealousy reared at the thought of her sharing an intimate moment with any other man. That was a first, too, the crippling panic that he might lose her.

She laughed, the teasing sound stirring the hairs at his nape. "If we discuss this now, I doubt we'll be in any state to question Mr Coulter."

"Perhaps you might call at Fitzroy Square and dine with me tonight?"

"Just dine?"

"And explore why this attraction has robbed me of my senses."

Before she made a reply, the carriage rumbled to a halt outside Coulter's townhouse in Wilson Street. Beatrice surveyed the facade while pushing her fingers firmly into her gloves.

Bower climbed down from the box and opened the carriage door. "The gentleman in question is home, sir. According to Mr Cole, the suspect has a mop of orange hair, a mop that appeared at the upstairs window a moment ago."

"Thank you, Bower. Wait with Sharp. We'll call you if we need you." Despite Daventry's suggestion, Dante doubted they'd get past the threshold with a beast like Bower in tow.

Dante approached the house but did not need to raise the brass knocker. A pretty young woman opened the door, though she had the jaded eyes of one whose appetites were far removed from her wholesome demeanour.

"Good afternoon," she said, acting like a maid or house-keeper, yet she surveyed Dante's form as if he were a haunch of beef and she'd not eaten for a week. "May I help you?"

Dante reached into his coat pocket and removed the letter written by the magistrate, one they used as leverage on occasion to gain entrance where they might ordinarily be refused.

"We're here on behalf of Sir Malcolm Langley, Chief Magistrate at Bow Street, and wish to speak to Mr Coulter."

The woman took the letter and peeled back the folds, but it was obvious from the way her gaze flitted about the page that she couldn't read.

"I know who they are, Miss Keane," the deep voice rumbled from within. "Show them into the drawing room, and I shall attend them shortly."

"Yes, Mr Coulter." Her teasing tone said her duties amounted to more than keeping house.

They were shown into an overtly masculine room furnished with dark oak and forest-green velvet, the sumptuous surroundings reminiscent of the private rooms found in exclusive gentlemen's clubs.

"Might I fetch refreshments?" Miss Keane said as if she'd repeated the question ten times in front of the looking glass this morning.

"I shall take tea," Beatrice said.

"And I'll have the same."

Miss Keane gave a coy smile and left the room.

"Keen?" Beatrice whispered. "She has the look of a woman who enjoys frolicking in the broom cupboard. No doubt she'll ask you to come and inspect her bristles."

Dante laughed, more so because he detected a hint of jealousy in her tone. "The man keeps company with the demimonde. I imagine Miss Keane fulfils various roles and has more than a healthy appetite for work."

Beatrice snorted. "She seemed keen to strip you bare and devour every inch."

"That task is yours, love, after you've dined with me tonight."

"Perhaps we might skip dinner."

A look of barely restrained lust passed between them. Had they been in the bedchamber of the hostelry, they'd be tugging at each other's clothes, panting with need. And yet when she smiled, he felt something else—a tug of a different kind.

Coulter marched into the room, his copper-coloured hair capturing their attention. The dark circles beneath his eyes spoke of a life of dissipation. He came straight to the point. "Mr D'Angelo, what brings you to Wilson Street?"

The fact Coulter knew Dante's name came as no surprise. "Allow me to introduce Miss Sands. She is conducting an investigation into the murder of Mr Babington, and I am merely her assistant."

With an appraising eye, Coulter scanned Beatrice as if she were a rare artefact in a museum. "Her assistant? Lucky devil. Though I'm not sure why you think I know anything about the murder of a man I've met twice."

Beatrice gestured to the plush velvet sofa. "May we sit?"

"By all means."

A maid arrived and set down the tea tray. She curtseyed to her master and batted her lashes like a harlot at the Blue Jade. The gentleman's gaze remained fixed on her plump posterior until she'd left the room.

"We seem to have come unstuck." Coulter gestured to the silver teapot. "I'd have had Bridget pour, but she has a terrible case of the shakes when asked to perform in company."

"I'm more than happy to serve tea while my colleague asks questions," Dante said, aware that this reprobate would go to any lengths to tease them.

"Most gentlemen would refuse."

"I'm not most gentlemen," Dante countered.

Beatrice cleared her throat. "Mr Coulter, you say you barely know Mr Babington yet you grew up together in Lancashire."

Dante suppressed a groan. Yes, they had agreed to tackle the matter directly, drag answers from Coulter if need be, but he expected her to begin with facts, not supposition.

When Coulter made no reply, she said, "Perhaps you're unaware of Mr Babington's penchant for fraud and theft, though considering he stole items from your home, I highly doubt it."

Based on the sudden thrum of excitement in the air, the gentleman found this female enquiry agent more than intriguing.

Coulter stared intently. "Miss Sands, you have a rather vivid imagination, one which could be put to much better use than probing a man for information."

The comment roused Dante's ire. He'd hoped for an opportunity to knock the smirk from this devil's face. "Answer her question. Tell us what Babington stole from the locked drawer in your study."

Tell me why you had my mother's brooch! Damn you!

"You know what Babington stole, else you wouldn't be here." Coulter's arrogance seemed forced. "Though I caution you to forget about Babington, forget your personal vendetta, for it will only end in misery."

"Is that a threat?" Dante's pulse soared.

Coulter pushed to his feet. "Not a threat, a warning from someone who has suffered while pursuing the truth. And as there's nothing more to say on the matter, I bid you good day. Miss Keane will show you out."

He made to leave, but Beatrice quickly said, "Daphne D'Angelo died while pursuing the truth. Do you not owe it to her, owe it to your nephew, to bring the culprit to justice? Or are we to assume from your bitter reply, from the evidence stolen from your home, that you had a hand in her death?"

Nephew?

Dante's mind reeled from the shock. Had he missed something? Had her uncle named Coulter as the illegitimate man claiming kinship with the countess, or was this more supposition?

Coulter froze.

Why wouldn't he? Beatrice had practically accused him of murder!

But Coulter did not swing around in a violent rage, cursing them to the depths of hell. He stood still, shoulders sagging as he heaved a breath.

"Mr Coulter, my father died alongside Mr D'Angelo's parents. We are committed to finding the man responsible and will not stop until we succeed."

"Not stop until you're dead," the man muttered.

"Yes, if that is the price of justice," Beatrice said confidently.

Coulter turned to face them, his conceited mask abandoned, replaced by a tortured expression that drew attention to the deep crinkles around his eyes.

"You're wasting your time. You'll never find evidence to prosecute the person responsible, and in the process, you'll lose a damn sight more than you'll gain."

Dante firmed his jaw. "If that's true, if you know so much yet had nothing to do with the murders, how is it you're still alive?"

Coulter cursed beneath his breath.

"You may as well tell your story, sir," Beatrice added.

Silence ensued—their whole case hanging in the balance.

In a somewhat plaintive mood, Coulter glanced around the sumptuous drawing room as if he were to sail to India and never return to his precious homeland again. His mocking snort was aimed at no one in particular.

"Happiness is like a spectre in the night," Coulter said cryptically as he dropped into the chair. "You may creep out of bed, follow it across the landing, try to capture its essence, but you will always return disappointed."

Dante tried to make sense of the man's ramblings. "Chasing happiness is chasing the unobtainable."

"Indeed. A man must embrace his unhappiness, deal with problems with an air of detachment. But how does one do that when one has suffered a great injustice? How does one find peace when one continues to breathe life into their insufferable tale?"

The nightmares, the constant memories, the hatred for the world, all fed the belly of the beast—the story of the past.

"Peace comes when you realise you have power over your thoughts," Beatrice replied. "That your thoughts control your destiny."

A ghost of a smile touched Coulter's lips. "I listened to the inner voices urging me to run and hide. But I should like to be free of this burden, and so I will tell you anything you wish to know."

For a moment they sat there, not saying a word.

One question burned in Dante's mind. "You had a brooch belonging to my mother, a cheroot case of my father's. How did you come by items stolen moments before they met their demise?"

Coulter relaxed back in the chair, water filling his hazel eyes. "Because it was my carriage that arrived at the scene, D'Angelo. I saw both blackguards flee, saw the bodies sprawled on the roadside, saw the boy clinging to his mother, trying to shake her awake."

A boulder-sized lump formed in Dante's throat. He tried to recall his rescuer's face but could remember nothing other than how it felt to have his heart ripped from his chest, have his world come crashing to the ground.

"When I gave chase, the murdering devil dropped his loot."

"Why did you not hand it to the local magistrate?" Beatrice asked.

"The magistrate would have assumed it was highway robbery, not a murder orchestrated to keep a secret."

Dante considered the man who bore no resemblance to his mother. "You visited my mother at Farthingdale." It was obvious now.

Coulter nodded. "You must understand, my whole life has been a lie. I was a young man, full of hope, and with a burning passion to uncover the truth."

"You have reason to believe the countess is your mother, sir?"

"I am the illegitimate son of Lord Summers and the Countess

of Deighton. I was raised in Lancashire by a distant cousin of the countess, told of my real lineage moments before my adopted mother took her last breath."

While Dante had no reason to dispute the claim—many aristocrats sired children with their lovers—it was hardly a motive to commit murder.

"My mother visited the countess on the day she died. I presume she went to discuss the fact, offer proof you were her half-brother."

Coulter frowned and shook his head. "Not half-brother. The earl has never sired a child with any of his mistresses, though I have it on good authority he tried. The countess wished to marry Lord Summers, but her parents insisted she marry the earl. Her affair with Lord Summers began before her marriage and continued until he died ten years ago."

Dante took a moment to absorb the information. "You think my mother was Lord Summers' child?"

"Yes, and so is the current Earl of Deighton. They were both fortunate enough to be born with their mother's dark hair." Coulter brushed a swathe of burnished copper hair from his brow. "The countess was visiting Lancashire when she gave birth to me. Had I been born with ebony locks, she might have taken me home. But I have Lord Summers' colouring, and so she invented a story of a stillbirth and paid her cousin to care for me."

They spent a few moments lost in thought. Strange how one twist of fate could wreak untold havoc on the lives of so many.

Dante studied the libertine who might be his uncle. "So, explain how you're alive and my parents are dead. If I understand you correctly, you're insinuating the countess hired someone to murder her daughter, possibly to ensure her eldest son inherited the earldom."

"It has to be the reason they all perished." Coulter pursed his lips and frowned. "But if you know what Babington stole from me, then you know I'm alive merely because I blackmailed the countess."

Beatrice looked confused. "Mr Babington stole Daphne's

brooch and Alessandro's cheroot case. I don't see how either of those things would give you any hold over Lady Deighton."

Coulter sat forward. "I speak of the letters."

"Letters?" Beatrice and Dante said in unison.

"The letter sent to my adopted mother. The one signed by the countess, detailing the financial provision made for me." Coulter waved his hand impatiently. "Another, thanking her for taking care of the burden. The letters Babington stole from my desk."

"Mr Babington made no mention of any letters," Beatrice said.

Now Dante knew why someone had ransacked Babington's home. Realising the letters were more valuable than a brooch, had Babington tried to extort money from the dowager? Had she hired someone to do away with Babington and retrieve the evidence of her infidelity?

One might consider the current earl a suspect. No man wanted to lose an earldom, be named a baseborn son. But Dante's uncle rarely ventured to town, preferred a quiet, peaceful life in Hertfordshire with his wife and growing brood. Dante would only visit the Earl of Deighton when all other lines of enquiry failed.

"Does the dowager know the letters were stolen?" Dante said. Was that why Coulter offered the warning upon their arrival? "Do you fear she might seek to silence you?"

Coulter flopped back in the chair. "The woman is the devil incarnate. I'd put nothing past her."

"Sir, are we to assume you found an ally in Daphne? When she visited the countess, did she present the evidence on your behalf?"

"I lent Daphne the letters because she wanted to confront her mother, accuse her of hypocrisy."

Suspicion soured Dante's mood. If Daphne had the letters, how did Babington steal them from Coulter's drawer? "But my mother died hours after visiting the countess and must have had the letters on her person."

"The countess denied writing the letters, called them forgeries, and threw Daphne out. She met me at an inn out of town while en route to Farthingdale. It's how I happened to be on the road that night. I took supper at the inn, frolicked with a serving wench, but couldn't shake the feeling of impending doom."

Beatrice cast Dante a sidelong glance before saying, "And so you rode after them but—"

"Arrived too late," Dante finished.

Coulter dragged his hand down his face. "If only I'd have left the inn earlier, gone with them, done—"

"You would have been killed, too," Dante said, for he was experienced enough to know when a man spoke from the heart.

"I visited the countess after Daphne's death, told her I had the letters hidden in a safe place, that if anything happened to me, they would be published in the *Herald*."

Beatrice gave a weary sigh. "And you never sought justice for Daphne?"

"No, Miss Sands. I blotted out the memories with wine and women and would have taken the secret to my grave had you not knocked on my door today."

Dante understood the man's need to bury his guilt. And without catching the countess in the act of murdering her daughter, or with no substantial evidence to support the claim, no court in the land would agree to a prosecution.

"I pray you will find it in your heart to forgive me," Coulter said. "Forgive me for confiding in Daphne. Forgive me for rescuing you from your nightmare, D'Angelo, only to send you back into the clutches of hell."

Morbid thoughts of the past filled Dante's mind, and he could do nothing but incline his head in response.

"Just one more question." Beatrice waited for Coulter to nod. "If you knew Babington had stolen these things, why did you not seek satisfaction?"

"I knew someone had stolen the items and only suspected Babington. It wasn't until you called today that I was able to make the connection."

"I see." Beatrice seemed satisfied.

Dante pushed to his feet. He needed air, needed to be away from here. "We shall not take up any more of your time. No doubt we'll have further questions. I trust we can call again."

"Of course." The fellow stood and considered Dante with keen interest. "Babington did not steal all the items the villain dropped that day. I have your father's pocket watch if you'd like it."

Dante tried not to gasp or cough, but the surge of emotion choked him. "Yes, I would like that."

Coulter gave a weak smile and left the room.

Beatrice was at Dante's side in seconds. She rubbed his upper arm. "What a wonderful surprise. Did you not keep anything of your father's when you sold Farthingdale?"

He shook his head. The thought of touching his parents' belongings had caused unbearable agony.

"Do you regret not taking a small memento?"

Holding his mother's brooch had brought the memories flooding back, not just the harrowing ones of that fateful night, but happy memories, too.

"I regret it more than I could ever explain in words."

She pressed her forehead to his upper arm and sighed. "I left my mother's dresses behind, too. But it's different for me. I have no memory of her."

He might have taken her in his arms, lost himself in her mouth, but Coulter returned with the treasured possession.

"Here, take it." He thrust the watch and chain into Dante's palm. "I've wanted to give you this for a long time, but—"

"I understand." Dante curled his fingers around the cool metal. "We'll let you know the results of our investigation. And if you think of anything else that might prove pertinent, you can find us at our office in Hart Street. Covent Garden, not Bloomsbury."

Coulter considered Beatrice with a libertine's interest. "So, men pay you to solve their problems, Miss Sands."

"People pay me to solve crimes, sir."

Dante was torn between embracing the fellow who might be his uncle and delivering a swift upper-cut to his jaw. "And I am tasked with beating those who overstep the mark."

Coulter laughed. "Ah, an intrepid duo. I see it now."

Beatrice straightened her shoulders. "I have one question

before we leave. Do you know why Alessandro hired an enquiry agent?"

The man thought for a few seconds. "To gather evidence against the countess. To force Lady Deighton to admit her failings. And because they feared the truth might get them killed."

CHAPTER 15

THEY SAT in the carriage outside Mr Coulter's townhouse, silent, Dante's mood subdued as he considered the pocket watch resting in his palm. Sharp shuffled in his box seat, waiting for instruction. A few times, Mr Bower cleared his throat, a gravelly grunt to get their attention.

"Is something wrong?" She'd thought Dante would be beaming with joy upon being reunited with his father's watch. Hearing the story, learning of his potential connection to Mr Coulter, must have taken its toll. "Dante, we knew it would be difficult, but we've learnt so much today."

Without warning he reached across the carriage, took her hand and placed the timepiece in her palm. "This isn't my father's watch. It belonged to Henry Watson. He bought it in London during our visit. I recall my father telling him he should have had his initials engraved into the shield emblem embossed on the case."

Tears welled. Tears for the man who couldn't wait to return home yet met a grisly end on the roadside one winter's night. Tears for the man seated opposite, who had every snippet of happiness snatched from his grasp.

Beatrice slipped the watch into her reticule. Later, when alone in Howland Street, she would take time to study the object, run her fingertips over the surface, hug the instrument to her chest.

"I'm glad it belonged to your father," Dante said, though his shoulders bore the weight of his disappointment. "You have nothing of his. And I know your heart is pounding with excitement though you're trying desperately to hide it from me."

She'd made a pact never to lie to him. "I'm both sad and delighted."

"I find myself equally conflicted."

The need to cross the narrow space and comfort him took hold, but he reached into his pocket and removed what appeared to be the chitty found in Mr Babington's study. After a brief glance at the receipt, he rapped on the roof and instructed Sharp to take them to Holywell Lane, Shoreditch.

"Shoreditch?" She could think of only one reason he would want to go there. "You mean to visit the shop where Mr Babington pawned his diamond ring?"

"Babington pawned other items, yet this was the only receipt he kept. Clearly he had every intention of returning to the pawnbrokers. I want to know why."

"But that was four months ago. I doubt the pawnbroker agreed to such a lengthy loan term. And if he did, the interest would be colossal."

One might question why he pawned a diamond ring in Shoreditch and not in a more affluent part of town. But then he'd probably stolen the ring from someone in Mayfair.

"You're probably right, yet the receipt is burning a hole in my pocket."

"Every day, we get closer to finding the fiend, closer to solving this case." Closer to separating and going their own way in the world. "I wonder what my next assignment will be. I pray it's something less taxing, like finding a lady's missing pug."

"Finding a daft dog won't be thrilling enough for a woman who courts danger." A muscle in his cheek twitched. "Perhaps we should ask Daventry if we can work together again. We complement each other in many ways."

"We do."

"And I enjoy your company." He shifted in the seat, rubbed a hand along his powerful thigh. "I enjoy your company immensely, as I hope to prove after dinner this evening if you feel inclined to accept my invitation."

Her pulse fluttered in her throat. "I enjoy every moment spent with you, Dante. Just make sure I don't have to pull a pistol on Bateson to gain entrance."

"Does that mean you'll come?"

"Isn't that up to you?"

Her brazen comment left him grinning. "I could make you come now."

"I'd rather you strip me bare when you do."

With it being a little less than a mile to Shoreditch, it was better to focus on the case and not the sparks of sexual tension that would have them writhing on the seat, desperate for physical contact.

"How do you feel about Mr Coulter?" She had found his story credible. When giving his account, she'd seen the sensitive man, not the pleasure-hungry rake. "Do you believe his tale?"

"I want to believe him. His story fits with everything we've learned so far, but I cannot find it within myself to trust him."

"No, you find it hard to trust anyone other than your friends at the Order."

"And you," he added quickly. "I trust you, Beatrice."

Oh, Lord! The need to touch him, kiss him, devour every aspect of his being came upon her again. She had spent the morning struggling to think of anything but how wonderful it felt to hold him inside her body, to feel full with Dante D'Angelo.

But they spent all their time journeying from one place to another, questioning suspects, never having a chance to examine whether this unique friendship had a future.

"You're the only person I trust, Dante."

The only person in the world she loved.

The smell hit Beatrice first. Having spent months living in a tavern in a grim part of town, one would think she'd be accustomed to the stench of stale sweat and musty clothes, to a room so thick with tobacco smoke it irritated the throat.

Mrs Crockett puffed on her pipe and continued to choke them with her filthy habit. "Diamond ring? Diamond ring!" She cackled, the shrill sound enough to send birds scattering. "Wait! Let me nip upstairs and search through my jewels, see if I've misplaced the bugger."

Dante slapped the receipt on the counter. "It quite clearly states that he pawned a diamond ring at Crockett's Emporium, Holywell Lane, Shoreditch. You will check your records, and you will do so now, madam."

The woman with thinning grey hair drew her black shawl around her shoulders and appeared suddenly frailer than when she'd hurried to greet them at the door.

"I've got used petticoats, plates and pots, will give you a shillin' a piece if you have any spare, but I ain't never had the funds to give a loan against a diamond ring." Mrs Crockett glanced at the note. "Maybe when I marry that sultan who's asked for my hand, things might be different."

Another loud cackle made Beatrice wince. "A man is dead, Mrs Crockett—stabbed to death in the street—and this note was on his person. Perhaps he had no intention of recovering the ring. Probably had a gaming debt to settle and so pawned his mother's precious jewels."

"I hear you, dearie. But I told you. I ain't loaned against a diamond ring." She squinted and looked at the chitty. "Besides, two months is the maximum loan term, not four."

Beatrice sensed Dante's anger bubbling hot like lava. Soon it would erupt, spill over and destroy everything in its wake. She glanced at him. A warning to approach the matter from a different angle.

"Madam," he began calmly, having heard her silent plea, "my parents were murdered in front of me when I was eight years old. I've spent a lifetime searching for the man who shot a woman while she clutched her child's hand." He paused, closed his eyes briefly. "So I ask you, I beg you, please search your records and put me out of my misery."

Mrs Crockett considered the man at the counter. Her gaze drifted over the elegant cut of his coat. "Fate's cruel hand reaches far and wide. Even touches the nobility."

"We all have a tragic tale to tell, Mrs Crockett. Everyone faces their own form of hardship." He gestured to Beatrice. "My colleague found herself destitute. For her, solving this case is a matter of survival."

Mrs Crockett took another puff on her pipe and then placed it on the counter. "A sad tale is like a blade to the heart. Next, you'll tell me she has three little mites who haven't eaten for days." Tutting to herself, she shuffled towards an open door at the back of the shop and called, "Fetch me the ledgers for June and July."

A muffled voice echoed from the back room.

"Bring them to the counter. Lazy mare. They're too heavy for me to carry." Muttering under her breath, Mrs Crockett returned to reclaim her pipe. "Some of these young uns don't know the meanin' of hard work. Spends all day preenin' herself, struttin' about the place like the world owes her a livin'."

A young woman appeared, head bowed, her curly sable locks hanging loose, obscuring her face. She carried two thin books a child could have managed, placed them down on the grimy oak surface, but avoided making eye contact.

"What's the matter with you, girl? Crick in the neck?"

"No, grandma," came the mouse-like whisper.

Mrs Crockett snatched the receipt found in Babington's study and thrust it at her granddaughter. "Check this against the ledger for June, and then July if you've no luck there."

The young woman took the note with her shaky hand and opened the first book.

Beatrice glanced at Dante and arched a brow. He appeared equally suspicious. Why would a woman who'd spent the morning tonging her hair, whose dress clung to her hips, a woman who clearly adored attention, struggle to look at them?

"We've reason to believe he stole the diamond ring." Dante watched the woman intently as she flipped through the pages.

"We apprehended Babington in the process of stealing a ring from an elderly widow."

"Yes," Beatrice said, "he confessed just before he escaped custody and some devil stabbed him in the street. Mr Babington had stolen many items of sentimental value, and we assume one of his victims sought revenge."

The faint *pat, pat* was that of teardrops hitting the page.

"Jane?" Mrs Crockett touched her granddaughter's arm. "Are you cryin'? What the devil's wrong with you? You're not havin' a fit of the vapours again?"

Jane's shoulders shook. The distressed woman looked up from the ledger, tears streaming down her face. "Please, Mr D'Angelo. I—I don't know anything about the stolen rings."

This attractive woman knew Dante?

"Ah—I see." Dante considered Jane's fine features. "Everything is a little clearer now."

"It ain't so clear to me," Mrs Crockett grumbled.

The muscles in Jane's throat worked tirelessly as she tried to speak. "You remember the gentleman I told you about, Grandma." She wiped her eyes with the back of her hand. "The one who agreed to set me up as his m-mistress, give me an allowance, enough so you could close the shop, and—"

"I told you. I don't want to close the shop."

"But it's too much for you, and—"

"I've seen you at Babington's parties," Dante interjected.

The dark-haired beauty nodded. "My friend is mistress to Lord Stanwick."

"Stanwick?" Dante raised a brow. "The man keeps a harem."

Jane shrugged. "That's how I met George."

Mrs Crockett suddenly cursed like a drunken sailor. "You bottle-headed fool! These stiff-rumped gents are all the same, rotten to the core. They'd steal your dying breath given half a chance." She grinned at Dante. "No offence, sir."

Jane dashed away her tears. "George loves me!"

Beatrice felt a stab of sympathy and didn't have the heart to correct her use of present tense. Poor Jane wished to escape her lowly station and the clutches of her controlling grandmother. What option did she have other than to use her God-given gifts?

The old woman raised her hand as if to slap sense into her granddaughter's head, but glanced at Dante and thought twice. "Oh, it's all fancy talk, sir. The girl has been seduced by a scoundrel and cannot be blamed for the mistake."

"Babington has never kept a mistress, never wished to be financially responsible for any woman. He played games, toyed with people, discarded them like pawns, and would never have made a commitment to your granddaughter, madam."

"You're wrong!" Jane slammed her hand on the ledger to object. "He gave me the diamond ring as proof of his loyalty."

"Diamond ring?" Mrs Crockett snapped. "What diamond ring?"

"It's likely stolen," Beatrice said, saddened by the woman's naiveté. Stolen from another one of Babington's victims. "And if it was a gift, why give him a receipt from your grandmother's shop?"

Jane's cheeks flamed. Tears filled her eyes.

"Tell us," Dante said in a remarkably cool tone. "Babington is dead. If you wish to dissociate yourself from his criminal deeds, you must tell us what you know."

Jane glanced at her grandmother, fear marring her porcelain complexion. "I gave George twenty pounds for the ring. It was a token gesture. A joke between us. But I made him take the receipt because I had to write it in the ledger."

Mrs Crockett's penetrating stare proved more terrifying than her rants and curses. "You gave him twenty pounds?" she said in a low, steady voice. "Twenty pounds? Twenty bloody pounds!"

While the young woman pleaded with her grandmother, tried to explain that she had put the money back when she'd sold the ring to buy new gowns, Beatrice attempted to understand Mr Babington's need for funds.

Failing to come to any conclusion, she glanced at Dante, shrugged and mouthed, "Why?"

"It's about the game." Dante drew her aside and dropped his voice to a whisper while the two women continued their verbal tussle behind the counter. "Babington liked dicing with danger. He liked manipulating people. No doubt he kept the receipt because he found it amusing that he'd earned twenty pounds from a woman of little means."

"That's so cruel."

"There are as many wicked men in Bloomsbury as there are in the rookeries. But Babington's evil streak is the reason a man murdered him in the street."

Mrs Crockett's high-pitched screech caught their attention. "Box? What box?"

"The box George gave me for safekeeping."

"You totty-headed ninny. It's probably full of stolen rings. What's the odds he was settin' you up to take the fall?"

Dante cleared his throat. "Under the circumstances, if Babington left a box here, we will have to take it with us and submit it as evidence."

Mrs Crockett wagged a wrinkled finger. "I ain't no fool. What's to say you won't take the box, fill it with stolen goods and blame my Jane? The magistrate will want to hang someone for the crime, make no mistake."

"We will open the box here," Beatrice said, trying to bring an element of calm to the situation. "We will record the contents and sign our names to the document. Then there can be no errors, no false accusations."

After a moment of contemplation, and sensing her back was to the wall, Mrs Crockett demanded Jane fetch the box.

"She's a foolish girl, sir, but there ain't no crime in that."

Dante's countenance softened. "I'm happy to testify she knew nothing of Babington's misdeeds, though she will need to make a statement at Bow Street."

"And I can arrange to sit with her while she does," Beatrice added.

"You may trust Miss Sands will ensure Jane is treated fairly." Dante fixed Beatrice with an admiring gaze while speaking to the pawnbroker. "She is honest to a fault and strives to save those who find themselves scrambling in the darkness."

Mrs Crockett's mocking grin showed her rotten teeth to advantage. "Happen you would say that seein' as you're in love with her."

ADELE CLEE

The comment caused Beatrice to catch her breath, but Dante looked as if he'd had the wind knocked out of his sails.

"People round 'ere trust no one," Mrs Crockett continued. "You're just another nabob out for his own ends."

Jane returned, cradling a small metal box as if it were a babe. She shook it—the faint rustle proving Babington hadn't filled it with stolen jewels—and set it down on the counter.

"Where's the key?" Beatrice asked, but knew full well Babington had kept it.

"We don't need a key." Dante reached into his coat pocket, removed the length of wire and the strange implement he'd used to break into Babington's desk drawer, and fiddled about in the keyhole.

Mrs Crockett tutted. "See. Crooks. The lot of 'em."

It took Dante seconds to open the box. They all craned their necks to peer at the contents. Beatrice knew the significance as soon as she laid eyes on the folded paper.

"Letters!" Mrs Crockett complained. "That's it! Letters! Though I suppose I should be grateful I'm not lookin' at a pile of robbed rubies."

Dante removed the letters and read them quickly. "They're the letters Babington stole from one of his victims. Find me some paper and an ink pot, Mrs Crockett, and I'll sign to say that's the evidence we've removed from your property today."

Mrs Crockett seemed keen to be rid of them. Like a sprightly young miss, she hurried to the back room and returned with quill and ink.

Dante took the paper Jane found under the counter and wrote a brief note about the evidence presented. With the absence of pounce, Mrs Crockett blew gently on the document, hitting them with the stench of her stale breath.

"I imagine they will want your statement at Bow Street within the next day or so." Dante slipped the letters into his pocket. "We'll send word when you're to make yourself available."

And with that, Dante bid both women good day.

He captured Beatrice's elbow and guided her out onto Holywell Lane. They had barely closed the shop door when they heard Mrs Crockett berating her granddaughter.

Beatrice accepted Dante's arm, and they strolled along the narrow lane to where the carriage was parked on Curtain Street.

"I didn't mention it inside the shop," she said, "but were there not three letters in the box?"

"The other was a letter to Coulter from Lord Summers' secretary, stating that should anyone make false accusations regarding the integrity of a peer, he would find himself embroiled in a lawsuit."

"Poor Mr Coulter. Neither of his parents wished to acknowl-edge him." Was their disregard the reason for his lack of morals, or had Daphne's death altered him irrevocably?

"Indeed. No doubt it accounts for his licentious ways." Dante understood how painful memories dulled a man's conscience.

"We may not have had our fathers in our lives for long, Dante, but we've never had cause to doubt their love." The men would never have forsaken their children to maintain their repu-tations. Well, at least she hoped the same was true of Henry Watson.

"In some twisted way, we're the lucky ones," he said, this newfound gratitude signalling a shift in him. "But finding the letters at Crockett's Emporium presents a problem."

They would need to submit them as evidence. The men at Bow Street would learn of Lady Deighton's infidelity, of Lord Summers' indifference to his illegitimate son. One crooked constable out to feather his nest would sell the story to the broadsheets, then it wouldn't be long before the Earl of Deighton's lineage was the talk of the *ton*.

"You have a responsibility to do what is right." She hugged his arm in a gesture of support, and because touching him brought immense comfort, and because she couldn't shake the gnawing feeling someone was watching them. "We must present the evidence regardless of how it affects those in your family."

He remained silent. The creaking of carts making their way along the lane, and the screams of children chasing wild dogs, did little to fill the void.

They'd reached the carriage before he spoke. "I'll call at Bow Street tomorrow and submit them as evidence."

"It's the right thing to do," she said, glancing quickly over her shoulder. "And I will feel happier when they're in the hands of the authorities."

Happier when she knew no one stalked them from the shadows.

Happier when she knew no one had cause to murder them in the street.

CHAPTER 16

THE MANTEL CLOCK struck the hour, seven chimes that sounded like the ominous peal of a death knell. For fifteen minutes, Dante paced back and forth before the fire in the drawing room. The letters he'd slipped inside his coat pocket for safekeeping weighed heavy, a burden he did not wish to carry. One glance at the hearth, and he contemplated scrunching the paper into a ball and using it to stoke the flames.

The need to be rid of the evidence had nothing to do with protecting the grandmother he despised. Nor did he care if the world learnt of his tainted bloodline. No. His parents had surely died because of the letters, slain at the roadside, and he couldn't help but fear the dowager's lackey had followed them to Shoreditch today.

Dante glanced at the clock, every *tick* growing infinitely louder.

Beatrice was to arrive shortly. Every fibre of his being longed for a night of stimulating conversation, for more passionate kisses, for another chance to sate their lust and sleep, bone-weary, in each other's arms.

If only he could shake the twinge of trepidation.

If only every muscle wasn't strung as tightly as a bow.

The crack of something hitting the boards in the dining room rang through the house like the clap of pistol fire. Indeed, he imagined hearing another shot outside, then cackling laughter, imagined darting into the street to find the razor-teethed fiend looming over Beatrice's blood-soaked body.

"Bateson, I've decided to walk to meet Miss Sands." Dante snatched his hat from the stand and was halfway out of the front door when he stopped abruptly. Should he leave the letters or keep them on his person?

"Very good, sir." Bateson held the door open, waiting for Dante to make up his mind. "It's cold, sir. Perhaps you should consider taking your greatcoat."

"Hmm." Devil take it! He should have delivered the letters to Bow Street, not brought the damn things home.

"Your coat, sir?"

"No. A brisk walk amid the chilly night air will do me a world of good."

"As you will, sir."

The atmosphere outside did little to calm Dante's nerves. A low fog crept through the streets, a ghostly mass stealing through the darkness, its spectre-like fingers ready to slip into his pocket and rob him blind.

Dante stopped on the corner of Howland Street, scanning the long shadows for signs of movement before giving himself a mental boot to the backside. Where was the man who didn't care if he lived or died? Where was the man who taunted the devil?

"Dante?" Beatrice's voice reached him through the darkness. She appeared beneath the soft glow of the lamplight. "It is you. Is something wrong?" Slight panic tinged every syllable. She glanced behind.

"No. I thought I would walk to meet you." He didn't want her to worry.

Moving a little quickly, she closed the gap between them and clutched his arm. "No. You're worried, worried that whoever killed Mr Babington will be looking for the letters. You came to offer your protection."

Dante couldn't help but smile. "Can a man have no secrets?"

"You have more than your share of those," she teased.

The world seemed brighter in Beatrice's company. The night

sky was more magical than monstrous. Like fog, fear dissipated as if it lacked substance.

"I presume Miss Trimble knows you're dining with me."

"She advised I bring Bower along to play chaperone." Beatrice laughed. "When I refused, she cautioned me about what can happen between a man and a woman when they've consumed too much wine. Then she taught me a manoeuvre should I need to free myself from the clutches of a lustful rake."

"Let's hope you weren't paying much attention."

During the brief walk to Fitzroy Square they made idle conversation, discussed the dinner menu, whether she liked the theatre, how she came to own a pocket pistol. Dante could have strolled through the streets until dawn, listening to her tales about the drunkards from the Bull in the Barn, watching her eyes brighten when she laughed.

You think you have what it takes to keep a scoundrel entertained for an hour?

Beatrice Sands could keep him entertained for a lifetime.

"Don't be alarmed, Bateson." She handed the butler her cloak. "I have my pocket pistol but have no intention of murdering your master."

Bateson inclined his head. "No, miss."

"And this might look like conventional attire." She gestured to the splendid cornflower-blue gown that showed the swell of her breasts to perfection. "But beneath, I'm wearing gentleman's trousers."

"I would expect no less, miss." Bateson turned to Dante. "Would you care to go through to the dining room, sir, or shall I serve drinks in the drawing room?"

"I believe Miss Sands is famished, Bateson." And Dante wished to get all formal conversation out of the way so he could focus on more pleasurable pursuits. "And our new footman in training is eager to earn his keep."

Bateson struggled to maintain his indifferent expression. "He is somewhat of a determined fellow, sir, rather excitable at times."

Curiosity danced in Beatrice's eyes.

Not wishing to ruin the surprise, Dante distracted her by

guiding her towards the dining room. "Tell me you're not really wearing trousers beneath that gown."

"What, and spoil the suspense?"

Were it not for the fact his staff had gone to a tremendous effort at such short notice, he would have skipped dinner, set his mind on seduction. But they had the case to discuss, and he was desperate to see her reaction when he presented his gift.

She stepped into the room lit by thirty candles, positioned so the light was soft and warm, caressing the rich red walls with gentle strokes.

"Heavens, you must have purchased every candle in London."

"Not quite." He captured her gloved hand, pressed a tender kiss to her palm. "I've spent too long in the darkness, Beatrice."

Her gaze slipped slowly over him. "Far too long."

"I took the liberty of seating us close together."

"So we might talk?"

"Yes, and the new footman has short legs."

Confused, she looked at the strapping figure dressed in black and gold livery standing statue-still behind the chair. "He looks perfectly formed to me."

Dante bit back a chuckle. "That's Thomas. The new fellow is considerably smaller, but I'm confident he will grow into the position."

Beatrice considered Dante through narrowed eyes. "You're being rather mysterious. From the boyish glint in your eyes, I can tell you're enjoying this game."

"I enjoy teasing you and hope to earn a few gasps and sighs tonight."

She arched a coy brow. "Will you be keeping a record?"

"I shall probably lose count rather quickly."

"Mathematics not your strong point, or are you easily distracted?"

"In your company, I'm always distracted." He led her to the table, and the footman pulled out her chair. Dante sat opposite, for he wanted to stare at her without gaining a stiff neck. "Thomas, perhaps it's time to call your assistant."

Thomas cleared his throat. "Yes, sir."

The man tinkled his bell. The thud of hurried footsteps in

the hall resulted in Bateson telling the boy to walk slowly, but the dining room door burst open and Scupper appeared.

The urchin had begged a penny from Dante almost every day for the last month. And yet it had been the boy's innocent comments earlier this evening that made Dante stop and take notice.

You all right, guv'nor?

Dante had been so lost in thought he'd almost barged into the boy. For some reason, he told Scupper about his impending meeting with the dowager, that he'd not spoken to the matron in years.

When you're hungry, best not to think about the pain in your belly.

They'd agreed Dante would think about a better day, when he might be so full he would struggle to breathe. And then the boy said something that took Dante's breath away.

Happen you should keep your penny tonight, guv'nor. Spend it on a piece of plum cake at Mrs Gladwell's bakery down near the timber yard. Go to bed with a full belly, then it don't matter wot happens tomorrow.

"Beatrice, this is Scupper, who on rare occasions agrees we may call him David." Dante gestured to the boy who looked younger than his eleven years now that Cook had washed his face and combed his hair. "But only when entertaining guests."

Scupper managed a bow. "Good evenin', miss."

Beatrice seemed more surprised by the urchin than she had the thirty lit candles. "Good evening, Scupper. So, you've come to work for Mr D'Angelo."

The boy nodded. "As a footboy, miss, though wot I'd really like is to work with horses."

"Mr D'Angelo is remarkably flexible." She threw Dante a mischievous grin. "I'm sure he needs a new groom."

"As a man who is flexible, it would serve me well if you were trained in various duties." More importantly, it would improve the boy's prospects should he be inclined to leave.

The child's excited eyes brightened the room more than the array of flickering candles. Dante felt the heat of it deep in his chest.

Thomas took the boy to collect the soup tureen. The second they left the room, Beatrice jumped out of the chair and rounded the table. She cupped Dante's cheeks and captured his mouth in a searing kiss that had him hard in seconds.

Just as quickly, she tore her lips from his, hurried back to her seat and gasped a breath. "Heavens. It's rather hot in here."

Hot? It was so damn hot he needed to loosen his cravat.

"So, you do find benevolence an attractive quality in a man."

She arched a brow. "Your act of kindness makes me want to rip your clothes from your body and kiss every inch of you."

"Then tomorrow, you may find me scouring the streets looking for urchins to save." Though if it was a matter of trading kindness for kisses, he'd have to buy a bigger house.

"Perhaps I might reward you for your good intentions."

Damn. He couldn't wait to get her alone upstairs, feel those soft thighs gripping his hips as he plunged slow and deep.

"Shall we forget dinner and go to bed?"

She trailed her fingers across her decolletage. "While I find the thought more than appealing, there are a few things we should discuss. Namely how you intend to deal with your grandmother."

Like an Arctic blizzard, the comment cooled his heated blood. "Tomorrow, I shall submit the letters as evidence at Bow Street, have Sir Malcolm read them before I take them to Berkeley Square and confront the countess."

Thomas and Scupper returned, and the boy watched the footman serve vermicelli soup.

"You intend to go alone?"

"I think it's for the best." He would not put her through the torture of hearing the dowager's vile diatribe. "She will use you against me. Insult you to the point I will lose all rationale." And yet he needed her there, needed her calming influence. Did not want to deal with things alone anymore.

"Dante, words are the weapons of the weak. Drunken men have called me despicable things. I'm more than capable of dealing with a verbal assault, and as your colleague, I must insist on accompanying you tomorrow."

Scupper made an odd retching noise. "Tell me they ain't worms?"

Beatrice glanced at her dish and laughed. "They're noodles."

The boy raised his chin in acknowledgement, but seemed oblivious to the footman's fierce glare and gesticulation instructing him to keep his young mouth shut.

"The lady's right, milord. There's no tongue as foul as that of a man wot's downed three quarts of liquor."

Dante couldn't help but smile, though Thomas looked ready to murder the boy. "I'm not a lord, Scupper, but I thank you for your counsel."

They continued the conversation while sipping their soup, and despite Dante admitting he feared the countess would exact revenge on them both, he eventually agreed Beatrice could accompany him.

"Old Bateson said the lady's got a pocket pistol," Scupper announced while removing her dish. "Said she'll shoot me in the arse if I drop the plates." He laughed. "I bet she ain't scared of a few threats."

Beatrice beamed. "Exactly so, Scupper."

Thomas took the boy aside and told him not to speak while serving.

"He reminds me of you," Beatrice said when Scupper withdrew.

"Because of his dark hair and mischievous grin?"

"No, because he says what he wants regardless of the consequences. And he is remarkably astute. How did you come to hire him?"

Dante told her about his conversation with Scupper. "Lucius Daventry saved me. I realised I have the power to save someone, too."

"Have I told you I find your benevolence arousing?" she said just before the help returned with the serving platters.

"Yes, but hold that thought for another thirty minutes."

Upon Beatrice's request, Thomas described the dishes in the vast bill of fare. "Pork à la Boisseau, lamb cutlets in piquant sauce." He gestured to the sumptuous array of food. "Sirloin of beef."

Scupper's eyes grew as wide as saucers. "Wot's that green thing wot looks like a spear?"

"Asparagus," Dante said.

Scupper scrunched his nose, but his gaze turned ravenous at the mention of pigeon pie. "Will you eat heverythin'?"

"Not everything. Cook will find a use for the rest."

"Why make so much?"

Beatrice grinned. "Scupper makes an excellent point."

"Sometimes a man doesn't know what he wants, what will satiate him, make him happy, until it's thrust before him in all its tempting glory."

But Dante knew exactly what he wanted, and it wasn't piquant sauce. He wanted to make love to Beatrice daily. He wanted to dine with her every evening, take strolls in the park, laugh at her amusing stories, feed her confectionery.

"Roasted rat would make you happy if you ain't eaten for a week."

The boy's comment brought Dante crashing back to reality. There were always people in worse predicaments, and despite his harrowing experiences, he lived a privileged life.

"Would you care to serve me lamb cutlets?" Beatrice said to the boy. "It doesn't matter if you spill any."

"I've been practising with my spoons," Scupper said proudly.

For the next fifteen minutes, they ate their meal and discussed all aspects of the case, everything that had happened thus far.

Beatrice dabbed her lips with her napkin. "May I ask you something?"

"You can ask me anything."

She paused. "During our journey from Rochester, when you finished giving your statement, you said one man relished the prospect of killing people, while the other appeared nervous."

After a night of passion, it had been easier to give his account.

"Yes. One man had no conscience. One wavered on the cusp between good and evil. I'd be dead if he'd not argued to save me."

"And the local magistrate recorded it as a highway robbery?"

"Yes."

She frowned. "Correct me if I am wrong, but the rogue shot my father without asking for his purse. Either they knew he was armed and shot him before he drew a weapon, or he was of no consequence to them."

"My parents were robbed before they were murdered." The cold-eyed devil had taken pleasure ripping the ring from his father's finger, from fondling his mother while— "Wait. The villain molested my mother before shooting her. I assumed it was part of their evil game, but perhaps he was only interested in finding the letters."

"Did they say they were looking for the letters?"

"No. They said very little. The nervous one rummaged through the luggage, which is why the magistrate believed it was a robbery." Dante recalled seeing clothes strewn about the muddy thoroughfare.

"Did you hear an accent? Did they sound similar?"

Dante shrugged.

"Were the coves the same age?" Scupper added while clearing away the serving platters. "One might 'ave been his son."

"No, I got the impression they were both in their twenties."

"Wot about their horses? You can tell a lot from a man's horse."

It was not something Dante had considered, and he rarely thought with a logical mind when reliving the tragedy.

"It was dark." He didn't want to close his eyes and picture the men astride their mounts, but he did. "One horse seemed of good stock, the other a shabby beast hired from a cheap post-house. Both men were competent riders."

"Dante, if they followed your carriage from London and changed horses en route, surely they'd have the same quality mounts."

"Unless one was a gent with more blunt to spend," came Scupper's sensible reply. "Then he might have paid for the better horse."

"Well, it's something to think about." Beatrice informed Scupper she would like the compote of pears and dessert biscuits. "I know you're reluctant to visit the earl without proof Mr Coulter's letters are genuine, but he may hold vital clues to the case."

She meant the heir to the earldom might have hired a

middle-class cutthroat eighteen years ago to destroy any evidence naming him as Summers' bastard.

"Let's see what my grandmother has to say when we visit tomorrow. I'm confident she is the one to blame." Dante paused to inform Thomas he fancied a slice of nougat and almond cake. "On second thoughts, I'll take the letters to Bow Street once we've seen the countess. I suspect we will need them as leverage, and there's a chance Sir Malcolm will insist on keeping them."

Beatrice licked compote from her spoon while lost in thought.

Dante watched her tongue slip over the silver metal, and while he imagined them flinging off their clothes and jumping into bed, he knew she was plagued by questions about the case.

"You said my father gave Alessandro his pistol. Did Alessandro not fire at the assailants?"

"He tried to fire, but the mechanism jammed. I believe there was a fault with the weapon."

"A fault?" Her soft voice trembled. "A fault?"

Dante dismissed the servants, but Scupper lingered at the door. "I hope you catch 'em, sir, give 'em a right old punch on the muzzler."

"He means mouth," Beatrice said, swallowing rapidly as if she might cry.

"I'm familiar with the term." The bare-knuckle boxers at the White Boar used it frequently. "I give you my word, I'll do a damn sight more than that." Dante smiled at the boy. "Run along and finish your duties, and then Cook will give you supper."

The boy left them alone, though the tension in the room was palpable.

Dante thought he understood Beatrice's dilemma. "I doubt your father knew there was a problem with the weapon."

She winced as if she'd swallowed something foul. "Dante, I fear my loyalty to my father is misplaced. I fear the crime had nothing to do with the countess, and my father sought to plan a robbery and use the money to pay his debts. A robbery that went horribly wrong when his accomplices turned traitor."

The first tear fell, then another, and she covered her face with her hands.

Dante stood. He threw his napkin down, rounded the table and drew her out of the chair. "Beatrice, please don't cry." The sight tore at his heart. "Lorenzo said my father was an excellent judge of character. Alessandro would not have hired a man without references."

"There m-must be a way we can check with Mr M-Manning." She choked on a sob. "Check to see if he lent my father money. Oh, Dante, why would my father want to hire a horse if not to ensure he wasn't in the carriage when the villains stopped it on the road?"

Dante wiped the tears from her cheeks with his thumbs. "So he might return home to you."

"What if that's why he climbed down from the coach first?" She clutched the lapels of his coat, ignoring his reasoning. "Because he knew the men aiming the pistols. What if he paid the coachman to stop at the common?"

Yes, there was a slim possibility Henry Watson had betrayed his employers, but the evidence against the countess was insurmountable.

"If it's true, Dante, I would have to resign my position. Mr Daventry won't want a murderer's daughter in his employ." Through red-rimmed eyes, she met his gaze. "And you, you will come to despise me, come to see me as a physical reminder of your pain. I'd have no choice but to leave, leave London."

Leave!

It seemed blind panic was contagious.

The mere thought of her abandoning him, of being alone again, had his heart pounding so hard it might burst from his chest. Then he started ruminating about how much it would hurt to lose her, feeling the agonising ache as if he'd woken one morning to find her gone.

"Your father is innocent." He felt the truth of it deep in his gut.

"I'm not so sure." She cupped his cheek. "Whatever happens, being with you has made me happier than I've been in my entire life. You must go forward, Dante, with hope in your eyes and gratitude in your heart."

Why the hell was she talking like she'd packed her valise, like she clutched a mail coach ticket destined for Plymouth? Like this was goodbye?

He wanted to tell her to stop being irrational, but he did the only thing he could to ease his sudden wave of insecurity.

He kissed the salty taste of her tears from her lips—a chaste melding of mouths meant to lower their racing pulses. A gentle caress meant to chase away their doubts and fears. But the kiss only served to heighten their need for each other, to rouse lust from its slumber, to leave them desperate to pour every inexplicable emotion into a physical act that would prove how good they were together.

She tore her mouth from his on a gasp. "Quick, Dante, lock the door."

Hell, this woman drove him wild. "Let's go upstairs, love. Take our time," he said, though his body ached to take her now.

From the urgent way she pushed his coat off his shoulders, from her roaming hands and aroused pants, she needed to feel him push inside her body.

"I can wait no longer." She reached down and tugged the buttons on his breeches. "I need to ease this craving for you before I go out of my mind."

He glanced over her shoulder, contemplating how a rampant coupling in a dining room might play out. "On the table it will be quick, rough, not the slow writhing or the sensual tangle of limbs you enjoyed, not making love."

"I may lack experience, but is it not always making love when two people care for each other?" Her hand slipped lower, gliding over his erection. "Make love to me quickly, here on the table. We can go upstairs later."

Damn, he was fit to burst and had never received such a tempting proposal. Indeed, he was at the door in seconds, turning the key in the lock, racing back to continue this wildly erotic liaison.

Beatrice pushed the plates aside to make space.

"Bunch your skirts to your waist, love." He unbuttoned his breeches with an urgency that heightened his arousal. His cock sprang free. Hot. Throbbing.

She gasped, her greedy eyes devouring every solid inch.

Relief washed over him when he noticed her white silk stockings, not men's trousers. "Hold your skirts." He braced his hands on her waist and lifted her onto the table.

After a little shuffling, a little repositioning, he took himself in hand, watched the head of his cock ease into her tight channel.

Their gazes locked.

A slow moan breezed from her lips as he pushed deeper.

"You were made for me," he uttered, lovesick as well as lustful.

"We were made for each other, Dante."

He reached under her gown to clutch her hips, became fixated on her heaving bosom, the way her mouth formed a perfect O as he pushed to the hilt. He could languish inside her for hours, spend his leisure teasing, stroking, exploring. But there would be time for that later. Now, she wanted it hard. She wanted to feel full, wanted to come as he slipped in and out of her.

With that in mind, he slid his hand between her legs and massaged her sex.

She reacted instantly, opening her legs, moaning his name, making him drive harder.

The china rattled on the table, every *clink*, *clink*, *clink*, mirroring his desperate pounding. He stole a quick look at the candelabra, praying Thomas had inserted the candles fully and one wasn't about to topple onto the table and set the room ablaze.

"Dante!" was all she cried as she came apart.

He gave her a few seconds to swim in ecstasy before rocking into her with fierce thrusts, holding nothing back. Strange. He was still fully clothed, yet every plunge into her wetness stripped off another layer, exposing him, the real man, not the construct of his past.

Lost in a frenzy, he kissed her open-mouthed, sucked her earlobe.

"Don't leave me," he heard himself say against her throat as he powered deep into her body. "Stay. Stay with me."

"I can't stay with you tonight," she panted, misunderstanding his plea, though she gripped his buttocks like she had no intention of ever letting go. "Miss Trimble will tell Mr Daventry I failed to return home."

"I'll say you're sick, and I had to put you to bed." He drove into her, into her again and again. "I'll say you have a fever. I'll have to strip off your clothes, bathe your skin with my mouth."

"That won't cool me down." Another moan escaped her, louder this time. "Harder, Dante."

But he was undone.

An obscenity burst from his lips. He withdrew just in time, took himself in hand and spurted over her stocking and the top of her thigh. The power of it tore a guttural cry from somewhere deep inside. A cry that went beyond physical satisfaction.

"Forgive me." His heart pounded in his chest. "I'll buy you new stockings."

"I don't care about the stockings." She stroked a lock of damp hair from his brow. "It was quick, but was it making love?"

He smiled. "Yes."

Sex with her wasn't just about the build-up, the euphoric release. It was about the contact, the closeness, the connection. It was about these unfamiliar feelings of affection, of permanency, of love.

CHAPTER 17

REMINISCENT OF THE night Beatrice attempted to gain entrance to Dante's house, the dowager's butler proved just as reluctant to invite them over the threshold.

"I cannot let you in without an appointment, sir."

Dante muttered his frustration. "Sherborne, as Lady Deighton's grandson, I am confident her instructions do not apply to me."

Why did Dante not thrust the letters at the snooty fellow and be done with it? But for some reason, he wished to tighten the man's coil and watch him unwind.

Sherborne stared through perfectly straight spectacles. "I'm afraid they do, sir. The night you left to live with the Italian gentleman, Lady Deighton gave orders you were never to set foot in her home again."

Dante sighed. "That was ten years ago. Besides, the dower house is in Duke Street, is it not? This house belongs to my uncle, and the only reason my grandmother lives here is because his lordship hasn't ballocks big enough to throw her out."

Unfazed by Dante's comment, Sherborne raised his chin. "Might I suggest you write and request an audience, sir?"

Beatrice's patience had worn thin. She'd barely slept, had spent the night pacing the room, wavering between lustful thoughts of Dante and worries about the daunting task ahead.

The need to lay the blame at the dowager's door, and not her father's, weighed heavily, too.

"Sherborne," Beatrice began calmly, "tell your mistress we've come about the letters Daphne D'Angelo brought here the day she died. Tell her we've been to see Mr Coulter and that if she refuses to see us today, our next call will be at the offices of the *Herald*."

Dante gave an arrogant sneer. "I'm sure my grandmother would prefer not to have her secrets sprawled across the front page of the broadsheet."

The man's face remained cold, stone-like, though fear flickered in his eyes. He strolled away as if he had a lifetime to waste, not years he could count on one hand.

"Dante, you need to approach this as an agent, not a man with a personal vendetta. What if Lady Deighton is innocent of any wrongdoing?"

But he had already found the dowager guilty, had donned his black cap and delivered the sentence. For Dante's sake, she hoped the dowager was innocent, else he would always be troubled by the past. But then the blame would fall to Henry Watson, and Beatrice's hopes and dreams would be left in tatters.

"Innocent?" Dante snapped as they waited like begging guttersnipes at the door. "She made my life a living hell, and I'll never forgive her for that."

"No," Beatrice agreed, hoping the dowager might say something to make amends. "Still, we should try to remain civil."

"The woman hasn't a civil bone in her body, as you will soon discover."

Sherborne returned, his pasty cheeks flushed. "If y-you will kindly follow me." The butler seemed unnerved and had probably received a veritable ear-bashing.

They were led through the hall to the dayroom at the rear of the house, which by definition should have been a bright place overlooking the garden. A place filled with natural light where one's spirits were uplifted. Yet, with the heavy curtains drawn, the room was dark and dismal. An anteroom to hell.

The Dowager Countess of Deighton stood near the marble

fireplace, her penetrating gaze finding them in the dimly lit space. Dressed in black as if in mourning, and with her white hair piled high in a style fashionable forty years earlier, the lady cut a menacing presence.

A woman wearing a drab mauve dress, with bony features and scraped back hair, hovered in the background like a member of a sacred order. A fanatical zealot so loyal to her mistress, she would sacrifice herself to further the cause.

"Leave us, Sherborne. Our guests will not be taking refreshment." The dowager glanced at her emissary, one flick of the head a silent instruction.

The servant stepped forward. "My lady would like you to sit." She gestured to the chairs positioned awkwardly near the far wall, put there to ensure they felt unwelcome.

Beatrice glanced at Dante. On the surface, he appeared the strong, capable man she had fallen in love with. Indeed, every taut muscle said he was desperate for a fight. Yet she saw the terrified boy who'd witnessed the worst of horrors, been denied love and any form of compassion.

Her heart ached to console him.

But anger reared.

Beatrice curtseyed to the dowager. "Good morning, my lady. Thank you for agreeing to see us."

The servant—with skin stretched so tight over her cheekbones it would be impossible to smile—said, "My lady says you left her with little choice. She asks me to remind you that blackmail is a crime."

"A crime?" Dante sneered at the dowager, hatred in his eyes.

"Help me move the chairs closer, Mr D'Angelo. Lady Deighton must be hard of hearing, which is why her maid speaks on her behalf."

"Who is this?" The dowager pointed at Beatrice. There was to be no greeting for her grandson, no questions about his health or where he'd been these last ten years.

"Miss Sands," Dante replied coldly. "She is an enquiry agent working with Sir Malcolm Langley to solve the murder of George Babington and the murder of my parents eighteen years ago."

The dowager pursed her lips as if she had caught a whiff of something foul. "Well, you've your mother's blood and clearly like frolicking with riffraff."

Sensing Dante was about to explode like a firework at Vauxhall, Beatrice gripped his forearm. "The chairs, Mr D'Angelo. Please help me move them."

"You'll leave them there, gel," came the dowager's harsh command.

Beatrice inhaled a calming breath. "No. I am going to move the chairs so you can hear my questions and deliver your response. Or we can leave, give the letters to the relevant authorities."

The dowager's pale face positively glowed with rage. "You impudent creature."

Dante suddenly woke from his trance. The hurt child and the angry man gave way to the skilled enquiry agent.

"Insult her again, and I shall ensure our next line of enquiry involves proving Lord Summers fathered your children." Dante grabbed a chair and slammed it down closer to the countess. "You will answer our questions, madam, else I shall tell the world Benjamin Coulter is the son you abandoned."

The dowager made no reply but gripped the arm of a nearby chair as if it were a chicken's neck and she was about to wring it dead.

The servant looked at her mistress, confused. Her script only went as far as relaying the dowager's disdain.

Dante moved the second chair and invited Beatrice to sit.

They dropped into the padded seats. Dante fixed his gaze on his grandmother while Beatrice found her notebook and flicked to the relevant page.

After mumbling her annoyance, the dowager had her servant help her into the chair closest to the hearth. Ah, now she deigned to play the frail widow.

"Pour me a small sherry, will you, Mabel." It wasn't a question.

Beatrice forced a smile. "Let us know when you're ready, my lady, and we shall begin."

"Begin?"

"With our questions relating to the death of my parents and George Babington," Dante countered. "And the death of Henry Watson."

"I don't see what any of it has to do with me."

"Which is why we will ask questions, present evidence."

"Yes, you're a boy who likes to play in the gutter." The dowager peered at Dante. "A boy with tainted blood. A boy who works as an agent because he lacks what it takes to be a gentleman."

"If being a gentleman means I sire children with my mistress and discard them without thought, then I'd rather be a dock worker."

Beatrice couldn't help but jump to Dante's defence too. "If I may, it doesn't matter what the world thinks of us. All that truly matters is what we think of ourselves. Mr D'Angelo knows he is superior to most men of the *ton*."

The dowager's laugh revealed her contempt. "Ah, your strumpet fights your corner. How long before she is with child and your bloodline is as foul as sewage water?"

Shocked at the depth of the woman's vehemence and having to grip her notebook for fear of lashing out, Beatrice was beginning to understand how the dowager used insults as weapons.

"Your affair with Lord Summers is common knowledge," Beatrice said, reading from her notes. "We have evidence to prove you bore him a child while visiting Lancashire, that you paid a cousin to relieve you of the burden."

The dowager opened her mouth to speak, but Dante interjected.

"We have a letter detailing the financial provisions made, but you've seen these letters before. My mother brought them here when she questioned you about her lineage."

"This is preposterous!" Snatching the glass of sherry from Mabel, the dowager drank down the contents and demanded another. "It's all lies. Lies manufactured by that disreputable fellow to extort money. Blackmail, that's what it is."

"Disreputable fellow?" Dante challenged. "You mean your son, Benjamin Coulter?"

"Mr Coulter is not my son. Heaven forbid. He's the son of

my second cousin Wilfred. He's forged documents, forged my signature. The man wants money."

Beatrice cleared her throat. "Mr Coulter wrote to Lord Summers, and we have his reply. A reply written on paper embossed with his family crest."

Sometimes an agent had to manipulate the truth to gain a confession.

"Mr Coulter was collecting evidence to prove all your children were sired by Lord Summers," Dante added. "He visited my mother at Farthingdale, told her the truth. And you had her killed to prevent her from revealing your secrets."

"Killed!" The dowager thumped the arm of her chair. "Murder my own daughter? Oh, you've your father's wickedness in you, boy. I saw it the night the constable brought you here, and I see it now." She turned to the servant hovering at her shoulder. "Mabel, I said get me another drink!"

"You were being blackmailed," Beatrice said while the countess downed her sherry. "Not just by Mr Coulter, but by Mr Babington. He stole the letters from Mr Coulter, immediately saw their value and came to demand money."

If the dowager had worn an evil expression before, she looked downright devilish now. "That reprobate deserves to rot in hell. I told him the letters were forgeries, but he knew people would cast aspersions."

Finally! Something substantial to explain Mr Babington's demise.

"I paid that devil five hundred pounds. You can write that in your notebook, Miss Sands. Tell the magistrate I am the victim, not the criminal."

At the mention of the magistrate, Mabel's eyes widened a fraction. She shifted ever so slightly, but with obvious unease. The servant seemed devoted to her mistress. So devoted, had she taken care of the matter?

"Indeed, I am delighted he's dead," the dowager added. "Thrilled, in fact." She held out her hand. "Now, give me the forged letters so I may dispose of them accordingly."

Dante sat forward. "As an agent of the Order, I have a duty to present them at Bow Street. They're evidence in a murder investigation."

"As my grandson, you have a duty to protect your family."

"Had you made me feel like a member of your family and not a scamp you'd been forced to take in off the street, I might agree."

The dowager's light laugh faded quickly. "Dante, you were disobedient and unruly. A mischievous sprite lacking breeding and manners."

"I was a heartbroken boy, lost and alone. You denied me supper when I couldn't stop crying. You referred to me as 'the orphan' in front of the staff."

"I saved you, made you strong, tough. Look at you now."

"You made me angry, bitter. Made me feel I was at war with the world."

"Nonsense. Your mother pandered to your whims. That was the problem."

"It's called love," Beatrice blurted. "Daphne loved him, loved him and Alessandro, loved them more than her reputation or position in society." Before the dowager could reply, Beatrice fired another question. "How long has Mabel been in your employ?"

"Mabel? What has that to do with anything?"

The servant must be in her forties. The women shared a comfortable familiarity which must have been nurtured over many years.

"My guess is Mabel has served you most of her adult life."

"Mabel was here when I arrived eighteen years ago," Dante confirmed. "Mabel solves all your problems, does she not, Grandmother?"

The dowager's cheeks ballooned, reddened with outrage. "That's enough of this nonsense! As your grandmother, I demand you burn those letters now." She stabbed a finger at the fire blazing in the grate. "I demand your friends at Bow Street arrest Mr Coulter for fraud and defamation."

Dante jumped to his feet, his face twisted in anger. "Did you hire thugs to kill Babington? No doubt Mabel is familiar with the process considering she used the same method to kill our parents." He motioned to Beatrice. "No doubt you had my mother followed the moment she wrote to you to beg an audience. Instructed the men to obtain the letters and return them to you."

Mabel shot forward. "No! No! I would never have hurt Lady Daphne, sir. You must believe that. She was the kindest, dearest soul and did not deserve to die so tragically."

The comment had a noticeable effect on Dante. All anger dissipated, and he hung his head, whispered, "Yes, she was."

A sober silence descended—a moment to contemplate human fragility.

The dowager's sharp tone cut through the quiet. "Our parents?" Her suspicious gaze swept over Beatrice. "What do you mean?"

A prickle of fear raced across Beatrice's back. "My father was murdered, too, my lady. Henry Watson. He was hired by Alessandro to prove or disprove Mr Coulter's claim."

This time the silence landed with a thud. Shaking the room with an invisible force. Mabel looked at Dante, panic flashing in her eyes.

And then the dowager leant forward and set her hate-filled eyes on Beatrice. "You dare bring that murderer's spawn into my house! You dare accuse me of hurting my daughter when you're keeping company with the offspring of the person responsible."

Beatrice wished the ground would open and swallow her whole. Guilt slithered through her veins. She glanced at her gloves, imagining them stained red with the blood of innocent people.

Your father was a scoundrel who lost his way when your mother died.

Her uncle's words rang in her head.

"Shame on you, boy!"

Beatrice couldn't look at Dante.

She couldn't raise an argument because she feared it might be true.

"What proof do you have that Henry Watson was responsible?" Dante spoke like a professional agent, calm, exact, though she could sense his emotional turmoil.

"Proof?" the dowager scoffed. "Henry Watson was a gambler and a cad. Indeed, were I not so incensed, I might laugh at the irony of it all." She shook her head. "They sat there, too, Daphne and that fiend. Accused me of paying someone to attack my daughter in an alley. Demanded—"

"Someone did attack my mother. It cannot be a coincidence."

"If I'd had anything to do with it, I would have hired someone to attack your father, not Daphne. He's the reason my poor child is dead. He's the one who seduced her with his exotic ways, the one who hired that damn Watson fellow."

Beatrice found it hard to breathe, let alone think logically.

Instinct said Lady Deighton had not hired brutes to hurt her daughter. Had Mabel hired them to ransack Babington's home, hoping to find the letters? Probably. Had Mabel hired a brute to slay Babington in the street? Perhaps.

"Henry Watson conspired with my cousin's boy to bring about my downfall. They concocted the whole story so they might blackmail me for funds. Two devious men. Two wicked men. They're the ones responsible."

Dante stepped closer to his grandmother. "Lord Summers' letter suggests otherwise. Is Coulter your son? Answer me!"

The dowager's lips curled into a scowl. "Do you think I would admit to siring a child with a lover? Do you think I would sacrifice everything I've worked for all these years? Mr Coulter is the child of my cousin Wilfred. And you will never, never, hear me say otherwise."

After a lengthy pause, Dante bowed and stepped back. "Then there is nothing more to say. As an agent of the Order, I shall present the letters as evidence in the murder of George Babington." He turned to Beatrice and offered his hand. "We should go now."

Beatrice gripped his hand and stood. She wanted to look at him but needed to see passion and admiration in his eyes, not suspicion and doubt.

"You would embroil this family in another scandal?" A hint of fear marked the dowager's tone. "You would have people question your lineage?"

"You courted scandal when you jumped into bed with Lord

Summers. You made matters worse when you abandoned your son. When you disowned your daughter because she fell in love with a foreigner. My integrity is not open to manipulation. It's time we all faced the truth and dealt with it."

Was the last comment directed at Beatrice?

Was she to accept her father may have played a part in the tragedy?

"Goodbye, Lady Deighton," Dante said as he escorted Beatrice from the room. There was an air of finality about his parting words, which had the dowager calling him vile names as he marched along the hall.

Once outside, it took a moment to shake the oppression of that room, to grow accustomed to the daylight, to breathe freely again.

"I need to visit Coulter," Dante said tightly. "We should have questioned him about the attack in the alley. There's every chance my mother spoke to him about it considering it occurred within the vicinity of Wilson Street."

"Will you visit Bow Street first?"

Conversation felt strained, awkward.

He released a weary sigh. "I wish to dispose of the letters as soon as possible. We don't know if my grandmother had a hand in Babington's murder, and so it pays to be cautious."

"Indeed." A shiver ran the length of her spine. She glanced around the square, thought she saw someone watching them, but blinked and he was gone. "I shall accompany you. I wish to speak to Sir Malcolm about something, and—"

"Your father had nothing to do with the murders," he stated. "And I doubt he would risk his reputation for a brooch and cheroot case."

She managed a weak smile, but proving her father's innocence was of paramount importance. "We're due in Hart Street this afternoon." She hoped one of the men had something new to impart. "We'll visit Bow Street together, but I'll leave you to speak to Mr Coulter."

She hoped to follow another line of enquiry.

One Dante would object to most vehemently.

CHAPTER 18

"Visit Manning? Have you lost your mind?" Alice Crouch shuffled uncomfortably on the long oak settle in the crowded taproom of the Bull in the Barn tavern. She shouted for the drunken lout at the bar to shut his loud mouth before turning back to Beatrice. "It's said he can crush a man with the weight of his stare. You don't want to know what he'd do to a woman."

Beatrice rubbed her temple to ease the tension. "I've been granted permission to question him in the chapel yard at Newgate. Sir Malcolm has arranged for me to meet the prison chaplain but insists I'm not to go alone. I hoped you might accompany me."

Sir Malcolm had advised she take Mr Daventry, a constable or an agent of the Order. When she explained her dilemma, her fear the moneylender wouldn't speak to anyone if he thought they were acting on behalf of the law, he'd demanded she find someone else.

"Me?" Alice brushed a hand through her curly red hair. "Luvvie, I can't go, and you shouldn't go neither. Best stay away. The man's a wolf in human form. He'll see it as a challenge, seek to punish us in some twisted way. Yes. Best stay away."

"Then I shall have to go alone."

Alice reached across the table, her large bosom spilling onto the crude surface, and grabbed Beatrice's hand. "Don't be a fool.

Manning will take one look at you and imagine all the ways he might inflict pain."

"I've no choice, Alice. If I'm to keep my position as an enquiry agent, keep my room in Howland Street, I need to discover if my father had anything to do with the murder of Dante's parents."

Suspicion flashed in Alice's emerald eyes. "So, it's Dante now?"

"I love him." There was little point denying the fact, and it felt good to tell someone. Besides, time was of the essence. "It cannot be helped. But for both our sakes, I need to find out if my father owed Mr Manning money."

Alice sighed. "Did I teach you nothing? Did I not warn you to protect your heart?"

"Not knowing if my father is a hero or a villain is breaking my heart, too." She squeezed Alice's hand. "Sir Malcolm assures me Mr Manning will hang. While awaiting trial, he's lodging with the turnkeys to prevent him from running his operation from behind bars."

"Luvvie, I'd bet there's a turnkey or two on Manning's payroll. And I heard they were struggling to find anyone to testify against him."

Criminals like Mr Manning used fear as a weapon. Even Alice, the most formidable woman Beatrice had ever known, was scared to the marrow of her bones.

"You're right." Beatrice pushed to her feet. "I shall return to Hart Street and speak to Mr Daventry." First, she would call on the only other person in the world who might assist her. "You've been so kind to me, Alice. The last thing I want is to cause you problems."

Alice nodded. "You don't survive around here without knowing which battles to avoid. Where Manning's concerned, you close the shutters and turn a blind eye." She glanced through the dirty window to the carriage parked outside. "Tell Mr Bower if he fancies a drink and a little company of an evenin', my door's always open."

Beatrice smiled but could hear an internal clock ticking. She said goodbye to Alice, asked Mr Bower to take her to Howland Street, where she pleaded with Miss Trimble.

"Mr Daventry should be informed," Miss Trimble said in her matronly tone.

"Yes, he should, but these are exceptional circumstances. Sir Malcolm has arranged for the Reverend Jenkin to chaperone us." She grabbed Miss Trimble's hand. "Please. Mr Manning might speak to me. It's the only chance I have of discovering the truth, of bringing an end to this nightmare."

Miss Trimble's gaze softened. "I'll come as long as Mr Bower accompanies us. At least I won't have disobeyed all of Mr Daventry's orders."

A rush of relief had Beatrice throwing herself into the woman's arms. Miss Trimble's stiff body melted into the embrace, and the woman hugged Beatrice back.

The Reverend Jenkin was a young man with a wealth of golden hair. He possessed a kind, innocent face, and no doubt thought those with the darkest hearts could be delivered unto the Lord if they repented.

He met them at the entrance to Newgate, a gloomy gaol that cowered beneath the backdrop of St Paul's majestic dome—a visual heaven versus hell. The introductions were made. The chaplain read a list of rules: maintain a distance of six feet, give no name or personal information, nothing that might help Mr Manning find them.

Find them? Hopefully, the blackguard would remain within the grim walls until he swung from the gallows.

"The Lord will guide you." The chaplain cupped her hand. Not in the lecherous way some did when they craved human contact more than morning prayers, but in a genuine gesture of support.

A shudder of fear shook Beatrice as she stepped through the fortified entrance. Given a choice, she would rather sit across from Mr Manning than meet John Sands in a tavern.

They stopped at the Keeper's room, where the stern overseer repeated the instructions in a much graver tone, complained that an enquiry agent was no job for a woman, a prison no place for a lady.

"Wait in the chapel yard. The reverend will remain with you."

The chapel yard was a small outdoor space surrounded by a high stone wall on one side, the monstrous three-storey prison building on the other. It might have been a pleasant area were it not so stark, were it not for the beady eyes of inmates watching her through the barred windows littering the facade.

Shuffling, the thud of footsteps and the rattle of keys, preceded the screech of the iron door opening. Two turnkeys appeared, big, slovenly men clasping a prisoner by the arms.

Beatrice could only stare. She had expected to meet a beast of a man, a monster taller and wider than any human creature. But Mr Manning was short, thin, almost emaciated. With his pointed nose, straggly brown hair and spectacles, he looked like a crooked banker, not a man the whole of London feared.

Beatrice glanced at Miss Trimble. "Where do I begin?"

The woman tried to smile. Perhaps her bottom lip quivered because of the cold. "I have no notion. But he has something you want, and I imagine he will expect something in return."

With clumsy steps and a shambling gait, Mr Manning moved closer. His feet were in leg irons, his hands secured in shackles. He couldn't swat a fly, yet those frigid grey eyes could pierce a person's soul.

Beatrice spoke first. "Good afternoon, sir. Thank you for agreeing to see me." Not that he'd had much choice in the matter.

"A man can make time in his busy schedule for a pretty lady, Miss ... ?" The dull, monotone pitch implied weakness, but one could not mistake the sinister undercurrent rippling like a noxious substance beneath the surface.

"Understood."

"Misunderstood?" Mr Manning's lips twitched. "Misguided, I'd say." He looked to the Reverend Jenkin. "It will take more than this angel to save my black soul."

"I'm not here to do the Lord's bidding." She turned to the guards. "This is a private matter. Might you step away so I may speak in confidence?"

The turnkeys frowned. They looked at the reverend, who nodded.

"You heard the lady," Mr Manning jeered as the brawny fellows moved to stand near the wall. "Well, if this ain't the most entertaining day I've had in here."

"I'm glad you see it that way, as I wish to ask you questions about your business dealings eighteen years ago."

The man's gaze turned threatening. "And what is it to you?"

Her throat was tight with nerves. "Have you time to hear the whole story?"

"Can't see as I'm going anywhere soon."

She paused, recited the words in her mind before beginning. "My father was murdered in an attack near Hartley Wintney Common in Hampshire eighteen years ago. The other occupants of the carriage were killed too, though their son survived."

She stopped for breath.

"Go on," he prompted, rattling his shackles.

"I'm good friends with the son, but have reason to believe my father was in debt to you. That he arranged the attack to steal valuables but was betrayed by his partners in crime."

Mr Manning contemplated the information. "And this son won't be friends no more, not if he finds out you're the daughter of the man who killed his parents."

"Precisely." There'd be no more passionate kisses in candlelit rooms. No more making love until the early hours. "It was a long time ago, and I doubt you'll remember."

"I remember every man who tried to diddle me, missy. I have their faces etched into my eyeballs, carved with the blade I'd gut them with if they failed to pay. But why should I tell you anything?"

"Perhaps we might barter, trade information, sir."

What could a man like Manning possibly want?

"Barter?" He laughed, the sound wholly unpleasant. "What I want ain't possible with these shackles. Happen you could drop to your knees and show your gratitude. Take my cock in that pretty mouth of yours and suck it hard."

A year ago, the comment would have shaken her to her core,

brought tears to her eyes. After her experiences at the Bull in the Barn, she simply sighed.

"With the hygiene practices being quite lax here, I fear I must decline your charming offer. But perhaps you might like to hear my harrowing stories. Perhaps I might tell you how I've suffered, why I cry myself to sleep at night."

Mr Manning had no conscience. He liked inflicting pain, and no doubt liked hearing the sordid details too.

The reverend shuffled sideways, putting himself in her line of vision. He glared and shook his head by way of a warning.

"I'll need your father's name if I'm to remember anything," came Manning's cunning request.

"Henry Watson," she said, much to the Reverend Jenkin's dismay.

"Eighteen years ago, you say?"

"He lived in Hampshire, near Hartley Wintney Common. He worked as an enquiry agent and often came to town on business."

Mr Manning glanced up at the windows, at the grim faces pressed to the bars, and they scurried back like frightened rats. "I know the name, but he didn't owe me money."

"Then how—"

"Not before you tell me what's the worst thing that's happened to you." His gaze moved past Beatrice and settled on Miss Trimble. "The nightmare that keeps you awake."

Miss Trimble jumped to attention. "Who? Me?"

"There's something wicked hidden inside that stony shell." He seemed excited at the prospect of discovering her secret. Probably would have tucked a napkin into his collar and rubbed his greedy hands together were they not bound in irons.

Beatrice was about to reply when Miss Trimble suddenly said, "My husband tried to kill me."

Mr Manning's cold eyes glistened. "How?"

"Tell me how you know my father first," Beatrice interjected. "Should my chaperone find the topic too distressing, I will tell you about the terrible thing my uncle did." Though by Mr Manning's standards, a drunken grope was hardly horrific.

The reverend cleared his throat and reminded them that Christians should fight for the Lord, not make pacts with Satan.

"Henry Watson came to plead for clemency. Not on his behalf, you understand, but for a weaker man—his client."

His client!

Beatrice didn't know whether to laugh or cry. Thank heavens her father wasn't in debt to the moneylender, though he must have acted on Alessandro's behalf. Oh, the thought of telling Dante, of ruining his idealised vision of his parents, cut deep.

"You wish to know what my husband did to me?" Miss Trimble said coldly. "He drugged me, beat me and left me half dead in the woods."

Beatrice swung around to face Miss Trimble. How she hoped it was all lies to appease a monster. And yet she saw distress in the woman's eyes, saw her struggle to maintain her austere facade.

"Did he swing by the neck?" Mr Manning asked eagerly.

"No. I did not report the crime."

"Why?"

Questions filled Beatrice's mind. Where was this devil of a husband? How had Miss Trimble survived? But the overwhelming need to protect her from this gruesome fiend gave Beatrice a burst of courage.

"She has answered two questions in a row, sir. I imagine you're a man who keeps his word, and so do me the courtesy of answering mine."

Mr Manning kept his gaze fixed on Miss Trimble.

A little panicked, Beatrice said, "Do you not wish to see terror swimming in my eyes, sir?"

The man shook himself from his trance. "Oh, I'll save that for the next time we meet, Miss Watson."

His comment was like icy fingers to her spine. But she had come too far to be intimidated now. "When my father came to see you, was he acting on behalf of Alessandro D'Angelo?"

Doubts crept into her mind as soon as she'd spoken. Dante would know if his father had debts, and a wealthy man had no need to borrow from a moneylender. Could it be Mr Coulter, then? Was Henry Watson acting on behalf of his client's brother?

"No." He laughed. "You've one more question, then it's time for my nap."

Drat. She had wasted one asking about Alessandro and had revealed another name in the process.

"Whose case was my father pleading?"

"Whose case, you say? Why, that would be a whipster. A fox hiding in the warren." Mr Manning jerked his head at the guards. "I'm done here. I ain't saying no more."

"No! Wait!"

They stomped forward, gripped his arms, ready to haul him back to his cell.

"I need his name."

Mr Manning glanced over his shoulder as the turnkeys helped him shuffle towards the solid iron door. "I'll tell you that when I'm out of this hole."

The reverend waited until the villain was out of earshot before hurrying forward. "You gave him too much information. Did I not caution you about mentioning names and places? I shall have to report it to the Keeper."

"It's of no consequence now." She would just have to pray Mr Manning dangled from the scaffold sometime soon. "But do what you must."

The reverend continued muttering his concern while escorting them to the entrance, but all Beatrice could think about was being free of the stinking place, taking Miss Trimble home, making her tea and offering to listen to her harrowing tale.

"Sir Malcolm requested a rough transcript of the meeting," the reverend revealed. "And I shall ensure you're kept abreast of proceedings here."

He meant he would clang the death knell if Mr Manning were released.

Beatrice thanked him, let him bless her soul and recite a passage about courage from the scriptures. No doubt she would be in his prayers tonight.

Miss Trimble glanced up and down Old Bailey Street. "Where is Mr Bower with the carriage?"

The reverend followed her gaze. "A constable will have

moved him along, Miss Trimble. I suspect he's parked on Newgate Street."

They bid the reverend good day. Beatrice snuggled into her pelisse and walked with Miss Trimble towards Newgate Street. Neither spoke. Her horrific experiences clearly occupied the poor woman's mind, whereas Beatrice desperately tried to overcome her disappointment at not securing a name.

"You didn't need to answer his questions," she said.

Miss Trimble sighed. "No. But it felt liberating to say it aloud. Though I do not wish to discuss it further and must insist we tell Mr Daventry I invented the tale."

Beatrice did not wish to pry. "Of course."

"Mr Manning toyed with us. He had no intention of revealing the name of your father's client."

A whipster? A fox hiding in the warren?

"From the clues, we know the client is a devious fellow, cunning, though that applies to half of the men in London."

It was then that their carriage pulled up alongside them. Well, Beatrice had presumed it was Mr Bower until she looked atop the box and saw the jarvey. The shifty fellow sat hunched beneath the depths of a blue greatcoat, his wide-brimmed hat pulled low so she could see nothing but a bush of ginger side-whiskers.

The carriage door flew open, taking them by surprise. It was not as surprising as seeing the shiny muzzle of a pistol aimed in their direction, not as surprising as the occupant's identity.

"Get in!" He glared at Beatrice and cocked his weapon. "Climb inside, else I shall shoot your companion. Shoot her dead."

Dante withdrew his pocket watch and noted the time. He thought the mantel clock might be fast, for Beatrice was never late, and Bower knew Daventry hated tardiness.

Daventry caught Dante's eye, then dropped his gaze to the fresh cut on Dante's knuckle. "Does Miss Sands know we were to meet in Hart Street at three o'clock?"

"She had an errand to run, which must be the reason she's delayed."

So why did the knots in his stomach clench so tightly he could barely breathe? Why did he feel the need to murder someone? Was it merely that his blood still pumped wildly after putting Benjamin Coulter on his arse?

"Then we may as well begin." Daventry stood near the fireplace, surveying the agents seated on the plush sofas. "I questioned Babington's servants. They all despised him, though none of them recall hearing anything the night a man ransacked his property. However, I heard a whisper that the footman is the brother of Lady Deighton's chambermaid. I'll mention it to Sir Malcolm, unless you have any objection, D'Angelo."

"No. No objection."

His grandmother had made her bed, and she could damn well lie in it.

Cole placed his empty coffee cup on the low table in front of him and motioned to the leather case. "I've studied Henry Watson's notes. We're wrong to assume the caller visited Farthingdale before D'Angelo's father hired the enquiry agent. Mrs Pickering's statement isn't dated."

Dante sat forward. "Let me explain what I've discovered since leaving you yesterday. It will answer many of our questions, and then Sloane can give us Mrs Pickering's account."

They all nodded and gave Dante their full attention.

Where to begin?

So much had happened. They'd uncovered so many secrets and lies, and yet the most significant development was that Dante believed himself in love with Beatrice Sands. Love! He almost scoffed aloud. Yet he could not deny what was blatantly obvious.

"Coulter visited Farthingdale. He believes he is Lady Deighton's illegitimate son. As well as stealing the brooch, Babington took incriminating letters from Coulter's drawer, though he didn't know Babington was the thief until Miss Sands told him."

Dante told his colleagues about Coulter being the man who saved his life due to his timely arrival at the murder scene, about finding the letters at Crockett's Emporium, about the meeting with his grandmother.

They listened intently.

"After speaking to my grandmother, it occurred to me that I failed to ask Coulter about the attack on my mother."

"It happened two hundred yards from Coulter's front door," Ashwood stated.

"Yes, and now I know why." Dante flexed his fingers, clenched his aching fist. "Coulter is partly to blame. He was bedding Mrs Killen, his friend's wife. The woman confessed to her husband during a violent row. Enraged, Mr Killen stormed over to Wilson Street, saw my mother leaving and presumed she was another one of Coulter's strumpets."

"So he followed her," Daventry said, "did to her what he wanted to do to his wife." He paused. "Did Coulter not give chase?"

"Coulter didn't know Mr Killen was outside his house. He heard the commotion in the street but never gave it a thought. Mrs Killen told him what happened. The woman said she was finally free of her husband. That he'd come home, packed a valise, took all the valuables he could carry and booked passage to France."

"And so you hit Coulter," Daventry said.

"I hit him because he failed to mention it when I questioned him yesterday." And because someone had to pay for hurting Daphne D'Angelo. "And because he kept his mouth shut, even though he knew the identity of the perpetrator. He let my mother believe the countess was responsible."

They all fell silent while their logical minds assembled the pieces of the puzzle.

Ashwood reached for the pile of papers on the table. "Before Sloane speaks, there is something I need to tell you. Something I'd prefer to say before Miss Sands arrives."

Dante's heart sank.

He prayed Ashwood didn't have evidence against Henry Watson.

Ashwood flicked through the pages. "This is a list of names taken from a book found beneath the boards in Manning's house in Gower Street. For obvious reasons, Sir Malcolm has the original." He glanced at Dante. "Henry Watson's name is listed, so is his address in Winchfield. The village is located two miles from the murder scene."

Hellfire!

"So, Watson owed Manning money." If only the Lord would strike Dante down, so he never had to tell Beatrice the news she'd been dreading.

"They found account ledgers, but they only date back twelve years," Ashwood said. "We've no way of knowing if Watson struggled to pay his debt, or if there was a debt at all. The names were simply listed alphabetically in a book."

Dante looked at Sloane. He wanted to ask about Farthingdale. Had the new owners kept his parents' belongings? Might they let him visit, tour the house and grounds? He could manage that with Beatrice by his side.

"What did Mrs Pickering say?"

Sloane consulted his notes. "As Cole quite rightly pointed out, we were wrong about the incident at Farthingdale. I've sketched a timeline, but the crux of it is that Coulter came to see Daphne D'Angelo in December 1804. The gentleman gave his name and spent two hours there. Daphne escorted him to his carriage, and they agreed to speak again when Alessandro returned from Italy."

Dante was confused. "But in Mrs Pickering's first statement, she spoke of an argument, said my mother threw the gentleman out."

"That's a separate incident that occurred in the following September, three months before they died. Alessandro was in Italy. Mrs Pickering said he visited his homeland once a year, but had to make the extra journey because of a business matter. He'd already delayed the trip because your mother was struggling after losing their unborn child. They didn't expect to be blessed with another, and she took it quite hard."

Dante coughed. The choking feeling came upon him, as if he were being throttled from within. He glanced at the decanters on the drinks table. The amber liquid glistened against the crystal, but Dante closed his eyes to the temptation and let the pain wash through him.

The men were not ignorant of Dante's plight. They sat silently, waiting for him to gather his wits and catch his breath.

He met Sloane's gaze and nodded for him to continue.

"As I said, your mother received another caller while Alessandro was away. The gentleman refused to give his name. After an argument, Daphne threw him out. She told the house-keeper the man was a devil and a crook, and that she would write to inform Mr Watson. She said if he should call again, Mrs Pickering was to get the gamekeeper to fire a lead ball at the man's arse."

Dante managed a smile. Just like Beatrice, Daphne D'Angelo would have fired the shot herself had she a weapon. He glanced at the empty seat beside him. If he lost Beatrice, the void would be as huge as the one left by his parents—perhaps infinitely bigger.

"Was Mrs Pickering able to describe the caller?" Someone else must have learnt about Coulter's claim. What other motive could there be for blackmail?

"He was tall, a man of good breeding, though he arrived on horseback, not by carriage. Mrs Pickering took it upon herself to have a groom saddle a horse and follow the fellow."

"Was he local to the area?" Cole asked.

"The groom followed him to a coaching inn five miles away, learnt the man hailed from Hampshire but nothing more."

"Hampshire." Dante sat back, his mind assembling all the likely possibilities and coming up with only one. "Ashwood, see if Manning has John Sands listed in his notebook."

Ashwood scanned the pages before stopping abruptly. "Yes, John Sands of Winchfield. Forgive me, D'Angelo. I received this list an hour ago, and the sergeant at Bow Street only mentioned Henry Watson's name."

Had John Sands read his brother-in-law's notebooks, black-mailed Dante's mother to gain funds to pay his debt to Manning? It made sense. But how did the crook come to know Manning in the first place?

He might have voiced his opinion were it not for the fact

someone had taken to hammering the front door knocker repeatedly.

Mrs Gunning shouted for the person to wait as she marched through the hall, ranting beneath her breath. Then a muffled conversation ensued, but the female voice sounded panicked.

Miss Trimble burst into the room, and they all stood.

"Miss Trimble?" Daventry stepped forward and took hold of the woman's trembling hands. "What is it? Have you come from Howland Street?"

Her cheeks were red from the cold, and she fought to catch her breath.

"It's Miss Sands," she gasped.

Dante's heart missed a beat.

"We were outside Newgate, and—"

"Newgate!" Dante cried. "Newgate?"

"Wait, D'Angelo," came Daventry's instruction. "Let her speak."

Miss Trimble gave a quick recap of events leading up to the moment a man waved a pistol at Miss Sands and forced her into a hackney coach, then she described the attacker—described John Sands.

Dante's blood ran cold.

"I ran to Mr Bower who was parked on Newgate Street, gave him a description of the jarvey, and he gave chase. He told me to come to Hart Street, and he would send word as soon as he finds them."

Daventry gestured to the drinks tray. "Cole, pour Miss Trimble a sherry." He drew the woman to a chair and made her sit. "What time was this?"

"We met with Mr Manning at two o'clock."

Nausea rolled through Dante, making him dizzy, making him want to retch. John Sands must have lost his mind. Yet, he didn't think the man would kill his niece. No. Once he discovered the nets were closing in on him, he'd be more inclined to flee.

"What the hell do we do now?"

Daventry raised a hand. "We wait. We wait for Bower's note, then we act accordingly. Bower knows what to do in these—"

"Wait? I'll not sit here while Beatrice is in trouble."

"D'Angelo. I lost an agent, a dear friend, because I arrived too late. I arrived late because I acted too quickly, made mistakes. Trust me. With patience, we will prevail."

Every muscle in Dante's body was primed to fight, to hurt the bastard who sought to ruin his life a second time, sought to hurt the only person he loved. For there was no mistaking the facts now. John Sands had robbed his parents' coach. John Sands had shot three people dead for no reason other than to repay his debt to the man known as Mortuary Manning.

CHAPTER 19

THE HACKNEY COACH reeked of sweat, straw, leather and gentle-men's cologne. Not the strong sensual smell of Dante's fragrance, but cheap and woody. A hint of perfume tickled Beatrice's nostrils, too. Every fare left its imprint. Would the next passenger catch a whiff of fear?

Beatrice watched her uncle intently as the vehicle rattled through the streets. Her heartbeat thumped in her ears. Try as she might, she couldn't help but gasp each breath. She might have gripped the seat, but everything felt tainted, dirty.

John Sands had kept the pistol trained on her for the last twenty minutes, had almost dropped it when the carriage bumped through a rut in the road. His shaky hands and unkempt hair, tired eyes and creased clothes said he was anxious, distressed. A distressed man might fire by mistake, his finger pressing the trigger when agitated or in a temper.

She had not spoken, not raged at him or begged for answers.

The answers were obvious.

John Sands was involved in her father's murder. It wasn't a coincidence the attack happened near the common. It was planned that way. Had her father climbed out first because he knew his brother-in-law was a deceiving devil—or was Henry Watson involved, too?

And though it was time to play the game, use her skills as an agent to extract the truth, her fear of being alone with him left her trembling to her toes.

"Are we returning to Rochester?" Her voice rattled with nerves.

They were heading south on the Kent Road, that much she knew.

Her uncle met her gaze. Despite wielding a weapon, there wasn't a trace of his usual arrogance. "It doesn't matter where we go. After your meddling, Manning will hunt us down."

He should be more worried about Dante D'Angelo.

"You moved before. You can do so again." She'd hoped the comment would settle him, but he squirmed in the seat, couldn't sit still. "That *is* why we moved to Rochester? To escape Mr Manning?"

Panicked, he glanced out of the window as if longing to see the milestone for Dover. "You're not working as a governess. I've been watching the boy's house, waiting to see what he'll do."

The boy? He meant Dante.

"You know where he lives?"

"I made enquiries years ago. Margaret had nightmares about the child and wondered what happened to him." He cursed. "You're his whore. He's put you up in that house in Howland Street, got you to do his dirty work and visit Manning."

"I am not Mr D'Angelo's whore. I'm his friend. And he doesn't own the house in Howland Street. Besides, after your mistake at the Falstaff inn, you—"

"Mistake?"

"In a fit of temper, you mentioned Mr Manning. You presumed it meant nothing to me. That I was a governess seeking the truth, assumed I lacked the wherewithal to find answers."

And she would have struggled had it not been for a twist of fate.

"You hoped Mr D'Angelo would blame his grandmother for the death of his parents," she continued. "You hoped to bide time until Mr Manning's trial and execution. Then he could not name you as the man who owed him money eighteen years ago."

It was a logical guess. Cases were often won on conjecture.

His ugly sneer made him look almost like himself. "I know what the boy does in Hart Street. You hired an enquiry agent. That's how you met."

"Mr D'Angelo is by no means a boy." No, he was every inch a man. She'd give anything to feel his strong arms surrounding her, holding her tight. "But yes, I hired him to find the villains who murdered our parents."

"Did Margaret give you the money? Did she plan this before she died?"

Beatrice thought carefully before speaking. "Aunt Margaret wished to see justice done. She urged me to find answers, gave me the means to seek the truth."

Her aunt had rescued the random notes, but it was enough to lead Beatrice to Dante D'Angelo. Surely it was her aunt who'd kept the newspaper cuttings describing the crime, who hid them in a book, a book she'd purposely left askew on the bookshelf in the parlour.

Her uncle muttered to himself, called his wife a liar, a deceiver.

"*You* were my father's client," she said, piecing together the clues. "He went to Mr Manning and pleaded for clemency because you couldn't settle your debt." She threw a lie into the pot. "My father begged for your life. Manning told me so."

John Sands lurched forward, wagging his weapon like a finger. "Do you know what Manning does to people who cannot pay? He tortures them to within an inch of their lives, thinks nothing of stealing wives and daughters and shipping them to brothels abroad. He slits the throats of the lucky ones."

Anger erupted. "Then why borrow money from him?"

"It was a gaming debt," he snapped. "I had no other way of paying. Blame your father. He's the one who brought me to London, thought it would be good for me to experience life in the metropolis while Margaret cared for you." He gave a contemptuous snort. "Now, look at us."

Mr Cole said Manning was known for his extortionate interest rates, which increased substantially the longer the debt was left unpaid.

"You cannot blame my father for your weaknesses."

"I wouldn't be in this mess if it weren't for him."

A few things occurred to her all at once. If he'd borrowed money, he would have given Mr Manning his address. If Manning had an address, he could have easily traced her uncle to Rochester. So the debt must have been paid. But it couldn't have been paid with the loot stolen from the attack because Mr Coulter found that.

"You cannot blame my father," she repeated, but tears were already welling as she contemplated what her uncle had done. "He was conscientious, diligent, made a will naming my aunt as beneficiary because he knew she would always take care of me."

"Like a lamb to the slaughter, he left me alone in that iniquitous den. They pounced within seconds of him leaving the tables. Goaded me to bid more, play harder, questioned my integrity."

Seasoned gamblers knew how to play against weak, arrogant men.

"But you found a way to settle the debt." Bile bubbled up to her throat. The realisation she had lived with a murderer all these years made her want to scrub her skin till it bled. "Didn't you?"

The truth would come at a price.

It meant Uncle John would have to do away with her, too.

"Manning told you?" Panic flashed in his eyes. His face turned ashen, and his hands shook so violently she feared he would accidentally press the trigger.

Oh, her heart was breaking, yet she managed to say, "Mr Manning enjoys seeing his victim's face contorted in pain. When I told him I was Henry Watson's daughter, he couldn't wait to torture me with the truth."

John Sands scrubbed his hand down his face. Beads of sweat formed on his brow, though it was so cold in the carriage her fingers and toes were numb.

"I don't know what he said, but it wasn't my fault."

"He said it was your idea."

"To steal valuables, not shoot the occupants. I met Manning the day your father came to town to question the countess." He stared at a point above her head, lost in the memory of the past.

"Told him I had a plan to get the money, told him I intended to follow your father home and rob his wealthy clients."

The mind was a powerful thing. She wanted to crumple to the carriage floor and cry until there were no more tears left to shed. But the logical part of her brain kept firing questions, constructing possibilities.

Two men held up the coach. Two men fired.

One man was nervous. One man had no conscience.

Had John Sands and Mr Manning committed this evil act together?

"But Mr Manning had another plan," she said, testing her theory.

The pathetic man trembled in his seat. He covered his mouth with his hand and made a weak, wailing sound. But no tears came. No apology. No pleas for the Lord's forgiveness.

"When Manning told me what I owed with the added interest, I'd have had to rob Coutts bank to clear the debt."

"And so you remembered that my father had named Aunt Margaret as his beneficiary." A tear slid down her cold cheek. "Claiming his property and selling the house was your only option. Manning accompanied you on your quest. You shot my father, shot a devoted couple in front of their young son."

A sob caught in her throat.

A pain ripped through her heart.

For Dante D'Angelo.

The victims were in a better place, but life was a form of purgatory, and Dante was the only one suffering.

"Good God! I didn't shoot those poor people. Manning did. The man's a blood-thirsty loon. He shot them for the thrill. Would have shot the boy, too, had I not intervened. I saved that boy."

And when Dante finally caught up with him, he'd wish he hadn't.

"You killed my father for money?" Beatrice clutched her abdomen and rocked in an attempt to ease her pain. "I've lived with you all these years and never knew." She felt physically sick. "Did Aunt Margaret know?"

"Do you think I wanted to kill Henry? I told Manning I'd

changed my mind, but the devil said he'd shoot Henry if I didn't." He reached across the narrow space and tried to grab her hand, but Beatrice jerked her arm away. "Manning would have killed us both had I not fired the shot. Then he would have come for you and Margaret, taken everything."

"So you killed my father to save me? Am I to embrace you as the hero?" Anger gave her a sudden burst of strength. "Did Aunt Margaret know?"

"We were trying to protect—"

"Did she know!" Beatrice yelled.

"Yes, she knew!" he shouted just as loud. "She knew, but her only thoughts were for you."

And that was why Aunt Margaret rescued a few measly notes and hid them in the chest. She could not meet her maker without leaving a clue that might lead to the truth. But after years of being controlled by John Sands, she'd lacked the courage to make a full confession. Instead, she had left it all to fate.

The hackney stopped at a turnpike next to the Green Man coaching inn. Beatrice had to push all emotions aside and focus on making her escape. She was the only person who knew the truth about Manning, and John Sands would likely shoot her than risk her telling Dante the tale.

The road narrowed slightly after the turnpike, leading them past a patchwork of fields and farmland. One could smell the nauseating stench of the tanneries banking the meadow, could see the men at work in the grey stone building in the distance.

"Where are we going?" she asked nicely—survival being her priority, not vengeance.

"To a place where Manning's men won't find us. Now he's told you the truth, he'll kill us both, and so our only hope is to flee to France."

"France?"

"We'll be safe there. I'll protect you. We can get back to how things used to be after Margaret died." He spoke as if he had not committed a heinous crime. Not murdered her father in cold blood.

En route, there'd be many opportunities to slip away. But the carriage creaked to a halt at an inn further along the road—the Nelson's Head.

"Why have we stopped?"

Two men in aprons, their shirt-sleeves rolled to their elbows despite it being late autumn, approached along the lane and entered the inn. It would be easy to attract their attention once inside.

"I hired a post-chaise in Rochester to bring me to London. Paid the driver to wait here for my return. He'll take us home and then on to Dover. I paid O'Shea a ridiculous sum to ferry me around town these last two days, but his duties end here."

Two days? Then he had followed them to London after the meeting at the Falstaff inn. Indeed, she realised he wore the same clothes, not the same arrogant grin.

He waved the pistol at her. "Wait inside the coach until I return. O'Shea's been instructed to shoot you if you attempt to leave." He alighted, left her alone with her thoughts.

What a shame she didn't have her pocket pistol, but she had left it with Mr Bower. Weapons were not allowed through the doors of Newgate. Still, for Dante's sake, she would test O'Shea's mettle. The fool wouldn't risk the noose to kill a stranger.

Would he?

CHAPTER 20

BOWER'S NOTE had arrived thirty minutes after Miss Trimble had given her emotional statement, brought by a boy in a hackney who'd been promised a sovereign if he delivered it safely. Bower's instructions were clear. Cross London Bridge, take the Kent Road and head towards Rochester.

Rochester? John Sands was a damn fool. That's the first place anyone would look. Which meant he was stopping for supplies— clean clothes and money—before heading south to Dover. Good. Being an hour behind, they would catch him at the house.

During the agonising wait in Hart Street, Miss Trimble repeated Manning's words verbatim. Dante couldn't believe Beatrice had taken it upon herself to confront the moneylender. He should have been livid, but he understood the clawing need to uncover the truth. Daventry had expressed his own fury, a fury directed at Sir Malcolm for putting the case against Manning before the life of an agent.

And so they'd commanded the use of Sloane's carriage, were rattling at breakneck speed along the muddy thoroughfare, had made ground by taking Waterloo Bridge and meeting the Kent Road in Walworth. By Dante's calculation, they were now only thirty minutes behind Bower. Assuming he hadn't stopped or taken a detour.

Dante glanced at the passing fields while seized by a sense of

ADELE CLEE

foreboding. The sun had dipped just below the horizon. Vibrant streaks of gold and red lit the sky. But soon darkness would swamp his world—just like it had on that lonely road in Hampshire.

Ashwood, Cole and Sloane sat in silence, their large frames squashed inside the conveyance. Daventry sat atop the box with Turton. He'd sworn never to lose an agent again. Swore no man or woman would ever die on his watch.

"We'll find her," Sloane said, "alive and well."

Dante glanced at Sloane. "Shoot me if we don't."

The panic, the pain, must have been evident in his eyes.

"You're in love with her," Ashwood stated, his sigh tinged with relief.

"I cannot bear the thought of living without her," he choked. "I cannot bear the thought of going home to an empty house, of not seeing her wearing her ridiculous trousers, swigging foul brandy."

When Cole frowned, Sloane said, "Miss Sands uses various tactics to pull our friend out of the doldrums. Vinegar posing as brandy being one of them."

"She's clearly in love with you," Ashwood said. "She's done everything in her power to help you find the devil who shot your parents."

"She's the most incredible woman I've ever met." Dante covered his eyes with his hand for a moment before sucking in a sharp breath and letting anger overcome his fear. "I'll kill that bastard if he's hurt her."

Based on Miss Trimble's account, John Sands was the fox in the warren. No doubt he feared Manning had told Beatrice the truth, hence why he'd kidnapped her outside Newgate. Silencing her had to be his motive. And yet the clod had left Miss Trimble behind.

They stopped at the turnpike. Dante lowered the window, tried to ignore the foul stench emanating from the tannery some distance behind the tollhouse, and listened to Daventry's conversation with the collector.

"Have you seen anything unusual?" Daventry continued sharply. "The woman is being held against her will."

The middle-aged fellow pushed his fingers under his hat and scratched his head. "Only the hackney coach. They don't often come this far from town, but he must have dropped his passengers at the Nelson's Head 'cause he came back the ways ten minutes ago."

"With an empty coach?"

"It looked empty. Oh, and there was that burly fellow who said he was in a rush. Complained he'd had to stop while the shepherd herded sheep across the road. And I had to make him wait at the gate as I was desperate for a piddle."

Burly fellow? Perhaps he meant Bower.

"Where's the Nelson's Head?"

The collector pointed. "Just along the road."

Daventry thanked him, and Turton paid the toll.

The fellow moved to open the gate, but the crack of a gunshot in the distance had him practically jumping out of his frayed coat.

"Lord Almighty!" the collector cried, clutching his hat to his head.

Dante's heart stopped, but somehow he pushed the carriage door open and vaulted to the ground. He raced to the gate, knocked the collector aside, and squeezed through the narrow walkway for pedestrians.

Daventry followed behind, as did Sloane, Ashwood and Cole.

"The shot came from across the meadow, near the windmill," Daventry said before instructing Ashwood and Cole to visit the Nelson's Head and make enquiries there. "I'll not have us all tearing across fields when Miss Sands might be at the inn."

But Dante took to his heels, regardless. Every fibre of his being told him to head to the windmill. The collector said the hackney had passed through ten minutes earlier. Beatrice would have escaped at the first opportunity.

Daventry and Sloane charged across the meadow, slipping and sliding on the sodden ground, but neither man was as fast as Dante. It was his life hanging in the balance. His love trying to escape a murdering fiend.

Dante crossed the first field—twenty yards ahead of Daventry—vaulted the low stone wall and darted towards the mill. The white slatted sails creaked with each revolution, the leisurely rotations at odds with the violent churning in Dante's stomach.

The gate leading to the mill was open. Some distance to the right stood a horse and cart, split sacks of grain littering the ground. The horse must have bolted upon hearing the shot. Indeed, there was another full grain sack on the tree-lined drive, abandoned by an equally fearful fellow.

Dante gestured for Sloane and Daventry to keep out of sight, scout the area.

Sloane pulled a knife from a sheath hidden inside his boot and indicated he would go left. There wasn't a man in London as skilled with a blade.

All was quiet, except for the rustle of the wind, the creak of the sails and the faint grinding of the millstone. Had it not been for the deserted sacks, Dante might have cursed his mistake and darted back to the Nelson's Head. But then he heard someone whisper his name from behind the hedgerow at the end of the drive.

Bower peered above the shrubbery and pointed to the open mill door.

Dante edged closer.

"Miss Sands ran into the mill, sir," Bower whispered. "The devil followed her. He's got a pistol, but I don't think he means to kill her. I shot him, nicked him on the shoulder, but I've brought nothing with me to reload." He pointed to a cottage on the right. "The miller and his family are hiding there."

"Does he have a single barrel or a side-by-side?"

"Looked like a single barrel."

Good. John Sands had but one shot.

Dante told Bower to remain outside, then crept towards the three stone steps leading into the mill. Grain sacks lined the walls of the entrance. Spots of blood left a trail all the way to the meal bin.

Dante stopped. Listened. Heard nothing but the ominous whirring of cogs and the grinding of stones.

He fought the urge to call out, to tell Beatrice not to worry, and proceeded to climb the wooden staircase to the next level.

But there was no sign of John Sands there. No sign of a coward cowering in the corner. The blood trail led to another flight of stairs, and it was clear he'd taken Beatrice to the upper gallery, an exterior balcony used by the miller when he needed to climb the sails and adjust the cloths.

Tension coiled in Dante's stomach. One slip from the gallery and a man would plunge eighty feet to his death. Still, there was nowhere else to hide, so the devil must have climbed to the top.

The sky was more dark grey than blue, with just a thin gold band clinging to the horizon. The wind ruffled Dante's hair. The sharp nip in the air pinched his cheeks. A quick look over the railings was enough to test a man's sea legs.

Bower was on his feet below, Sloane beside him, calling and pointing to a spot out of Dante's view.

"I know you're there, you murdering bastard," Dante shouted. "Only one of us will make it down alive. I suggest you show yourself so we can get this over with."

Dante saw a mud-splattered boot first, then a leg and a body as John Sands edged his way around the balcony, his back flush with the pointed roof.

"It wasn't me!" the blackguard cried, clutching his injured shoulder with one hand, holding his pistol in the other. "I didn't shoot your parents. Manning did."

Manning? The comment struck Dante like a blow to the back, taking him by surprise, knocking the air from his lungs. It took a few seconds for him to gather his wits. And then the scene appeared in a vision before him: John Sands and Manning, two mismatched men astride mismatched beasts.

A host of questions bombarded his mind, along with the sudden realisation that he cared about one thing, one thing only.

"I'm not here to avenge my parents. I'm here to avenge my wife."

Sands looked confused. "Wife?"

"Where's Beatrice?"

"Wife!"

"Damn you! Where is she!" Panic, black and blinding, pushed to the surface. "If you've hurt her, I shall gut you like a fish. Ensure it's a slow, painful death."

But John Sands was just as alarmed. "Wife! You've sullied my little Bea?" He raised a shaky hand and aimed his pistol. "No. You can't be married. No. You'll not take her from me, do you hear?"

The twisted degenerate cocked his weapon. Based on his flared nostrils and bulging eyes, it was more than a threat. He meant to shoot.

But Dante had dealt with more terrifying men than this miscreant. They did not follow Ring Rules at the White Boar. A man might take a kick to the teeth if he took his eye off the game. And so one learnt to fight like the rogues on the street.

Indeed, with a perfectly timed flick of the leg, Dante knocked the pistol from John Sands' hand, watched it fly over the wooden railings and land on the ground.

"Now I've evened the odds, I'll let you have the first hit."

John Sands lunged, threw a weak punch Dante caught in his fist.

"I shall break every one of your fingers," Dante said, crunching the man's bones. "What have you done with her? Tell me where she is."

"I don't know." He wailed in pain and crumpled to his knees. "She ran inside the mill, but I've not seen her since."

"Get up!" Dante grabbed Sands' cravat and hauled him to his feet. He had to find Beatrice and would hand this devil over to Daventry. "I'm taking you into custody for the murders of Henry Watson and Daphne and Alessandro D'Angelo."

"No! It was Manning, Manning who shot them!"

"You can discuss it with Manning when you share a cell with him in Newgate." John Sands would be dead long before his appointment with the scaffold.

"Newgate! No! The man will throttle me in my sleep." Agitated, Sands thrashed about violently, fought and struggled to break free. "No! You can't. Not with Manning. No!" He pounded Dante's back with his fist, forcing Dante to release him.

The man was possessed by such a frenzy, he could barely keep still. He went to take another swipe at Dante, but swung too quickly, lost his footing and tumbled backwards. The crack of the wooden rail splintering preceded the harrowing cries as John Sands fell to the ground.

Bower and Sloane hurried to the body. But darkness was descending, and Dante's only thought was finding Beatrice.

"Beatrice!" he cried as he hurried down the rickety staircase. "Beatrice!"

Daventry met him on the ground floor near the grain sacks. "Quick, help me move them." Daventry grabbed a sack and dragged it away from the wall. "Miss Sands came in here asking for help. The miller hid her in a small cupboard and then took his family to the cottage."

"A cupboard?"

Dante quickly helped Daventry move the sacks to reveal a small cubbyhole no more than three feet high. He dropped to his knees and pushed the wooden panel aside. It was dark outside, hard to see, even darker in the tiny space.

"Beatrice?"

He heard heavy breathing, muffled sobs. He reached into the hole and moved the old sacks. Beatrice lay curled in a ball, trembling to her toes. He touched her.

"No! Get away!"

"It's Dante, love. Take my hand. Let me help you out of there."

"Dante?" came her whispered reply.

"You're safe now. I'm here."

She moved slightly, raised her head, stretched out a shaky hand.

He pulled her out of the filthy hole, wrapped his arms around her and held her so tight to his chest they both struggled to breathe.

Daventry tapped him gently on the back. "I'll leave you with Miss Sands while I deal with her uncle. We'll need to alert the coroner and the local magistrate. I expect we'll be here for a few hours."

Beatrice raised her head. "The coroner?"

Dante pushed a lock of hair behind her ear, stroked her tear-stained face. "Your uncle is dead. He fell off the gallery. But he's got a wound to his shoulder, and the magistrate will want to know why."

More tears fell, and she pressed her forehead to his chest. "Forgive me, Dante." She sobbed into his cravat. "I shouldn't have gone to see Manning without telling you. But Miss Trimble—"

"Hush, love. It doesn't matter now." He looked at Daventry. "Manning shot my parents. John Sands was his accomplice. Perhaps you should send Ashwood to fetch Sir Malcolm. If we're to give lengthy statements, I'd prefer to do it once."

Daventry nodded. "Ashwood can take Sloane's carriage. Bower will need to remain here and explain why he shot a man." He glanced at Beatrice. "Miss Sands might like to visit the miller's cottage. His wife is making tea."

"We'll be along shortly."

Daventry left them alone.

Dante held Beatrice close. He closed his eyes, said a silent prayer of thanks, and let his love for her consume him until he could contain it no longer.

"Beatrice."

She looked up at him.

"I'm in love with you."

She swallowed, blinked back fresh tears. "You are?"

"I'm so in love with you it hurts, hurts to think I might lose—"

She pressed her finger to his lips to silence him. "As we're bartering for information, know that I'm in love with you, Dante. I'm so in love with you it's like a bright light burning inside me."

He felt the light, too, so warm and comforting. It chased away the darkness, brought with it hope and infinite possibilities.

"I told your uncle you were my wife, and I hate lying."

A smile tugged at her lips. "He cannot hold it against you. Not anymore."

"But it felt so good to say the words." He paused, took a second to take a breath, to look back along the rocky path and appreciate how far he'd come. "Marry me. Let me take care of you always."

She reached up and cupped his nape, pulled his mouth to hers and kissed him so deeply his heart swelled. "Yes," she whispered against his lips. "I want to be your wife, the mother of your children. I want to take care of you always."

They held each other for a while, wallowed in a rare moment of happiness.

Beatrice looked up at him, a little forlorn. "It's all over now. The case is solved. We've no need to work together."

He kissed her softly on the mouth. "You're wrong, love. Our work together has only just begun."

CHAPTER 21

THE MORNING LIGHT found its way through a crack in the curtains. Dante covered his eyes with his arm, silently moaning so as not to wake Beatrice. But his brain fired into action, the events of last night bouncing back and forth in his mind.

They'd not arrived home until midnight. Daventry and Sir Malcolm had dealt with John Sands' death, but the laborious task of giving statements had taken longer than expected.

Afterwards, Beatrice had agreed to come to Fitzroy Square to explain what she had learned from her uncle. Together they'd sat before the roaring fire in the drawing room, swigging brandy while discussing the case. They'd made love there. Made love in bed a little later, and she had agreed to spend the night.

Dante feared he'd not let her out of his sight again. But it was unhealthy to concoct stories about future events, unhealthy to live life as if awaiting a tragedy. And so he would do as Beatrice suggested and make the most of every moment.

Thankfully, he'd woken with a throbbing erection, and so he turned on his side, ready to run his hand over the gentle flare of her hip, hoping his betrothed might like to take advantage of his excited disposition.

But he was alone in bed.

He rubbed his eyes, came up on his elbow and scoured the

room. A quick scan of the floor and his heart sank. His clothes were scattered about the place, hers nowhere to be seen.

He jumped out of bed, slightly panicked. So much for avoiding unhealthy stories. He imagined she was an early riser, but it was almost midday. He imagined a worried Miss Trimble hammering the door, but they had told their friends of their intention to marry. Surely no one begrudged them a little privacy.

He grabbed his clothes, shook out the creases and dressed quickly.

What if she'd left? What if she couldn't live with the fact her uncle was responsible for the death of Dante's parents?

You will come to see me as a physical reminder of your pain.

But they'd discussed it last night.

And then the chamber door creaked open, and the love of his life slipped into the room so as not to wake him.

She almost jumped out of her skin when she turned and saw him looming.

"Good Lord! You gave me a fright. I thought you were asleep."

"I woke in an affectionate mood, hoped you might give me another chance to express my abiding love."

She glanced at his breeches and smiled. "I'm sure an opportunity will arise again shortly."

"No doubt." He only had to think of her, and blood rushed to his loins.

She set a package down on the chair. "Are we going back to bed, or shall I ring to say we'd like breakfast?"

"I'd not planned on leaving this room today."

"Good." She began unbuttoning her pelisse, stripping for him until she stood in nothing but her chemise.

He followed suit, removed every item of clothing until naked.

Beatrice considered him with an appreciative eye. "Don't you want to know where I've been?"

Dante glanced at the brown paper package. "Home, I presume."

She nodded. "A note arrived in Howland Street for me this morning. Bateson has one for you, too, from Sir Malcolm." She paused, stepped closer and touched his chest. "Dante, they found Mr Manning hanging in his cell. Somehow he located a length of rope. Somehow he tied it to the bars and hung himself."

Hung himself?

Manning would never have taken his own life.

"More like someone wrapped a rope around his neck and throttled him until he was dead. There'll be an investigation." Though who the hell would want justice for Mortuary Manning?

A conversation he'd had with Daventry and Sir Malcolm in the miller's cottage flitted into his mind. Both men had assured him Manning would never see the light of day. Both men assured Beatrice there would be no need to spend sleepless nights fearing Manning might call.

"Do you feel cheated?" she said, stroking his chest. "Did you want to see him stand trial for murdering your parents?"

"They couldn't have tried him for the crime. There's no evidence other than your testimony, and I refuse to put you through the distress of seeing Manning in court."

No, everything had worked out for the best.

She came up on her toes and kissed him. "Let me give you my gift before we climb back into bed."

Dante arched a curious brow. "Gift? It's not the silver tea tray, is it?"

Clearly excited, she hurried to the chair and retrieved the small rectangular object. "A tea tray big enough for one cup? No. It's something Mr Bower helped me find. He's spent two days trailing around every trinket shop in Bermondsey."

"Trinket shop?" A lump formed in Dante's throat. "Not the trinket shop where Babington sold my father's cheroot case?"

"Thankfully, the owner had taken a liking to it and kept it for himself. I've paid far more than expected. The man described Mr Babington perfectly, so I'm sure it's the right one."

Dante stared at her, his heart ready to burst.

"Mr Bower meant to give it to me yesterday, but what with all—"

He kissed her, kissed her like she was the air he needed to breathe.

When he straightened, she had tears in her eyes.

"Please open it. If it's not the right one, you'll be disappointed."

"I won't. My mother gave my father the gift because she loved him. I recall the look on both their faces when he opened it." He looked down at the wrapped case. "Love prompted you to give me this gift. Regardless of what it is, I shall treasure it always."

He wiped a single tear from her cheek and set about ripping the paper.

He had not cried since he was eight years old, yet the thought of losing Beatrice had drawn a tear from his eye. Seeing the hunting scene painted on the case, seeing the image of his father sitting proudly on his mount, brought another tear trickling down his cheek.

"Is it? Is it the same one?" she asked eagerly.

Dante inhaled deeply and scrubbed his hand down his face. "Yes, it's my father's case." He slipped his arm around her waist, pulled her close, and she lay her head against his shoulder. "My mother used to say he loved those hounds more than anything. But she knew he would never love anyone the way he loved her."

"Mr Sloane told me Farthingdale is for sale. Perhaps you might like to purchase a house in the country."

For a heartbeat, the idea seemed appealing. But he'd spent his life living in the past. "I would rather focus on our future, rather we started anew, let our parents rest in peace."

"We need to let them go now," she agreed.

A vision of him clutching his mother's body flashed into his mind. Perhaps a part of him would always be the heartbroken boy at the roadside. Perhaps a man was the sum of all his experiences.

He kissed her hair, inhaled her scent. "Were it not for the tragedy, we might never have met." He could not bear the thought of that either. And so he made a vow to stop inventing stories.

She sensed his disquiet. The dainty hand on his chest began moving in caressing strokes, healing his scars, soothing his fears. She dipped fractionally lower each time, her fingers grazing the hard contours of his abdomen until she dared to slide her hand down the length of his cock.

"Come to bed," she whispered. "Let's spend a few hours here, and then you can take me to Gunter's. You can feed me lemon ice despite the fact it's cold outside."

This woman knew how to flood every dark memory with a ray of sunshine.

He turned to face her and smiled. "Pineapple mousse would be my choice for you, my love."

She laughed. "And why is that?"

"Like you, it's soft and sweet and so deliciously tempting."

"And for you, Dante, I shall choose a pyramid of macaroons."

"Because they're hard and smooth on the outside, soft in the centre?"

She looked deep into his eyes. "Because you love them, and I love you. And I wish to spend every day of my life making you happy."

"I love you," he said, his chaste kiss of appreciation quickly becoming a rampant mating of mouths, a mating that lasted well into the afternoon.

Highwood, Bedfordshire
Evan Sloane's country residence

"How does it feel to be married to Dante D'Angelo?" Sybil Daventry asked as the wives of the men who worked for the Order huddled together in Mr Sloane's drawing room.

Flutters of excitement made Beatrice silently chuckle. She'd been Dante's wife for three hours and had worn a permanent grin ever since. "He's everything a woman could want in a husband." Everything a woman would want in a lover and a friend.

All the women glanced across the room at their respective husbands and nodded.

"I imagine they're discussing Mr Craddock's trial." Vivienne

Sloane sipped her champagne. "At the very least, he'll get seven years transportation."

If only Mr Craddock had gone to the authorities when Mr Babington blackmailed him. But the fear of debtors' prison made men lose all rationale.

"The gossips say he killed Mr Babington, but the witnesses described a thin man who was fast on his feet." Beatrice had read numerous reports in the broadsheets stating that Mr Babington had ventured all over the country, using aliases to dupe unsuspecting people out of funds. The wider the news spread, the more victims came forward. "The man had a lot of enemies."

Sophia Cole touched Beatrice gently on the upper arm. "I imagine you're relieved now the case is over. At the same time, you're probably missing the thrill of the chase."

"It's exciting until you have something to lose," she said, wondering how she would cope when Dante was given his next assignment. "How do you sleep at night knowing they place themselves in danger?"

Sybil Daventry sighed. "Lucius takes his responsibilities seriously. He ensures they're trained to defend themselves, instinctively knows when to pair them together on a case. And they're all extremely skilled agents."

As if hearing his wife's praise, Lucius Daventry glanced at Sybil, and his hard exterior softened. He inclined his head, devotion and respect swimming in his dark eyes.

"But you work for the Order, Beatrice," Eva Ashwood said, stroking her abdomen in such a way one knew she was with child. "How will Dante cope when you're faced with a new client?"

Dante wouldn't have to worry. She had decided to take another role in Lucius Daventry's organisation. The master of the Order had saved her, and now it was her turn to save someone else.

"Rather than accept a new case, I'm to assist Miss Trimble. Four new ladies are moving into Howland Street this week, all women without prospects or funds." But she suspected Miss Trimble needed her the most.

Sybil nodded. "My husband is paying for them to stay at the

Clarendon Hotel. I believe one of them caught a pickpocket loitering in the lobby."

Eva's eyes widened. "Will they all be agents?"

"I believe so. Lucius agreed to follow Dante's advice and consider their assignments carefully. They already have a potential client. Lord Devereaux wants to hire an agent, but Lucius told him only female agents were for hire. Told him the men only work to help those without funds."

"Lord Devereaux?" Sophia wiggled a brow. "The man can click his fingers and have anything he wants. Why would he need to hire an agent?"

"I have no idea."

Eva chuckled. "Do you know, Sybil, when one considers the fact all the gentlemen of the Order are now married, one wonders if your husband is skilled in matchmaking."

They all laughed.

And yet Beatrice couldn't help thinking there was some truth to the theory.

"If that's the case, he'll fall foul with Lord Devereaux," Sophia said. "The man has a new mistress every six months, though they all look remarkably similar."

Sybil suddenly gasped. "Quick, Beatrice. Your husband is prowling towards us like a panther in need of an afternoon bite."

"I'll lay odds he wants you to inspect the broom cupboard," Vivienne whispered. "Or he's lost his sapphire stickpin and needs your help upstairs."

Beatrice smiled. "It will take an hour to search the room thoroughly."

Dante approached, looking extremely handsome in his dark blue coat. He bowed. "Ladies. I've come to steal my wife."

"Have you lost something, Dante?" Vivienne teased.

"My mind if I'm to be parted from Beatrice a moment longer."

The ladies sighed.

Dante offered his hand. "Mrs D'Angelo, might I invite you to take an afternoon stroll?"

Beatrice couldn't wait to be alone with him. She'd not spoken to him properly since yesterday afternoon. And since making their vows, their friends had monopolised their attention.

She gripped his hand. "I'd like nothing more than to spend an hour alone with you, Dante."

He led her out into the hall and drew her into his arms. "Am I mistaken, or do your friends assume we intend to do something other than walk?"

"They know we're in love, know we can barely keep our hands to ourselves."

He bent his head and kissed her. Their first proper kiss as husband and wife had heat pooling in her belly.

"Tonight, we'll have hours to indulge our passions, but let's walk together. I feel like we've not spoken for days."

His comment warmed her as much as his kisses. "Then let me run upstairs, fetch a pelisse and change my shoes. Vivienne said there's a pretty spot by the lake. Perhaps we can walk there."

He nodded. "I shall wait for you on the terrace."

She hurried to their chamber and returned momentarily.

They strolled down to the row of mausoleums, the burial place of Mr Sloane's ancestors. They talked about the ladies who were moving into Howland Street, about Mr Craddock's trial. He revealed the conversation he'd had with Lucius Daventry.

"I've been assigned a new case."

Her heart dropped as fast as a brick in a water barrel. "Dante, promise me you'll be careful."

"You haven't asked what it is."

"Tell me it's not finding Mr Babington's murderer."

"No, love, that's an impossible feat. There are too many suspects, Mabel being one of them." He paused. "She came to see Daventry three days ago, but he refused to let her speak."

Good Lord!

"Did she come to confess?"

Dante shrugged. "Daventry told her that good people commit foolish acts in the name of duty. That the world was best rid of a man like Babington, and it was likely someone else with a gripe hired an assassin."

Mr Daventry's thoughts would have been for Dante, too.

He'd been hurt enough and didn't need society pointing the finger. Didn't need his name involved in a scandal.

"Mabel kissed his hand and thanked him," Dante continued. "So, no. I doubt anyone will be hunting for Babington's killer."

Beatrice was both relieved and apprehensive. "Then what's your new assignment?"

He laughed. "Lady Dalton's maid was arrested for theft. The servant says she can prove her innocence."

"What's so funny about that?" she said, thankful it wasn't a case of murder.

"Nothing, except she's accused of stealing the lady's dog."

"Her dog?" It sounded like a case for one of the ladies at Howland Street. "Not a pug?"

"Indeed, but this pug was wearing a diamond collar."

Beatrice started laughing and couldn't stop. Dante laughed, too, laughed until tears streamed down his face.

"You may need my help," she said, catching her breath. "Pugs can be pesky creatures."

"My sparring practice at the Wild Boar will have prepared me sufficiently."

They continued walking, both chuckling periodically, though a woman's life hung in the balance, and Dante would most certainly save her.

He stopped suddenly and took hold of her hands. "There's something I want to give you. A gift I hope you will accept."

"A gift?" She couldn't think what it might be.

"I know we said we'd stop looking to the past, but it's the only thing I have of hers, and she would have wanted to give you something on your wedding day."

Emotion bubbled to her throat when he removed Daphne's brooch from his pocket. Tears filled her eyes when he placed it in her palm.

"It's yours, Beatrice. Given to my mother by a man who loved her more than life itself. Given to you by a man who cannot believe his good fortune. A man you pulled from the darkness. A man who loves you to the depths of his soul."

The lump in her throat made it hard to speak. "I shall treasure it always."

They kissed, pressed their foreheads together and whispered words of love. When they parted, Dante chuckled again. "Perhaps we should play a trick on your new friends. Hide in the study, bang the desk and make amorous noises."

She thought about Miss Keane and laughed. "There's always the broom cupboard, but I'd rather you didn't tell them you were inspecting my bristles."

THANK YOU!

I hope you enjoyed reading *Dark Angel*.

It's the end of the series but not the end of the Order.

Why does Lord Devereaux need to hire an agent?
How will he fare when he realises the woman who's been
assigned to help him is someone from his past?

The Devereaux Affair
Ladies of the Order - Book 1

More titles by Adele Clee

To Save a Sinner
What Every Lord Wants
The Secret To Your Surrender
A Simple Case of Seduction

Lost Ladies of London

The Mysterious Miss Flint
The Deceptive Lady Darby
The Scandalous Lady Sandford
The Daring Miss Darcy

Avenging Lords

At Last the Rogue Returns
A Wicked Wager
Valentine's Vow
A Gentleman's Curse

Scandalous Sons

And the Widow Wore Scarlet
The Mark of a Rogue
When Scandal Came to Town
The Mystery of Mr Daventry

Gentlemen of the Order

Dauntless
Raven
Valiant
Dark Angel

Ladies of the Order

The Devereaux Affair